Tinnin

30 Mar 2023

To; Haley

It is a privilege for me to present a copy of "Tinnin" to you. Thank you for all the ways you have helped us. Delene joins me in wishing you well in future endeavors.

Jasper

Tinnin

A Family History Novel

JASPER S. LEE

ARCHWAY
PUBLISHING

Archway Publishing books may be ordered through booksellers or by contacting:

Archway Publishing
1663 Liberty Drive
Bloomington, IN 47403
www.archwaypublishing.com
844-669-3957

Cover Image Credit:
Shepherd Plantation House
Patsy Cannon of Athens, Georgia

ISBN: 978-1-6657-3238-3 (sc)
ISBN: 978-1-6657-2830-0 (e)

Library of Congress Control Number: 2022919804

Print information available on the last page.

Archway Publishing rev. date: 1/12/2023

Contents

Dedication

With great pride, I lovingly dedicate this book to my grand-daughter, Anna Delene. She is the person in my life who has many of the wonderful traits of the main character of this book, Ellen Loretta Shepard Lee. Anna Delene is the great-great-great granddaughter of Ellen. No doubt, Ellen would have adored Anna Delene.

Anna Delene, I wish you much success in life. May you enjoy learning about your ancestors and strive to make them proud in all that you do.

Acknowledgments

A number of people assisted in writing *Tinnin*. Some chose to consciously participate; others participated vicariously. Their contributions in this book came a century or so after their earthly demise. Others willingly participated in this book, as well as the earlier *Return to Tinnin*, published in 2017.

Among those who consciously helped in writing *Tinnin* are individuals who supported the work and helped to achieve an acceptable book. Emily Jahr of Savannah College of Art and Design is acknowledged for reading the manuscript and making useful suggestions. Thank you, Emily, for keeping my words straight and proper. You have always enthusiastically stepped forward to do what needs to be done to get a book "right!"

Four individuals are acknowledged here for their services:

- Ronnie McDaniel of Danville, Illinois, is acknowledged for his copy editing and other suggestions that improved the initial manuscript. This gentleman is an accomplished editor who has helped me in many ways with a number of books. Thank you!

- Jacqueline Frost Tisdale of Starkville, Mississippi, is acknowledged for her assistance in reviewing the manuscript and making important suggestions. She had additional insight by having grown up in Clinton, Mississippi, where Tinnin is located.
- Wally Warren of Clarkesville, Georgia, is acknowledged for reading the manuscript and providing helpful suggestions. No doubt, his extensive public library work served him well as a manuscript reader.
- Morgan Anglin of Georgia College and State University in Milledgeville, Georgia, is acknowledged for reading the manuscript and providing useful suggestions.

Two professional genealogists are acknowledged here for their help with matters related to *Tinnin*:

- Anne Vanderleest assisted with considerable genealogical information and researching family history. She also served by reading and critiquing the book and providing useful suggestions for *Tinnin*. Anne is a genealogist who resides in Concord, North Carolina.

- Skip Duette, a professional genealogist, helped with a range of family history information and situations. His efforts helped assure that the author didn't stray. He resides in Clifton Park, New York. I am proud to call him Cousin Skip!

A special thank you goes to retired attorney Ann Tipton of Sautee-Nacoochee, Georgia. Her assistance in finding, interpreting, and reporting old Texas court records was very useful. Her guidance was especially important on matters of estate probation.

Appreciation goes to all individuals who participated unconsciously by saving old letters, business forms, farm records, and similar information. These old documents provided nearly two centuries of insight into personal family information.

Many family members and friends encouraged me with this undertaking. Foremost among these is my wife, Delene. I thank her for her patience and help by reading the manuscript to assure that the story was as it should be. Overall, it is her encouragement that keeps me going!

Special acknowledgments

Special acknowledgment goes to artist Patsy Canon of Athens, Georgia. Her wonderful artistic skills resulted in a compelling watercolor picture of the plantation house. Thank you, Patsy, for your enthusiasm and effort in painting a picture of the Shepard home on the plantation. (The house was constructed in 1857 and served as a home for several generations. It was raised in 1998 for a gated residential subdivision for the city of Jackson, Mississippi.)

Acknowledgment also goes to Cousin Ellen Miller Gabardi for her assistance with family information. Gatherings at your home to talk with relatives were special.

Additional acknowledgment goes to Sydney Hemphill of the Savannah College of Art and Design (SCAD) for the preparation of art used throughout the book and the portrait of the author as used on the cover. Sydney hails from Lafayette, Louisiana. No doubt, she will have a highly successful career as a book illustrator.

Preface

Tinnin is a historical novel about the life of a girl who became a young adult in the South during and just after the US Civil War. The main character is Ellen Loretta Shepard, a cotton plantation owner's daughter, who chose to marry a man named Jasper Henry Lee. This man had charisma and some ability for hard work but unknown personal qualities that made him suspect to her father.

After privately talking with Jasper, Ellen's father gained information that resulted in him being disliked even more. Her father felt he was inappropriate to join the family. Rejection of her Jasper lasted until his untimely death after six years of marriage. Good times and bad times highlight a life of romance, love, and forgiveness.

Written by her great-grandson, the story is based on considerable research into family history. DNA analysis of descendants was a part of determining genetic family relationships. Online searches and visits to historical agencies yielded useful information. The services of professional genealogists were used in doing advanced research related to the Lee surname. A Lee Family History was prepared and used as a source of information. Hideaway places in the attic of the family plantation home built before the Civil War had trunks belonging to ancestors that yielded a trove of old letters, invoices, and similar documents. These provided a great deal of intimate insight into the life Ellen (1847–1918).

To the author, Ellen was a smart, attractive young woman who could have made a better decision about romance. Interestingly, if she had made a different choice, the Lee author would not be here to brag about her.

Introduction

Tinnin is a sequel (or some would say an update) to the previously published biographical novel entitled *Return to Tinnin* (2017). Both were about the life and times of a girl who became a young adult during the US Civil War in the Confederate States of America. *Tinnin* contains much more family detail about the man she married than was available in the earlier book.

The main character is Ellen Loretta Shepard Lee. Good times, and some that weren't so good, highlighted her life. She approached the age at which she wished to marry when "good" men were in short supply. Many had been killed, severely injured, or had shipped away for military service. In a strong display of leadership and personal conviction for what was right, her father voted the Union ticket. How he voted, however, might have made them more vulnerable to the antics of the Confederate Army.

Considerable family research went into writing this story by Ellen's great-grandson. Family history information stored in old trunks and boxes provided a wealth of information. DNA analysis was much a part of determining genetic family relationships. Online searches and visits to historical agencies yielded useful information.

This story is factual. In some cases, the nature of the times required a display of "how it likely was." Readers may think of this as embellishment. The author used care to remain factual and present the situation as it was. Enjoy!

Ellen Loretta Shepard Lee
Born: September 7, 1847, on the Shepard Cotton
Plantation in Tinnin, Hinds County, Mississippi
Died: March 21, 1918, in Tinnin, Mississippi

1

Fearful Anticipation

It was Easter Sunday 1863. The Shepard family had gone to church that morning and was now hosting the preacher to enjoy lunch with them that day. Ma had done her best to prepare a delicious and abundant meal. A big question was always present about disruption by troops as they marched across the plantation to their next battle.

"Preacher Hoyle, it is so good to have you here with us for dinner on this glorious, beautiful Easter Sunday," Pa George Shepard said. "You certainly had a powerful message at Mason Chapel this morning on the principles of salvation and human love. It was the perfect message for Easter. I am so glad you didn't preach about saving souls from eternal life in the hot fires of hell. Some folks in the congregation needed to hear what you had to say about salvation and love. I was one of them."

Ma (George's wife, Sarah) added, "Preacher, you are amazing and a real blessing in our community. Here, have another piece of chicken. You know, the thighs and breast pieces are all gone. I am sorry we have only wings, necks, backs, gizzards, and hearts left. Of course, we have collard greens, stewed potatoes, and cornbread. And we have my family's favorite of lemon cake for dessert."

So went southern cooking on the Shepard Plantation that Easter Sunday in Tinnin, Mississippi. It wouldn't be long before all eyes of the family were on the year's new cotton crop.

As Ma started passing the platter of remaining fried chicken, the sounds of a horse's hooves could be heard rapidly coming down the long hill moving toward the house. Pa went to the porch on the front of the house. He faced the dirt trail, where dust was in the air from the hooves. The rider, somewhat out of breath, shouted to Pa George, "Union troops are on the way and will be here tomorrow. The company is about a hundred soldiers. And there may be more. Take steps to protect property and family."

After the message was delivered, the horse and rider sped back up the hill, kicking up even more dust. As many people as possible in the Tinnin community would be alerted by the horse rider about the future arrival of the soldiers, and the precautions that needed to be taken to assure minimum loss and damage. After all, they had already had Confederate and Union forces come through before, and both were about equally abusive.

Pa George knew what had to be done, but he didn't know that his oldest daughter, fifteen-year-old Ellen, had come to the porch behind him. Ellen, trembling and with tears in her eyes, said, "Pa, what are we going to do? The presence of troops scares me. Do you think one of them will take advantage of me? I've heard stories about how troops take advantage of young women. I want to save my specialness until my wedding night—that is important to me and what I have been taught as being right. And, Pa, some men at the Ratliff Store are already looking at me with a gleam in their eyes. You and Ma were married when she was fourteen, and I was born when she was fifteen. So—"

"Not in my presence will any soldier lay an inappropriate eye on you," Pa assured her. "I will shoot straight into the face of anyone who does so in a lustful way."

That soothed Ellen a bit, but she knew each soldier had a gun better than Pa's rarely used old double-barrel. Pa further said, "Don't let any of those scums at the Ratliff Store touch you either. I will speak to your Grandfather Ratliff about this." He owned the store, where some local people got their coffee, sugar, and the like."

Pa went back to the dining table with Preacher Hoyle,

where Ma and Ma's parents, Zachariah and Susan Tinnin Ratliff, were seated. Sarah had invited her parents to join them for an Easter meal with the preacher.

Ellen went back to the children's table with her seven siblings. (As the oldest child, Ellen was the unofficial leader of the children's table.) Pa announced what the rider had said. "And," he continued, "we just had a Union field artillery company here two weeks ago. They discarded bullets and one cannonball. Why again? Most likely, they're headed to the battle of Vicksburg."

Preacher Hoyle immediately said, "I have to go. It takes at least fifteen minutes on a fast horse to get back to my home in Clinton. I hope I don't run into the soldiers on the way."

He grabbed his worn Bible, ran outside, unhitched his horse, and jumped on its back. The horse went up the hill trail faster than the messenger who had brought the word about the troops.

Ma was disappointed that Preacher Hoyle had left so quickly. "You know," she said, "he didn't even say thank you, have a prayer, or anything. He ran. Maybe we need to think twice about inviting him to have a meal with us again."

Pa lamented, "Kind of like preachers around here. Maybe he was going to aid his own family. You know, if a preacher can't save himself, how can he save souls? He would have been safer if he had stayed here with us until the soldiers passed through."

Ma was also disappointed that she had put so much work into preparing the meal, including the lemon cake that had not been sliced for serving. She had spent Saturday butchering two fine young chickens and getting the food cooked for the meal. Of course, Ellen and others of the older Shepard children had helped some with the collard greens, corn bread, and other fixings. But, they likely would not see Preacher Hoyle again because of the havoc caused by the arrival of other troops.

Ma saved the leftover fried chicken in the pie safe overnight. Not much there but a neck, back, wing, heart, and half a gizzard. The preacher and the Ratliff and Shepard families had, earlier for Easter lunch, eaten the good pieces, including the wishbone, breast pieces, thighs, and drumsticks. Ma had a thought in the back of her mind about hunger among the soldiers, however. Could she find a way to build goodwill with the soldiers?

Preacher Hoyle was an itinerant minister who served at Mason Chapel, a small congregation that pretty well followed the beliefs and practices of the Methodist Episcopal Church. The church met in a small frame structure with a couple of privies outback. Several posts for hitching horses were in front.

The church house was near the clapboard schoolhouse in the Tinnin community, so the privies were also used by schoolchildren and teachers. Just like the Tinnin community, the church congregation was small—not many white folks in the community were brave enough to venture out to church, as lots of bad stuff was going on due to war and racial tensions. The situation was far more perilous than one preacher could solve.

Preacher Hoyle also served a couple of other tiny churches within a few miles of Clinton. The schoolhouse near Mason Chapel served as a social center in the community.

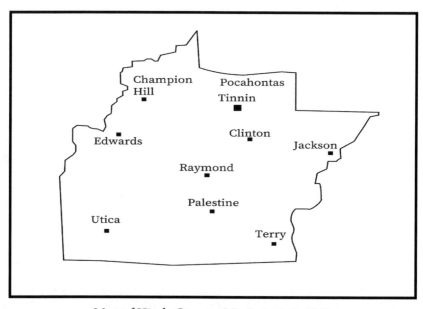

Map of Hinds County, Mississippi, in 1860

On his way to Clinton, Preacher Hoyle ran into the company of soldiers (they stormed Clinton before venturing to Tinnin). The soldiers stopped him and looked him over good. They asked if he had money, and, yes, he did from his preaching that morning at Mason Chapel.

Private O'Reilly took his meager earnings and stuffed it in his pocket.

Since the preacher had a fairly good-looking horse, the soldiers decided to keep it and let the preacher go. As the preacher protested that he would have two miles to walk, they pointed guns at him and told him to get going. One soldier was heard to say, "A good horse is far more valuable than a half-baked preacher." One took the preacher's Bible out of the saddlebag and threw it at him; Preacher Hoyle picked it up because it had some sermon notes.

Preacher Hoyle was not accustomed to this kind of treatment. He was so overcome with fear and having to walk that his heart pounded excessively. The pounding was so great that he fell from a heart attack. A stranger passing through found his half-dead body, put it behind the saddle over the horse he was riding, and rode to the local town marshal's office. The only doctor was next door and, fortunately, saved Preacher Hoyle's life.

This, however, did not slow the movement of the soldiers.

* * * * *

Back at the Shepards, the children were asked to join Pa and Ma and Grandparents Ratliff at the adult table. It was already after 3:00 p.m. Time was wasting. Dinner had been delayed until the preacher arrived following his morning sermon that lasted until 1:00 p.m., and then it took a few more minutes for him to tell everyone goodbye and ride to the Shepard home.

A serious conversation ensued. Pa told the family what the rider had said. The girls cried; the boys were too young to be concerned. Everyone was given a responsibility in preparing for the troops. The Shepards had to protect their limited possessions.

The slaves were a bit confused by word-of-mouth rumors. Some thought that they were already free because of the 1862 Federal that would abolish slavery in the U.S. It had no impact on those who lived in the Confederate States of America, where slavery was still practiced. Most of the Shepards' slaves continued to live on the plantation until 1865. But when troops came through, they did not come around to help with the problems that were created. Overall, life was stressful, even without the thought of soldiers coming. Farmwork and life began to change with rumors about the abolition of slavery. It would be 1865 before the major impact of abolition would be felt on the plantation. (But Pa, with his Indiana upbringing, knew abolition was the right thing to do.)

Pa continued with the plan, which involved hiding things deep in the forest of Shepard Hills, in the attic of the house, and in the ground. The work had to be done before dark that day, with the anticipated arrival of the soldiers the next morning. There was some fear that the soldiers would arrive in the darkness of night, and this was even scarier.

Everyone in the family got involved. Ellen was responsible for the draft animals, which were to be tied in thick, brushy hollows in the hills. These included pairs of horses and oxen, along with a mule. She led them one by one to an area filled with small trees, vines, and bushes.

Ellen's sisters Georgia Ann and Sarah were responsible for taking the cured meat (about 150 pounds altogether of hams and bacon sides) from the smokehouse to the attic of the house. Several trips up the ladder were needed. A few small pieces were left in the smokehouse, just in case the soldiers demanded some meat. It would be there for their taking. The ladder leading to the attic was cut into pieces and burned for heat in the fireplace, leaving no easy way for the soldiers to get into the attic.

Ellen's sisters Mag and Rachel were responsible for burying the gunpowder in the ground near the stable in a pottery container that would keep it dry. Other small household things were tucked away in places not readily visible. Naomi and James helped with this. Since Ira was only two years old, he wasn't given a responsibility.

Ma Sarah, her mother, and daughters Ellen and Mag helped quickly clean the table and kitchen. Then Susan and Zachariah departed for their home. It was located in the heart of Tinnin near the Ratliff Store and about a mile away.

Nothing was done to protect the loose chickens, penned pigs, and pastured cows. They would be left vulnerable to the soldiers' whims (if they could be caught). But Naomi, who was six years of age, asked about their dogs, Ritz and Bummer, as well as the barn cats, Oscar and Lucille. Pa said to let them stay loose, adding, "Ritz is the best dog." He'd had some training; Bummer had turned up as a stray with mange and a bad eye—which made him kind of mean. It was hard to defend him, even though he was a good watchdog—one eye and all. "As for the cats," Pa instructed, "let them continue their rat patrol of the corncrib. We don't need the rats to get our corn."

Pa had a certain confidence that he could handle the situation with the soldiers. After all, when voting was held on whether or not to secede from the Union and form the Confederate States of America, Pa had voted the Union ticket. He had moved to the South from Indiana as a very young man in 1841, searching for opportunity. Many of his values had been shaped by his parents and others in the Midwest. Of course, he had slaves until they were granted their freedom on January 1, 1863, by US President Abraham Lincoln. (Of course, the South was not in the Union at the time, and the order had little immediate effect.) Pa lost a small fortune of investment when emancipation occurred. He felt that his vote for the Union ticket on the secession matter resulted in some people in the community never again trusting him.

He had worked hard to gain his plantation holdings of 1,200 acres (some with government grants from the Choctaw cessation). In 1857, he had built a large home for his family. Various outbuildings supported his family and plantation life. He did not want his property taken or destroyed. He wanted a good future. The future was looking promising until the US Civil War began. The farm was almost in a direct line between Jackson and Vicksburg—a major route for delivery of farm products to the promising foreign markets by way of Vicksburg and its connections to ports in various countries.

Easter Sunday night, no one slept well (except baby Ira, who was still breastfed at age 2). Through the night, there was always a listening ear for the sounds of soldiers. The sun began to rise over Shepard Hills on the Monday after Easter. No sign of the soldiers yet. Morning chores were to be done—milk the two cows (Ellen's responsibility) and gather any eggs that were laid early (Mag's responsibility).

After the chores were done, everyone was to come into the house. Of course, the sighting of any soldier in the distance was plenty reason to immediately come inside.

Regardless, everyone made it through the night and went about doing what needed to be done.

2
Scary Soldiers

It was now the day after Easter. No one knew if or when the soldiers would arrive.

Pa George Shepard did not know that they had camped less than two miles away on a hillside just south of a place called Kickapoo. This meant it wouldn't take long for the soldiers to go down the dirt trail through Shepard Hills to the home. They broke camp and began moving north toward Tinnin.

About midmorning, a field artillery company began arriving. Commanded by Captain West, the hundred men made their way into the area surrounding the Shepard home. Men were walking with light weapons and packs, a few with injuries rode horses. Pairs of horses pulled four twelve-pounder field howitzer cannons. Captain West ordered the first lieutenant to have troops find a site for overnight setup.

Shepard plantation home
(Credit, Patsy Cannon)

The captain brought a squad (twelve men with light arms) with him to the front porch of the house. He fired a shot into the air. He banged on the wooden floor with his gunstock and shouted, "Everyone in the house, come out right now."

Pa, Ma, and the eight children came running out—all were very afraid. Loaded guns were aimed at them by four soldiers. Smoke from the shot fired into the air was still present. James was so scared he peed in his pants and cried. The family members were asked to get in a line near the middle of the porch.

Eight armed soldiers got on the porch. Then five of them went inside to search the house. The other soldiers stood in the yard and guarded the goings-on with pointed guns. The three soldiers remaining on the porch looked the Shepards over good. The captain asked questions about food, animals, gunpowder, and the like. Pa provided information but did not reveal where things were hidden. He told the soldiers about the barn, smokehouse, chicken house, and stables. He told them about foods in the smokehouse.

A very important question Captain West asked was, "Does a confederate soldier live here?"

None did. Pa said, "No."

This appeared to help the soldiers adjust to the family. This truthful answer might have saved both the lives and property of the Shepard family. The soldiers with raised, loaded guns lowered them. Stress was only slightly reduced.

While Pa was talking and all family members were distracted, one soldier, Private Cason, approached Ellen. She was a good-looking young woman and relatively mature for her fifteen years of age. He looked her over with lustful eyes and asked her, "What's your name?"

"Ellen," she softly replied.

He said, "I will see you later, Ellen," and moved on to other duties.

Ellen was frightened, but there wasn't much she could do except worry and think about what he might be up to if he saw her again. She thought about ways to defend herself from unwanted advances.

Pa told the captain that he had voted the Union ticket. That seemed to endear the captain and members of the squad to him—at least a bit more.

Conversation ensued. Pa, as he later shared with Ma, did learn that this company of soldiers had come from the Battle of Corinth to Jackson and then plundered the town of Clinton. They were now on their way to Vicksburg. First, they would gather just west of the Big Black River near the community of Bovina in Eastern Warren County. There, they would join with other soldiers, including those from Illinois, Indiana, and Iowa, under Generals Sherman and Grant to go take the city of Vicksburg for the Union in a major war event later known as the Siege of Vicksburg.

Those searching the house found a few things and took them. Of particular interest were food and beverage items, such as cornmeal, potatoes, coffee, and whisky. There was nearly a half barrel of Dexter whisky that Pa had brought back from Vicksburg—enough for several soldiers that evening. The searchers did not take the small collection of letters and other documents the family was keeping.

One soldier opened the pie safe and found the plate of leftover chicken and uncut lemon cake from dinner with the preacher. He and the other soldiers in the house immediately ate the chicken and spit bones on the floor. Of course, the soldiers who got the heart and half-gizzard had no bones to get rid of. But considering what they had been having to eat, the soldiers found the cold, leftover, fried-in-lard chicken to be very tasty. They decided to take the cake with them to their overnight camping site, just a hundred yards or so away in front of the house.

Most of the day was spent pilfering for things of value to plunder. It was then time to set up camp. A relatively level field site near the house was chosen to set up for the night. It was near a dug well with good water and in the fruit and pecan orchard. Being early spring, about the only thing available in the orchard was strawberries—and not many of them. The soldiers had packed a few tents and cooking items for camping along their journey.

Four of the soldiers decided to stay the night in one of the vacant shacks that remained after the slaves moved out. Old remnants of beds and a fireplace were available. Some of the other soldiers thought these four might have been gay, but this notion was not confirmed.

The soldiers weren't exactly in dress uniform, and nor were they freshly bathed. Body odors were strong and penetrating. Clothing was frayed and often dirty. A few had stains on their pants because of the diarrhea they had suffered. Their hair was scraggly and their faces unshaven for the most part. A few appeared sickly with colds and related ailments, such as ringworm and, perhaps, syphilis. Some had head lice and often scratched their scalps. In spite of all this, it was fortunate that the shots fired on the first day of encampment did not injure anyone. Overall, they were in better condition than the Confederate troops of a couple of weeks ago had been.

A few of the soldiers had gone over the house and outbuildings, searching for anything that would be useful. Small amounts of meat were taken from the smokehouse. Gunshots were heard from near the hog pen. Two seventy-pound pigs were killed; primitively butchered; and, after gutting, roasted over a fire in the encampment. The fire singed the hair off (creating a bad odor); crusted the skin; and, after a couple or so hours, cooked through the carcasses. One soldier took the livers from the two pigs, cut them into slices, and tried to fry the slices in hot lard. Now, it was time for the troops to eat.

Pa's Kentucky Dexter drinking and medicine whisky was confiscated. A few soldiers began drinking before the tents were all up. Staggering about and slurring their words were signs they were into it. One who'd particularly imbibed had too much and began throwing up. Sad. Not much was in the vomit except a few particles of the chewed chicken gizzard he had taken from the pie safe. He hadn't eaten since breakfast that day, except for the leftover chicken. Two soldiers had piccolos and began playing them. Some of the soldiers joined in by singing, clapping, and dancing about. Their euphoria was likely the result of being in a good camping site.

No one in the Shepard family rested well that night. Soldiers were at hand. Their behavior was unpredictable. Four soldiers stayed up to guard the encampment. One soldier had said he would see Ellen later, and that made her particularly fearful. Ellen made up her mind that she would defend herself as she needed. Also, there were Ellen's slightly younger sisters. Of course, Ma was only thirty-three years of age and still quite attractive. But everyone made it through the night OK. What would happen when daylight came?

The next morning, the soldiers were out and about at dawn. Fires were started for limited cooking of breakfast. No toilets were available; soldiers relieved themselves wherever convenient but never inside the camping area. Large leaves were used to wipe after, as the soldiers would say, "taking a crap." The camp was taken down in preparation for the march to the next site a few miles away. But the soldiers didn't leave immediately.

Shortly after taking down the camp, some continued searching around the outbuildings for things of value. One freshly dug site near the hog pen got their attention. The soldiers checked and found a pottery container of gunpowder under a small pile of freshly dug soil. This made some of them furious, particularly their commanding officer.

They returned to the Shepard home, fired three shots into the air, and called out much as they had on the previous day when they'd arrived. The family fearfully went onto the porch as ordered. Loaded guns were aimed at them. The captain shouted in terse terms about the gunpowder. The family hadn't told the soldiers about it (but they hadn't been specifically asked about gunpowder). What else was hidden? None of the Shepards spoke a word.

Several soldiers loudly stepped onto the porch. One was Private Cason, who walked straight to Ellen. He softly asked, "Remember me?"

Of course, she did. He'd struck fear in her on the previous day. Just when she said, "Yes," Private Cason stood behind her, pressing his body against hers. He put his right hand around her waist and pulled her more tightly to him. He reached around and put his left hand on her left breast. He stood tightly touching her body. Soldiers who noticed this ignored it; they did not step in to defend Ellen. Such troop behavior was not uncommon among both the Confederate and Union forces.

Just as he pulled her tighter and whispered in her ear, "You are a beautiful woman," she vigorously defended herself, pushing his left hand away from her breast and elbowing firmly into his gut with her right arm. This forced him back about a foot, just enough for Ellen, with all her might, to swing her clinched right fist, hitting him firmly in the crotch. He bent over, gasped for air, and stumbled to the edge of the porch. None of her family noticed, as they were distracted by the goings-on and threat of burning by the other soldiers. Ellen never told anyone about this except her mother. If Pa knew, he might have become irate and incited hard feelings and violence.

Just after Ellen had defended herself and Private Cason was on the edge of the porch, a big shout of "Fire!" was heard. Gunpowder had been thrown in a four-foot-long streak on the porch floor. It was to propel a fire that would quickly burn the house. That frightened Private Cason, and he jumped off the porch.

Ellen was free of assault for now but concerned about her home and what might happen later. She had heard reports of other women and how soldiers had taken advantage of them.

Pa pleaded not to set the gunpowder on fire. Ma pleaded the same. The children were sobbing and begging. Ellen and her just younger sister, Rachel, screamed, begging the soldiers not to burn the house.

Anyway, the persuasion by Ma and Pa and the children was sufficient. Pa even reminded the soldiers of what he'd said yesterday about voting the Union ticket. The captain ordered that the soldier not to ignite the gunpowder. The house was spared. Before departing, the captain left a warning: "If this house is ever painted or made fancy, we will come back and burn it to the ground. No Confederate soldiers are to ever live here."

That warning by the Union troops was heeded for more than the next hundred years. In fact, no member of the military ever lived in the house; nor did any member of the family serve in the military. It was always Pa's teaching that peace was better than war. He often wondered about the good of the US Civil War. He had always felt that slavery wasn't right. He was more progressive than most Southern white folks, considering his Midwestern orientation. Pa agreed with US President Lincoln's Emancipation Proclamation that had taken effect on January 1, 1863.

The family rested a little better as the soldiers began their march toward Champion Hill for their next camping site. Some food was gone. All of Pa's Dexter whisky had been taken (the previous night's imbibing might have helped save the house). Two pigs had been prepared by the soldiers and eaten on-site. The horses and other animals hidden in the thick woods of Shepard Hills were still there. Maybe these would be the last troops to come through.

Ritz and Bummer had stayed hidden under the house next to the base of the big chimney. They hardly came out at all during any of the ordeal. But when the Union soldiers left, they did and wagged their tails at the Shepard children. This helped the family get over their ordeal. As for the cats, they went about their usual work of controlling the rat population in the corncrib.

The Shepard family tried to return to a calm state. They had been spared major tragedy. The house was not burned. Ellen was safe—all family members were safe. Life would go on in the post-slave era, but it was a time of poverty and deprivation. They never knew when another group of soldiers might show up. Actions of Confederate and Union military forces during the Civil War brought great havoc to Tinnin and the Shepard family.

Pa often shared with his family questions about war. He would begin with, "Why was war needed?" Ellen was always eager to hear his explanations; he sounded so reasoned and eloquent to her. Pa would say, "Humans are intelligent beings and should be able to settle differences in humane ways without war." He would say that war caused great human loss. It killed and injured people and destroyed what they had made through their efforts. Southerners should have agreed with the policies of their nation. Slavery was not justifiable in a moral society.

Another thing Pa did not like was the popular notion of guns. He wanted them used discretely and with caution, not flaunted or used as threats. He felt guns had been created primarily for one purpose—to give one human an advantage over another human or over an animal by threatening and/or taking its life. Of course, he and his family had been bullied by men with guns when the Confederate and Union forces came through Tinnin. He was glad no guns had been discharged by troops to physically injure his family. Soldiers had used guns to harvest some of the animals on the farm. He pretty well thought that anyone who carried a gun was insecure and did so in an attempt to enhance low self-esteem and bully other people. So, it was just as well that he had only an old double-barrel shotgun.

Pa's ability to lead such discussions was probably a product of his Midwestern upbringing. His views on his role as the head of household and his embrace of the fundamentals of education were also Midwestern in roots. There were likely times when Pa thought that if he had stayed in Indiana he would have avoided all the turmoil he had found in Tinnin, Mississippi. However, he thought of Tinnin as his home and the place he should live and seek wealth if any could be found.

Even with war threats and destruction, people in the Tinnin community found pride in where they lived. They felt there was good quality of life, but that thought was primarily associated with white people. Blacks, though they did not enjoy increasing equality in most regards, were adjusting and leaving with their not yet realized newfound emancipation.

The surrounding geography included hills with wooded areas that provided habitat for important meat wildlife, such as rabbits, deer, and squirrels. Though Pa was not a hunter, he would let others hunt on his land if they shared their harvest. Creek bottoms provided good lands for row cropping (except following a heavy sustained rain, when runoff water in the Bogue Chitto Creek would get out of its banks). Springs in the hills provided good-quality fresh water. The air was clean and free of the pollution found in cities where coal was burned and ironwork carried out. Overall, the Tinnin community was a beautiful and healthful place to live—if the troops would just stay away.

But it was spring, and crops needed to be started. This required work by each individual in the family who was old enough to work in the field. Cotton, corn, sweet potatoes, and pinder (the Gullah name for peanut) had to be planted as crops. The vegetable garden had to be readied and planted. Fortunately, a few winter vegetable crops had survived, such as collard greens and turnips; these were helpful in getting through rough times with troops. Before the recent troop experience, potatoes, cabbage, onions, radishes, and lettuce had been planted. Spring and summer vegetable crops should now be planted, which included okra, tomatoes, squash, field peas, and butter beans. A lot of hard labor was required, breaking the land with mule-pulled plows and using hoes to plant by hand.

Youngsters in the Shepard family who were approaching adulthood were unsettled by what they had witnessed.

Some were wondering if this war experience would ever end. And life was hard—lots of work and little income. Things should be better in the future. There would be ups and downs, as well as successes and failures. Pleasures in life had to be gleaned from simple things that didn't require money.

Children in the family began to think about their future. Would they have food? Clothing? Safety? Their experiences caused them to grow up quickly. School wasn't much of an issue—no one in the family went to school more than a few days each year. The Tinnin schoolhouse was not a very impressive place and usually had one teacher for eight grades. But in spite of the school situation, all of the older Shepard children could read and write to an extent—at least enough to get by.

Ellen dreamed of a future romance and life as a wife, mother, and homemaker. She had entered womanhood. She had to sort things out for herself. Sometimes, things looked bleak. How could she live a good life? She wasn't sure if a good life even existed for her.

The dream was of a loving, kind, and considerate man who would carry her away to a secure life of happiness with plenty to live on.

3

Finding Romance

Ellen and all of the Shepard family adjusted as best they could following their ordeal at the hands of the Union soldiers. Now, if the Confederates would stay away and let the family and farm heal. And they did, as the Union forces had pretty well depleted the will of the Confederate soldiers to fight for a losing cause.

The fall harvest of 1863 had been made. Eleven bales of cotton worth about $375 had been picked and ginned. Production was considerably down from a couple of years ago when the farm still had plenty of labor. Beyond the money for the cotton, there wasn't much cash income available. Self-sufficiency was very important. Grow potatoes, corn, beans, greens, okra, squash, and other foods. Raise a few animals, particularly pigs for butchering and chickens for eggs and meat. Not much was gleaned from hunting game; the Shepard family was never much into hunting. They tried to use some of the new Federal reconstruction programs, but that wasn't easy. Times were hard.

With the harvest done, Ellen had a little spare time. She did some knitting and general things around the house. Her thoughts began to wonder about a larger world. Ellen and her first cousin, Susan Ratliff, were about the same age and shared some of the same interests in getting a man. Since their homes were a mile apart, they often got together and talked about what they wanted in a man and assessed local young men in terms of their dreams.

Except for an occasional outing at a church, singing or for a barbecue, they didn't have contact with many men in the Tinnin Community who were eligible or met the standards they had. Susan and Ellen would typically find fault with the local young men—needs a bath, not considerate, poor personal skills, lack of education, little potential for income, dishonest or not trustworthy, and immoral by the standards of the day. Some might drink too much whisky or carry on close relationships with women they deemed inappropriate for the man they wanted.

Thanks to a friend, Susan was about to help change their lack of men. On the second Friday in November, Susan walked over to Ellen's home and told Ellen she and her friend, Beatrice, were going to Brandon on Saturday.

They would spend the night with the family of an aunt, attend a brush arbor party on Saturday evening, and return late Sunday. They invited Ellen to go with them. But before she went, Ellen wanted to know more about their activities.

Other than the experience being a good outing, the incentive was that there were a few young, single men in Brandon. They had come there to help reconstruct the town and railroad, which had been damaged by soldiers in the war. Susan explained to Ellen, "These men have jobs and make money." Now that was appealing. Each wanted a man who had sufficient income to provide for life's needs.

During the war, there had been very little money among the people. But she didn't know much about the education, morals, and personal backgrounds of the men—they had come from all around. Maybe they were dodging military service with the Confederate or Union forces, or maybe they had just gotten out of prison, or maybe they had deserted a wife and family in another state. Anyway, Susan, Beatrice, and Ellen decided they would go and check out the situation. They wanted to have a weekend of fun!

Susan said the fare on the train from Clinton to Brandon was one dollar each way. They would need two dollars. Susan would have her younger brother, Robbie, drive them to the Clinton depot in the family's wagon and return on Sunday to get them. That sure sounded good to Ellen. She had turned sixteen in September and was approaching the age of major interest in men—and particularly, men who had jobs and made money. She also wanted her man to have all of his body parts, such as not missing a leg or an eye.

So, Ellen got permission from her Ma and Pa to go— not always easy. She told them her cousin had invited her to go with her and a friend. She didn't tell them there were possibly some single men of interest. She packed a few things, including a fairly fancy dress and her "prettying-up stuff." She pretty well had most everything ready to go on Friday night.

Saturday morning arrived, and the wagon driven by Susan's brother came but about five minutes late. Susan and Beatrice were in the wagon. Ellen, always conscientious, was concerned they might be late arriving at the depot and miss the train. She mentioned it. Robbie popped the reigns on the horses rumps to speed them up. They arrived at the depot in Clinton nearing 9:00 a.m. and caught the 9:23 train to Jackson; it continued on to Brandon.

The train arrived in Brandon at 12:28. Susan's aunt was there to meet them. She took them to her home where they refreshed and prettied up a tad before going to the barbecue, singing, and dancing at the local Presbyterian church. (It was a tad more liberal about such activities than the local Mason Chapel in Tinnin and defined sin, whatever that was, a little differently.) Ellen was very pretty and womanly after getting ready. She was enough to tempt any man's eyes.

A small crowd was there when they arrived at the church on Government Street in Brandon. More people were arriving. Ellen was a tad shy at first. She was experiencing a lot of new things. The aunt introduced her to a few people. She got some of the barbecued goat, a baked sweet potato, and a cornpone. She, Susan, and Beatrice took their plates over to an empty table outside to sit.

Men in the crowd had been admiring the young women, particularly good-looking Ellen. Three men got their food and sauntered over to sit with the women. The one who sat by Ellen asked her name; she shyly said "Ellen. What's yours?"

He said, "Jasper," and asked, "Where do you live? Do you like this barbecue?" Those and others such questions guided their conversation.

Both Ellen and Jasper instantly felt some sort of attraction to each other. They continued to sit at the table and talk after they'd finished eating. Susan and Beatrice had left the table with the men they were sitting with. Ellen had overheard Beatrice's man say there was some fresh, soft hay in the stable on the other side of the church building where folks put their horses when in church. Both couples were soon nowhere to be seen.

Ellen wasn't sure about what was next with Jasper.

She kept remembering what her mother always said. "No young man good enough to marry wants to marry a used woman."

Apparently, Jasper had some of the same feelings, but Ellen didn't know about his past activities and experiences with women. Maybe he was trying to woo her along. Ellen carefully structured the conversation and activities in a "safe" direction. She kept remembering what her mother had taught her about proper relationships between men and women.

Ellen wanted an honest man of high morals for a long-term relationship. She wanted a loving husband who would care for her, protect her, father her children, and be kind. She wanted a good provider.

Ellen and Jasper kept sitting at the table and talking. War had created so much destruction and uncertainty, and it was always on her mind. A time of calmness with an interesting man was good.

Ellen told Jasper a little about herself. She began by telling him about her family and that she lived with her parents and seven younger siblings. Next, she spoke about her home and farm. The farm had 1,200 acres of hills and creek bottoms. They planted cotton (their main source of money), corn, and other southern crops. She talked about the little community of Tinnin where they lived. She told Jasper that he needed to come see it for himself, and he said he might.

And what about his background?

Jasper told Ellen that he was in Brandon working to upgrade railroad structures to the East that had been damaged by Confederate troops as they'd left. These structures were toward a little town known as Pelahatchie. The Confederates did not want Union troops to find a useable railroad. On the other hand, they did not want to completely destroy the rails, as they might need them in the future. Jasper got paid at the rate of $1.75 a day and was provided boarding in a nearby boarding house, known as Sister Annie's.

The music was beginning to start under the brush arbor by the church building. The music was provided by an elderly man with a fiddle, a young woman playing a washtub, a man with a guitar, and former slave named Sam playing a beat up old piano. There were some chairs around the music group and an open area where dancing could be done.

Jasper took Ellen's hand and asked her to go over near the music. This was something new for Ellen—no man had ever taken her hand and asked her to go with him any place. She smiled at him. They arose from the bench seat at the table and walked together holding hands to a spot under the brush arbor. She had a certain feeling of infatuation or something about her that she couldn't readily explain to herself in her mind. She looked at Jasper and tried to size him up. He was kind of tall and relatively thin but with ample muscles. He was whiskered, and his clothing needed care, though it appeared relatively clean. He did not have a body odor, as did soldiers she had experienced earlier. His teeth looked OK. Jasper didn't appear sickly. He was well tanned and had calloused hands and blue eyes.

One big question Ellen had was his age. How old was he? With his slightly graying hair, he kind of looked like he was as old as her Pa. But she thought he couldn't be. She was reluctant to ask. So, she asked where he was from.

And he replied, "Another state back to the east here."

Then she asked how long he had been in Brandon.

He replied, "Going on three weeks."

Ellen told him that where she lived was in the Tinnin community of Hinds County. She was in Brandon with friends.

Just as Ellen was getting up courage to ask Jasper his age, the old man with the fiddle announced it was time for a singing. The songs were mostly religious—church hymns such as "Rock of Ages" and "My Faith Looks Up to Thee." Other songs included "Goober Peas," "I Wish I Was in Dixie," and "Yellow Rose of Texas." This last one would be of particular note in their future, but Ellen and Jasper didn't know it.

Ellen knew some of the words to the songs; Jasper knew a few. They both enjoyed trying to sing. She observed that he knew the words of songs from the South better than those of the North. Of course, Ellen's Pa was from Indiana and had taught his family a few of the songs he knew from the North.

After about forty-five minutes, the fiddler announced that the singing was over and that the band would play more music. "Dance if you want to," he said. On the second number, Jasper tugged Ellen's hand, and they were up getting into the dancing. Some numbers were fast; others, slow. After a couple of dances, they decided to walk outside. It was getting dark. They would walk into the woods near the church.

Just as they were going out the door, Beatrice and her man were coming inside. No eye contact was made. Beatrice had a couple of pieces of straw in her hair. They went to the dance floor and began doing their do. Susan and her man weren't to be seen.

Ellen and Jasper strolled on their way out, holding hands. After they had taken a couple of steps into the woods, Jasper said that Sister Annie's Boarding House was only a short walking distance. He asked Ellen if she would go to the house with him. She said yes. But yes made her quite nervous.

They entered the parlor at Sister Annie's and sat on a sofa. Across the room sitting on another sofa was a couple obviously falling in love or something—maybe not love but passion. Ellen had all kinds of feelings about this experience. She did not know what Jasper's next suggestion might be, but she kept holding his hand.

Ellen did not have to wait long for Jasper's next suggestion. "Want to see my room?"

She said, "Yes, I would like to briefly see your room."
All the while, flashing in Ellen's mind was her commitment to herself and her family that her "specialness"
would wait until her wedding night.

She saw his room, and, after quickly looking around,
said, "It's time for me to go back to the church to get with
my friends and leave."

Then Jasper said, "Are you sure?"

Ellen answered, "Yes, but let's hold hands and talk
some more." She did not want this to end. Something
about the situation made her want it to last a while longer.

When Ellen and Jasper got back to the Presbyterian
Church, both Susan and Beatrice were sitting with their
men at one of the barbecue tables. The band had stopped
playing for the night. Susan's aunt would soon be there to
pick them up.

Jasper told Ellen he would like to see her tomorrow.
Ellen indicated that she was staying on the edge of town
toward a community known as Gulde. "We will be leaving early to catch the train to Clinton and home," she
added. Jasper indicated that he would come early to talk
and tell her goodbye. Ellen indicated that she would also
like to see him.

She told Jasper goodnight and went with Susan and
Beatrice to get in the wagon to ride away. Ellen waived

at Jasper until they were out of sight—longer than usual because of the bright harvest moon.

Was Ellen excited! She had met a man for whom she had almost immediate feelings. She barely slept that night and was up extra early the next day to see Jasper. Of course, she didn't know if he was a man of his word and would show up. He did. Ellen rushed to greet him. They talked; she told him to write her a letter and to visit her in Tinnin. He agreed to do so (even though he wasn't much at writing).

The threesome caught the 11:32 a.m. train in Brandon for Jackson and Clinton. Robbie was there at the depot to meet them at 2:30 p.m. and drive them to their home in Tinnin on the wagon.

Thoughts kept going through Ellen's mind: Would she ever see Jasper again? Could she get him to come to Tinnin? Little did she know that Jasper had feelings for her. He immediately wrote and mailed a letter to her in Tinnin. She got it about the first of December 1863. He wanted to come to see her in late December. He said he thought he was falling in love with her. She wrote back and said it would be fine to come for a visit. "I can introduce you to Pa and Ma and my sisters and brothers."

After another exchange of letters, arrangements were made for Jasper to visit the day after Christmas. Ellen talked Pa into letting her use the wagon to go get a young man at the Clinton depot who she had met in Brandon.

She talked her sister, Rachel, into going with her. The horse and wagon with Ellen and Rachel arrived at the depot on December 26 about a half hour before the train.

The train stopped; passengers were getting off and on. No Jasper. Had he stood her up? And then he appeared with a small bouquet of gardenia blossoms. He was late getting off because he was helping an elderly preacher at the Women's Institute get off. Ellen thought to herself that Jasper was a kind man. She rushed to greet him. And they hugged. She had never hugged a man other than her father before, but this was a different kind of hug. There was a romantic feel to it. Jasper handed Ellen the gardenias; she smelled them and enjoyed the fragrance. She thanked him. Ellen introduced Jasper to Rachel, and they got in the wagon for the five-mile ride to their home.

They arrived at the Shepard home in Tinnin about 4:30. Bummer came from under the house to bark ferociously at the stranger. Rachel jumped from the wagon to calm Bummer by patting his head. She and Ellen knew he could be mean with people he hadn't sniffed before. Ellen and Jasper unloaded, and Ellen tied the horses, still hitched to the wagon, to a post. They all went on the porch. Pa and Ma came out; a couple of sisters peered out through a window.

Ellen introduced Jasper to her father and mother. She said, "I call them Pa and Ma; you can call them Mr. Shepard and Mrs. Shepard."

Pa welcomed Jasper, and the two men exchanged a few greetings. He asked him where he was from, how old he was, and what work he did to earn a living. Jasper said he was from back east, was thirty-six years old, and worked for the railroad. Some of those answers didn't sit well with Pa. Other questions went through his mind: What about previous marriages or communal relationships? Had he fathered children he didn't talk about? Had he been involved in crime? What work skills did he have? So many questions; so few answers. Little did Ellen know that she might never learn full details even after several years.

Pa, in a stern voice, asked, "What do you mean by back east?"

Jasper indicated that he had been traveling for quite a while. He had stopped in many places, where he'd worked a while and moved on. He said he often told people he was born in South Carolina. Pa asked about his mother and daddy and what they did. Jasper indicated he'd had no recent communication with them and gave no names. Most of these answers did not sit well with Pa.

Ellen said Jasper was here for a couple of nights and would be leaving three days from now. Ma indicated he could sleep on a pallet under the steps that go upstairs. "We have some dry, fresh-from-the-crib corn shucks in a large cotton pick sack."

Jasper, trying to be gracious, said that would be fine. Ellen was a bit taken aback, but she knew there were Pa,

Ma, and eight children in the house and no extra beds. So, she needed to be content. After all, she was trying to introduce a new person to her family.

Ellen told Jasper she wanted to give him a showing around. She took him into the house kitchen, sitting room, the bedroom for Pa and Ma, the bedroom for the girls, and the bedroom for the boys. The privy was out back and was a two-holer. Water could be drawn from the well. They went outside so Ellen could continue showing Jasper around. Their first activity was to store the wagon they had ridden in from the depot under the shed and release the horses into the lot. Afterward, they walked past the smokehouse, stables, hog pen, chicken house, and other outbuildings. Ellen said, "I want to show you the crystal-clear flowing water in the spring branch."

They walked across a small area of open pasture; simultaneously, they reached for each other's hand. Holding hands, they approached the spring-fed branch on the edge of the woods. It was flowing nicely. Ellen told him the water was very good and that they would sometimes drink it. She showed him where a gourd dipper was kept for getting and drinking spring branch water. Jasper tried it and agreed it was good.

At that point, they simultaneously embraced each other. A long kiss followed. Wow! Ellen was in love; maybe Jasper was in love. After a few moments, they continued their stroll, holding hands.

Ellen and Jasper were gone on what Ellen had called "Jasper's showing around." It took longer than Pa and Ma thought it should—unless they went to fields some distance away. But they didn't think the two were that interested in the fields. They didn't know that Ellen and Jasper were taking an innocent romantic stroll through the woods past the spring branch.

But it was getting late in the December afternoon, and they figured they had better soon get back to the house.

Ma was fixing supper with the help of Rachel and Mag. Georgia Ann was looking after Ira, the baby brother, who was only a little over two years of age and the youngest of the Shepard children. Pa was out gathering the last eggs of the day. He would soon be in the house.

As the family gathered for supper, each of Ellen's siblings met Jasper. He tried to talk to them a little. They were very interested in who he was, where he was from, what kind of work he did, and if he had been to school. After all, this was the first man Ellen had brought home. They sat down at the table; Jasper had a seat next to Ellen. The meal wasn't very scrumptious—fried salt pork meat, dried butter beans, corn bread, and baked sweet potatoes. Jasper ate and expressed appreciation for his meal.

Afterward, Pa indicated that he wanted to talk with Jasper. Though the weather was kind of cool, in the early evening, the two men went on the front porch. Pa again asked about Jasper's parents, where he was from, and what kind of work he did. The answers still weren't very satisfactory. However, Jasper indicated that he had great respect and growing love for Ellen and would talk more soon.

Pa assumed, and rightly so, that a courtship was developing between Jasper and Ellen. Answers from Jasper were few and not very informative. He would talk with Ma and Ellen later.

It was getting dark. The coal oil lamps were lit. The shutters on the windows had been closed and secured. A fire was built in the fireplace to drive away some coolness in the air. General chatter and watching siblings play lasted about an hour. Then Pa said it was time to go to bed. He also said to Jasper, "And you know where your bed is. Right?" The implication was that Jasper was to stay in the pallet of fresh, dry corn shucks and not approach Ellen. But Pa didn't know that his daughter might go into the closet.

Everyone was about in bed. Pa went and peed off the porch as he did each night but moved to a different place. The coal oil lamps were blown out. A few embers in the fireplace glowed and would keep overnight to start the fire in the morning (with the help of pine heart kindling).

After everyone was asleep, Ellen sneaked out of her bed and opened the closet door under the steps that led to the attic. Jasper was there but not asleep. She got down on her knees and rubbed the hair on his head, and they kissed. He put his arms around her; she didn't resist. She pulled the closet door shut and lay beside him. They kissed again; he rubbed her shoulder. Passion was high, but Ellen remembered that her "specialness" was for another time. They lay side by side and talked lowly for about an hour. Ellen then left and went back to her own bed without waking members of the family (the six Shepard girls all shared the same room).

Next morning, everyone was up. Jasper got a little sleep in the shuck and cotton pick sack pallet in the closet under the steps. Ellen wanted to take him around Tinnin and, especially, to see Ratliff Store (that her grandparents ran), Mason Chapel, and the shabby schoolhouse. Ellen asked Pa if she could borrow the wagon for this.

Pa said, "No."

Ellen became upset and pleaded, saying, "We will walk."

Pa softened his mind and let her borrow the wagon. But she promised to use it carefully and treat the horses kindly. She must also do the harnessing and unhitching after the wagon was back. She agreed to this.

She didn't have to do the harnessing and hitching all by herself; Jasper would help. In fact, he was quite skilled at it. Experience from some past times and places proved useful. He just needed to know the exact ways Pa wanted things done.

On their ride, they learned of a singing that evening at

Mason Chapel. They made plans to go and enjoyed it. The singing was a bit "churchier" than that at the Presbyterian church in Brandon. As Ellen's Pa has said, sin has a range of meanings—sin in one situation might not be sin in another. This singing might have been a little straitlaced for a couple who was falling in love. Or maybe it was more appropriate, considering Ellen's moral standards.

If someone wanted a liquid "something" before, during, or after the singing, it was available behind the Ratliff Store. Under the wagon shed, an out-of-towner from Bolton would be there with home brew. Somehow, the Ratliffs always paid no attention to what was going on under the wagon shed. Of course, it wouldn't have been there if some people hadn't wanted it. But Ellen and Jasper did not go there for a sample; several others at the singing did, and when they returned, their imbibing was quite evident.

That evening, Jasper slept on the same pallet of corn shucks in a cotton pick sack as he had the night before. Ellen came into the closet after all others in the family were asleep to tell him goodnight, thank him for the day, and remind him of tomorrow's early schedule. Passion was high, and the night ended with a big kiss.

Next morning, Jasper was up and ready to go to the Clinton depot and back to Brandon. It was time to say goodbye. Hugs and kisses were made. Jasper asked Ellen to come to Brandon. Ellen asked Jasper to come back to

Tinnin. Letters would be exchanged. They would work things out so they could have some time together!

Pa had his say with Ellen. He did not think Jasper would be a good fit in the family. There was too much age difference—he was thirty-six going on thirty-seven, and she was sixteen. He was more than twice her age. Ellen would explain the age difference by saying many young women married older men. Most of the time, the marriages worked as long as the wife followed the instructions of her husband. There weren't enough men to go around. The war had caused the deaths of many men, and others had been permanently maimed. How could such a marriage ever work? Pa thought Jasper was little more than a vagrant roaming around the South. He also thought there was a lot he didn't know about Jasper. He wanted Ellen to have a better man! But Pa didn't change Ellen's mind.

With passion as high as it was, a way would be found for Jasper and Ellen to be together again. So, in mid-January, Jasper made another trip to Tinnin. He was there three days. It was good hog-killing weather, and Jasper knew how to do what needed to be done. He worked side by side with Pa for a full day. Their work enhanced the family's meals with fried fresh pork tenderloin and pig's liver. The bladder was removed, drained of liquid, and hung up to dry in the wagon shed. Once it was dry, baby Ira could play with it like a ball. It would last until it burst, and that could be fairly soon with rough play.

And, as in past times, Jasper slept on the pallet made of corn shucks in a cotton pick sack in the closet under the steps. Of course, he and Ellen had time together. Ellen would sneak into the closet to kiss him good night. And on the last night, said she loved him. He said the same back to her.

Jasper found his way back to Tinnin at least four more times before the end of February. Their romance was moving fast. And Valentine's Day sped the romance along. Jasper came to see Ellen and brought her a small bottle of perfume. She adored it; she had never had perfume before. They embraced, took walks, held hands, and talked about a possible future together.

They reasoned that Pa and Ma had a big house that could be home to a young couple, and the 1,200 acres of farm land provided enough for them to get into farming. Life and work would be hard. But that was all they had ever known. They dreamed they would later get a house of their own and become more independent. Or as a newlywed couple, they could continue living in Sister Annie's Boarding House in Brandon. He could continue with his job, and she could seek work. But Jasper didn't like the notion of his bride living at Sister Annie's; some tough guys stayed there, and she might not be safe around them.

Jasper and Ellen never knew what soldiers would be doing and when they would pass through the area. The Union troops coming from Vicksburg were under orders to be very destructive. Any Confederates were fairly well demoralized because of the defeats they'd experienced. That, however, didn't keep them from being mean. It was best to avoid where soldiers might be, and that wasn't easy, as the line of movement from Vicksburg to the east was along the route of the railroad. Until the war was over and all matters about it settled, uneasiness would always be a part of life in certain areas of the South.

More plans were made before the Valentine's visit was over. Things had to be kept simple; there wasn't much money or time. Those plans would go into early March. And Ellen was not sure about the feelings of Pa and Ma, particularly Pa. He generally didn't feel that the young men his daughters had brought around would make good marrying material. He wanted the very best for his daughters.

Love was all about Ellen and Jasper. They were deeply infatuated with each other. But how could it be lasting? They hadn't known each other that long. There were many uncertainties. They didn't have education, personal possessions, or other things of worth. But they knew how to work and take risks. Ellen was smart, and Jasper was experienced; together, they could figure things out.

4

What Pa Told Ma (After a Private Talk with Jasper)

"Ma, I have something important to tell you," Pa said, "and you must never tell anyone—not ever!"

"What?" Ma replied. "What is it about? Is it good or bad? Has a man gotten to one of our girls? They are still quite young, you know. It must be serious. You know we have always privately talked with each other. Yes, I will keep it private."

"Listen, Ma. If a man had gotten to one of our daughters, I would organize a group to get him put in the county jail. When we were finished, he would no longer be a man. Understand?" Of course, Pa was talking about something he would never do. He felt that every man needed to have appropriate private parts!

Next, Pa began telling Ma some of what Jasper had told him. What Pa said was what he'd garnered from his conversation with Jasper on the porch, during their walk to the garden, and from the time they'd sat on the wood pile under the old black walnut tree near the corner of the yard. It was told to Ma with some clarification by Pa.

"This is serious stuff," Pa said, "I am upset that our Ellen says she is going to marry that man. Surely she can find someone better. I want her to have a man who is a good fit for our family. I told Jasper that we believe in being truthful, and that is what is expected of him."

Ma spoke up. "The way you are talking, it sounds like a big problem with this Jasper man. You know the war has taken so many men. Good, young men are in short supply. Our Ellen has feelings like most all young women. She wants a man to live with and have babies. But she needs a man who will treat her honorably. I once heard a preacher in his sermon say 'loving, faithful, generous, and kind.' That summarizes the kind of man Ellen should have."

Pa continued, giving a summary of what he had learned, as well as his personal assessment. He said, "I believe Jasper is a roving, no-good pioneer who may never settle down. However, he has a few useful skills."

Because they'd worked side by side butchering a hog, Pa had observed his competence in doing the work that was needed. "He knows how to slit a hog's throat for a good bleed and put the pig in a barrel of scalding hot water before scraping off the hair. He is a good scraper—fast and firm. He makes clean skin. You know we don't like cracklin's and salt meat with coarse hair stubbles. Those stubbles don't feel good in my mouth."

They also talked a bit about Jasper's upbringing.

"Jasper didn't have a papa at home. You know, that makes a big difference in how a boy develops. I don't think he understands how a decent, God-fearing family is supposed to live together," Pa said. "And he has always lived in a small house with a bunch of folks crowded together or in a makeshift place in the woods."

"He may never learn to be a part of a good family. That's what makes Jasper a bad choice to be the husband of our firstborn daughter. He knows how to scrounge for food in a forest and river bottom. He told me he has caught and cooked both possum and coon to keep from being hungry. I sense he may also have begged neighbors for food. He is close to being a deadbeat."

Ma responded, "He doesn't sound like a good person to add to our family. You don't think you are being too harsh on him, do you? Maybe we can convince Ellen there is a better man for her. But, gee, she has to find that better man first."

"Jasper is not a good example for our younger daughters either. What kind of man will they bring home? I have seen Mag with a short, fat man who has a wooden leg. I believe she calls him Sibley—or, rather, Mr. Sibley. You know how some men want women to say 'Mr.' Mag says he is her sweetheart."

"And, Rachel—have you noticed?—has been going riding in the woods and down to the creek with a man she says is her beau. Somehow, I wonder about the gardenia flower he brings her and the blanket she puts in his surrey before they ride. On some Sundays they go to church singings but not to preachin's. How can they hear what the preacher says from the Bible about being saved if they ain't there?"

"Ma, I asked Jasper some specific questions," Pa said, "and he told me a few things that helped me learn more about him. For example, he told me that his mother was a woman by the name of Sarah Lee. He said he was born to her in March of 1827. I recall he said the twenty-seventh day. They lived in a small log cabin with her brother Jordan Lee and his family in the Broad River bottom area of Richland County, South Carolina. He, just as his older brother, William, was given their mother's Lee family name."

"I pressed him about his father. He said his mother appeared to not be exactly sure who his father was, though his last name was likely Faust or Frost. Possibly the man was named Casper or Goss Faust. Jasper said that there was a large Faust family with several young men in the river bottom area.

"He said his mother was often quite friendly with some of the Fausts. He once saw her and one of the young men coming from beneath a clump of huckleberry bushes near the river. They said that they had been picking berries."[1]

"Jasper did say Sarah's brother, Jordan, was not his father. Any relations between them, if there had ever been any, seem to have been before her brother was married. Now that kind of stuff really bothers me! In this Shepard family, we don't approve of such. It is a sin in the eyes of God. People in the community will shun us if they ever hear such."

Ma interrupted, "Pa, are you saying that Sarah and Jordan had been acting as if they were married? That would be incest."

"No," Pa responded, "Jasper didn't say such with certainty. Jasper said he sometimes used the Goss name, rather than what he thought was his real name of Jasper," he continued. "What is Jasper hiding? Maybe he was trying to identify with someone. The name matter was never made clear to me.

"His brother or half brother (depending on who the father was) William, as Jasper told me, was born on

---

[1] Family Tree Y-DNA testing of descendants of Jasper Henry Lee in the year 2020 indicated genetic sharing of current generation Faust male individuals with the great-grandson of Jasper Henry Lee named Jasper Sloan Lee. The relationship existed though it was several generations removed.

September 12, 1812, when his mother, Sarah, was thirteen years of age. Some folks thought she was only twelve! He was her first child and the only one before Jasper.

"William was fifteen years of age when Jasper was born. William's father was also likely a Faust. A sister, Mary, was born in 1833. In each case, someone in the community helped her deliver the babies. I just wonder if they all had the same father and why there were so many years between their births. Maybe she wasn't as involved with men as she could have been."

Ma spoke up, "Why didn't that Sarah Lee woman have more babies? You know, women around here have a baby every year or two until they can't. In some cases, having babies kills the woman. No doubt, Sarah was lucky about the baby situation."

"Here's what I think," Pa said. "Though they always wanted to do better in life, times were hard. They weren't always well behaved. I don't think they practiced the teachings of the Bible as related to being good people. They sometimes sinned in bad ways. But without knowing what the Bible taught, they didn't know how wrong they were living." In those times food was often limited; I don't think they had enough to eat. Their clothing was made of animal skins and hand-me-down rags (occasionally something of silk).

Ways to get from one place to another were quite limited. They walked or rode a horse, mule, donkey, or ox. Sometimes, the animals were borrowed. Other times, they caught rides on wagons when other people were traveling.

Even though they wanted to be migrating pioneers, they had to stay where they were for a while because they didn't feel safe going farther to the west. The Indian situation had to calm down before they could cross Georgia and Alabama. The families were fearful, but they made it safely. They were afraid of physical attack—a big threat to their well-being, particularly in the Creek nation."

The time of needing a passport for safe travel was over in the 1820s and 1830s, depending on where you went and whose land you crossed.

"Jasper told me the situation as he understood it. Sarah and her children began migrating with a group from the Faust family into Alabama and Mississippi. They spread out in several directions," Pa said. "And they likely never saw each other again.

"Jasper told me they settled for a while in Tallapoosa County, Alabama, and then Talladega, Alabama, where Sarah's brother's son, Jordan Lee, Jr., was married in 1843. After a few years, Jordan, Jr., and his wife with four children split from the migrating group and went to Indiana. Contact was lost with him at that time; no one has heard anything since.

"Sarah's brother, Jordan Lee, died in 1847," Pa said, "based on what Jasper told me. No doubt, that left Sarah with additional responsibilities."

Pa continued, "Jasper told me that his brother William married Charity Suttle in 1834 in Perry, Alabama. Afterward, he and his new wife split away from the traveling group and went to Tennessee. A son, William Henry, Jr., was born in 1837. Charity died that year. William Henry, Sr., later went to Mississippi and Arkansas, and along the way, according to Jasper, he seemed to take and discard wives. He fathered children—as Jasper said, 'my nieces and nephews'—with those wives.

"Jasper said that, in another generation, it would be impossible to figure out the William Lee family! Of course, he hasn't seen or heard from his brother in several years. He relies on travelers to give him information but rarely sees anyone who knows anything."

Ma piped up with, "It surely sounds like a sinful, impure family to me. I just wish I had talked to Jasper. He gave you a lot of details, as you have shared with me. Maybe I could straighten him out."

Pa continued with something like, "There ain't no way of straightening him out. He is nearly thirty-seven years of age, and thinks he is very smart. You know, Ma, he ain't right for Ellen."

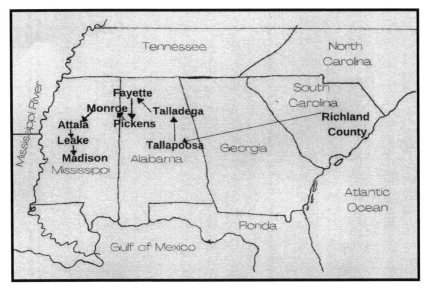

The migration route of Jasper Henry Lee from South Carolina into Mississippi with several members of his family as well as other families. (Note: Hinds County is adjacent to Madison County. Vicksburg is in Warren County, which is west of Hinds County on the Mississippi River.)

"Here's something else he told me," Pa continued. "After William struck out on his own, Jasper and his mother and sister migrated into northwest Alabama. I believe he said Lamar County. There he met a young woman whose family was, at that time, also on the move.

"The woman and her parental family soon crossed the state border line into Monroe County, Mississippi. In 1845 at age eighteen, Jasper married the young woman, whose name was Nancy Pickle (age twenty). Now, she was Nancy Pickle Lee.

"Jasper said that there were a fair number of Pickle family members around Monroe County. Some had small farms; others had stores and blacksmith shops. I believe they were mostly good folks.

"Interestingly, Jasper said he put up a $200 marriage bond to Nancy's brother George Pickle. Whatever happened to the bond is unknown. Governor A. G. Brown of Mississippi held the bond, as was state law at the time. But where did Jasper get that amount of money to secure the bond? Most women were free for the taking."

Pa told Ma, "Jasper was pretty open about how he and Nancy lived. He said he and Nancy lived in barns and cabins while they did farmwork. It was often hard, manual labor. In 1847, Nancy became pregnant. She gave birth to Sarah Isabelle Lee the following year. There was no question in Jasper's mind about who the daddy was— him! Jasper told me Nancy was a faithful wife.

"At that point and for some unknown reason, Jasper deserted his wife and baby daughter. Maybe Jasper had been unfaithful, and Nancy made him leave. Nancy and baby were apparently in dire poverty and returned to live with her parents, Jacob and Catherine Berry Pickle. This was a difficult time, but her parents came to the rescue."

Ma wanted to know what happened then.

"Gosh," Pa said, "it wasn't long before Nancy found another man who she knew only as Mr. Dill (maybe she was on a rebound after Jasper left). I asked Jasper if the former Pickle girl became a Dill."

The two chuckled.

"That sounded strange to me," Pa continued. "He assured me it was true to the best of his knowledge, though he had never met Mr. Dill." One wonders about the truth of this situation.

"Nancy and Sarah Isabelle stayed in Mr. Dill's small log cabin with meager possessions but survived. Plus, Nancy began having Dill-fathered babies. After three babies, Dill disappeared from their lives. Jasper didn't know much about this but said he would tell me if he ever learned anything.

"It seems that Nancy Pickle Lee Dill always had her eyes out for men," Pa said. "Jasper told me Nancy took Sarah Isabelle Lee and her new Dill babies and left for the county line area of Leake and Attala Counties, Mississippi. She knew a returned and decorated confederate Civil War veteran named William Jenkins who now lived there. His medals impressed her.

"Nancy and the veteran began living together, and she became Nancy Pickle Lee Dill Jenkins. The veteran had sons by a previous marriage, one about the same age as Sarah Isabelle. As life goes, Sarah Isabelle was beginning to sense she would like a man for herself. She and one of her mother's husband's sons supposedly fell in love and were married when she was fifteen years of age. After all, they were living in tight quarters and might have shared a corn shuck bed with other children and no telling who else.

"You know, Ma," Pa said, "Jasper didn't have any

recent information. He felt his daughter was with the Jenkins young man and now likely producing babies—that was the world in which she lived. He also felt that Nancy was having more babies. The way I figure it, there were eleven children fathered by five men living in their small house. One wonders if the babies knew the identity of their fathers!"

"Probably not," Ma said in her Southern vernacular. "But based on the way they lived, it don't make no difference."

"Jasper told me that, while his former wife was making a new life for herself and Sarah Isabelle (the formality of a divorce is unknown—they just parted ways), he was trying to put down Mississippi roots in Monroe, Attala, Leake, Madison, and Rankin counties.

"Jasper said he couldn't readily find a good place to stay. He solved that for a while when he met and married a woman named Mary Caroline Ross in 1850. She was from a family with some resources but not wealthy. She lived in a nice house for the early 1850s era. Of course, Jasper quickly moved in. Incidentally, according to Jasper, his new wife might have been someone he knew before leaving South Carolina, as she had been born in South Carolina.

"Ma, do you think Jasper is up to some of the same shenanigans as he has done before? It seems he was on the lookout for women who could uplift his status. Mary

Caroline was from a family with property—land, slaves, and money.

"As it went, his new wife died shortly after marriage. Another death in her family occurred at about the same time. Her only sister died. That left Jasper and his now deceased wife's sister's surviving husband, E. O. Regan, as administrators of the estate their wives' father had left. Jasper received a share of the estate, which gave him a bit more wealth than he had ever had before in his life. I think he ran through the money."

Pa told Ma, "Jasper became distanced from his mother and sister. Earlier, they had tended to follow along with him. In the end, he apparently lost track of them. Jasper was never able to tell me if they were still living and, if so, where they lived and how they made a living. Somehow, he purposefully or accidentally lost track of them. Maybe he was enjoying the proceeds from his second wife's estate and seeking another woman.

"Jasper now makes a little money working for the railroad. I believe that's at the Brandon station in Rankin County. He works repairing tracks damaged by war activity—both the Confederate and Union armies used the railroad. You know, those Rebels tore up a lot of stuff just to keep the Union soldiers from being able to use it.

"Ma, I hope he was truthful with me. Somehow, I believe he was. I firmly believe the lack of a good father around him as a child is part of his problem."

Pa explained to Ma how Jasper told him that he loved Ellen and would be asking her to marry him. "How can we stop this?" he asked. "As her father, I can't approve of this union. I don't want him to ever come to our house again. You know, Ellen is only sixteen years old (though she'll soon be seventeen), and Jasper is thirty-seven—more than two times her age. Is he a man who will be loving, faithful, generous, and kind?"

"Don't forbid him to come to our house. We must be reasonable," Ma said. "Forbidding him to come to visit us will only drive our family apart. Our daughter will be gone. We might never see her again. I have to go now and cook some corn bread and peas with stewed potatoes for supper tonight."

The conversation was over. Only time would tell if Pa listened to Ma and used moderation with Ellen and Jasper.

5
Families Joining and Dividing

The first of March was fast approaching. Ellen and Jasper shared letters. (Too bad they didn't have email, texting, and telephoning of today.) They had made plans for something big in their lives. Jasper was coming to Tinnin on the last day of February, and Ellen was to travel to Brandon on the morning of March 1. (In 1864, February had twenty-nine days—it was a leap year. They thought of it as a great time for lovers and marriage!)

Right after Valentine's Day and Jasper's return to Brandon, Ellen spoke to Pa. She waited until he was alone. She told him she and Jasper were in love and wanted to be married. Pa had a fit! He rarely cussed, but he did on this occasion. He said a lot of bad things about Jasper.

He wondered aloud about how they had the money to get married and go about getting life for the two of them underway together. And he ended with, "Hell no!"

Ellen thought, *How can Pa be so opposed to Jasper?* Maybe it was infatuation on her part.

The next day, Ellen again talked to Pa alone. She explained that she didn't think it was right for him to reject Jasper; she said he was a good man who had been so nice to her. She said Jasper was the nicest man she had ever met. He would come there on the last day of February to talk about marriage. Pa said there was no need for him to do so. His mind was set, and it wouldn't be changed; Jasper was not the right man for her.

Neither would Ellen change her mind; her mind was made up regardless of what her Pa said.

The last day of February arrived. Jasper rode the train to Clinton and, miraculously, hitched a wagon ride with a stranger to Tinnin. Pa had forbidden Ellen to take a wagon to meet Jasper. He had to walk down the long hill on the dirt road. Bummer started barking as soon as he came into sight. Ellen heard Bummer and went outside to calm him. She looked up the road, and there was Jasper! The barking had alerted Ellen to Jasper's arrival. Pa was out back tending to animals in the barn and did not see Jasper coming down the hill—probably just as well.

Ellen was thrilled. She ran out to greet Jasper, meeting him about halfway up the hill. She hugged him; he hugged back. Ellen was nervous when she told Jasper a little of what her Pa had said. Anyway, Jasper was at the Shepard home, and he and Ellen would do the best they could. Jasper thought that he loved Ellen so much that her Pa's feelings were not about to change his mind. He really didn't like the way her Pa was acting toward him. In the back of his mind, he kept thinking that Pa, being a man, could sense that some things were hidden and weren't being told. Jasper didn't offer any more information because they had previously talked in private.

Ellen invited Jasper into the house. He greeted Ma and the siblings who were present. Pa soon arrived with a few eggs in a basket. He immediately saw Jasper and exclaimed, "What are you doing here?"

Jasper was fairly blunt back, saying, "I came to ask for the hand of your daughter Ellen in marriage."

Pa was beside himself with anger and dropped the eggs. Rachel cleaned up the mess from the broken eggs.

Pa went on, "Just what else do you have in mind?"

Ellen stepped in, "Pa, Jasper is a good man. I believe he is right for me. I am in love with him. We plan to be married soon."

Pa and Ma appeared upset, but that didn't dampen the romance in the room. Pa stomped out to the porch to cool off. Ellen soon followed him.

Ellen said, "You and Ma always told me that a marriage should be a happy time that brings two families together. You also said that the time of courtship was more important than the wedding day. You know, I think you were likely right. We have been in courtship now for a few months—plenty long enough for us with our amount of love and commitment." It had actually been a little less than four months since they'd met at the Presbyterian church in Brandon.

"Please, Pa, Jasper is my man," Ellen continued. "As I have told you, we will be getting married very soon. Let's work this out so we are all happy."

Pa, beginning to cool a bit, said that this didn't sound good to him and that he feared for his daughter."

Ellen indicated that she wasn't afraid. "Pa, Jasper needs to stay here tonight. OK?"

Pa said, "No."

Ellen indicated that, if Jasper couldn't stay there, he would leave, and she would go with him.

Pa starred off the porch into the fruit orchard for a few moments. He relented and said, "Well, OK, he can stay here tonight. But he must leave first thing in the morning. He sleeps on the pallet in the closet under the stairway and you in your bed."

Ellen thanked Pa and said he would leave early the next day.

Ellen went inside and quietly spoke to Ma about what was happening. She confided that she could not understand Pa's attitude toward Jasper. She and Jasper loved each other, and they wanted to marry each other and spend life together.

Ma listened patiently and then said, "You know your pa. He wants good for his daughters; he wants the best for each of you. I suspect you should heed what he has said."

Ellen continued talking with Ma about thoughts for their future. She said she and Jasper could live in the house, work, and then get a place of their own. She also said another way for them to stay was for Pa and Ma to set aside certain land for them, and they would work it. Anyway, the farm was plenty large enough for another worker and to support one additional person. She reminded Ma that the slaves were gone and that the farm needed more workers to do what they had formerly done. Always promoting Jasper, Ellen indicated that he was a skilled farmworker who knew how to go about getting things done.

After a night of trying to sleep on a pallet of corn shucks in a cotton pick sack, Jasper was up early. The only family member up was Ellen. Jasper was preparing to leave. But no one knew that Ellen had come into the closet where Jasper slept on a pallet after all were asleep. They'd agreed she would be leaving with him. They would get a ride to the Clinton depot and catch the train to Brandon. They would go to the clerk's office to get a marriage license. Jasper had saved sixty-two dollars from his work; Ellen had only a couple of dollars.

So, Ellen was also discretely packing. She didn't want to alarm family members and create additional stress for them. It was soon time to go. Pa did not yet know that Ellen was also leaving. He spoke to Ellen, saying she could not use the wagon to take Jasper to the depot in Clinton. At that point, Ellen knew she had to provide more details.

"Pa," Ellen said, "I am leaving with Jasper. Our plans are to get married day after tomorrow in Clinton at the home of Chaplain Reverend Autry of the Institute for Women (Hillman College). We will get our license this afternoon at the clerk's office in Brandon."

Pa shouted, "*No!*"

Ellen indicated that, unfortunately, his thoughts didn't much matter at this stage.

Pa went further. "You ain't staying at this house—not ever. If you marry him, you leave here."

Ellen shed a couple of tears and accepted what her father said. In the back of her mind, she was wondering if her Pa really loved her. If so, how could he be so firmly against her marriage?

Ellen was beginning to realize that she might never see her ma, sisters, and brothers again. She hugged each of them and said goodbye. But Pa was too bitter for a hug.

Ellen and Jasper left, walking up the hill trail with, each carrying a few possessions. They walked to the home of her cousin, Susan Ratliff. Ellen knocked firmly on the door. Susan came to the door all sleepy-eyed. Ellen explained that they needed a ride to the depot in Clinton just as soon as they could get it. "We have a train to catch in about an hour."

Susan quickly got ready and had her brother join them as they hitched horses to the wagon and headed out.

As they rode to the depot, Ellen told Susan their plans. She asked Susan to go by and tell Ma what they were doing on her way back home in Tinnin. As they approached the depot, they went a hundred yards or so out of the way to Reverend Autry's home. There they met with him and said they were on their way to get a marriage license. He agreed to perform the rites of matrimony the next day at 3:00 p.m. in his home. Ellen said a few family and friends might attend but no more than ten people.

Afterward, Ellen asked Susan to also share the details of the wedding with Ma and Susan's own family; she wanted them to come to the wedding. She asked Susan if she would be her attendant and wear a Sunday school dress. Then Jasper and Ellen bought tickets for the train to Brandon. They boarded the train and waved goodbye.

The train arrived in Brandon just in time for Jasper and Ellen to go to the clerk's office on Government Street to get the license. The clerk was Henry Cole. He quickly issued a marriage license dated March 1, 1864. The license granted an authorized individual to celebrate the rites of matrimony of Jasper H. Lee and Ellen L. Sheppard (Ellen noticed that her last name had been recorded with an extra "p," but she didn't say anything).

Ellen and Jasper then went to Mulhollands Store just across the roadway to get a dress for her and coat and pants for him. Ellen got what she wanted—a simple white dress. It had a tiny waist and a bow on the back, and, she thought, it properly emphasized her feminine features. Jasper got a navy jacket and pants. Money was short; they would have to wear the shoes they had. They went to the jewelry area of the store and bought two-dollar wedding bands. Then it was to Sister Annie's Boarding House for the night. They had to share a small bed that night but Ellen remained true to wearing a white wedding dress.

They were up about the usual time the next morning preparing to catch the train to Clinton. And were they excited! Jasper walked about a quarter mile to the job office of the railroad and said he was quitting. He thanked them for allowing him to have the job. Of course, his job supervisor grumbled something about such a short notice. Jasper said he was sorry, but it would need to be that way. He told the desk clerk at the boarding house that he would not be back. He told the people at both places he was about to marry the woman of his dreams.

Jasper packed what little he had into a small, ragged suitcase. Ellen had what she'd brought the previous day. They wore their wedding clothes. Jasper folded the marriage license and placed it in the pocket of his coat—he didn't want to lose it.

After a half-mile walk to the depot, they bought tickets and boarded the 11:48 a.m. train to Jackson and Clinton. The train arrived in Clinton at 2:08 p.m.; fortunately, it was on time. They walked the short distance to the home of Reverend Autry on the campus of the Institute for Women, or at least what was left of it after Civil War destruction.

They arrived at the house a little early and waited under a tree in the front yard. Just before they were ready to go in, a wagon arrived with Ellen's cousin Susan and her brother and parents. Greetings were exchanged. Close behind was a wagon with Ma, Rachel, Mag, Naomi, and Georgia Ann. The other siblings stayed at home with Pa, who didn't want them to see the wedding. He didn't want Ma or the other children to go either, but Ma was firm and went. Jasper had no family or friends present. Maybe that was appropriate, as no one knew his family, much less anything about him.

Some residents in the Tinnin community held strong thoughts about Pa and the wedding. Sadly, Pa didn't come to the wedding of his oldest daughter. He was very upset. He felt Ellen was misjudging Jasper. He sent word for the newly married couple not to come to the house and that he never wanted to see Jasper again. This was heartbreaking to Ellen. A family divide had occurred. Ellen might never again see her parents.

Most everyone wore Sunday school clothes. Ellen freshened a tad in a side room and came out as a radiant bride. The bride and groom quickly reviewed details with the preacher. Jasper gave the preacher the marriage license (which he later signed and returned to the Rankin County clerk's office).

Reverend Autry performed the ceremony in the front room of the house. Being Baptist, he more or less used Baptist wedding vows. The ceremony was kept simple. Susan held the ring Ellen had for Jasper; Jasper held the ring he had for Ellen. After announcing why they were there, the preacher had a short prayer asking for God's blessing on the union between Jasper and Ellen. He then went into recitation of the wedding vows.

The reverend said, "Will you, Ellen, have Jasper to be your husband? Will you love him, comfort him, and keep him, forsaking all others to remain true to him? Will you honor him, submit to him, and strive to follow his direction as his helpmate? If so, say, 'I do.'"

Ellen said, "I do."

The reverend continued, "Repeat after me, 'I, Ellen, take thee, Jasper, to be my husband. And before God and these witnesses, I promise to be a faithful, obedient, and true wife.'"

Ellen repeated the vow.

Next, Reverend Autry spoke to Jasper. "Will you, Jasper, take Ellen to be your wife? Will you love her, comfort her, and keep her, forsaking all others? If so, say, 'I do.'"

Jasper said, "I do."

The reverend continued, "Repeat after me, 'I, Jasper, take thee, Ellen, to be my wife. And before God and these witnesses, I promise to be a faithful and true husband.'"

Jasper smiled at Ellen and happily repeated the statement.

The reverend called for the exchange of rings. Susan passed Jasper's ring to Ellen. Ellen repeated the words the reverend had asked her to say as she slipped the ring on Jasper's finger: "With this ring, I thee wed, and all my worldly goods I thee endow. In sickness and in health, in poverty or in wealth, till death do us part."

Jasper took Ellen's ring from his pocket and repeated the same vows as Ellen. He placed the ring on Ellen's ring finger. The reverend said a short prayer to end the ceremony. The bride and groom kissed and hugged. The reverend now pronounced them Mr. and Mrs. Lee. Ellen gleamed with pride. She walked over and hugged her mother and said goodbye. She also told her mother to tell Pa she loved him. It appeared that everyone present was happy. Jasper slipped the Reverend Autry two dollars gratuity for doing the ceremony.

As the small group was still gathered, Ellen quietly asked her cousin Susan to ask her parents if they could stay at their house that night. They talked with Susan's mother, and permission was given. Ellen and Jasper had no transportation, so they rode to Susan's home in their wagon with them—making the wagon kind of full. But it was exciting to the newlyweds.

At Susan's home, the newlyweds brought in their belongings and went to the room that was theirs for the night. It was a small, room isolated away from other family with a tiny, shuttered window. They got out of their wedding clothes and dressed to take a walk over to the Ratliff Store and otherwise look around the area. They held hands, hugged, kissed, and laughed. Anticipation of their future was exciting but nerve-racking. They did not know where they would be the next night. A bit later, they joined with cousin Susan's family for supper.

As the morning sun rose, the couple was up and about. They gathered their things together. As they were doing this, Ma arrived in a wagon with a few things that belonged to Ellen. These were going with her as she and Jasper ventured west. They were without a destination; they were going wherever the situation merited. Ellen again hugged her mother. She thanked her for bringing her things and told her goodbye.

Susan and her brother drove the newlyweds to the depot in Clinton, where they boarded a train to Vicksburg. A lot of things were in disarray, as the Union forces had surrounded Vicksburg and prevented the entry of food. This siege had resulted in near starvation and forced the Rebels to surrender. Union forces had then departed the area on their way east. The railroad was still operating, however. Some of it had been patched up following dam-age by military forces. Anyway, it was deemed safe for travel to Vicksburg. Ellen and Jasper told Susan and her brother goodbye. They bought tickets and boarded the train for Vicksburg.

In Vicksburg, the new couple found a room in a home with a woman widowed by the war, a Mrs. Cornweller. She was a sweet, nice lady of the Old South who could not figure out how the Confederates had allowed the Union forces to take Vicksburg—a major shipping city of the South (her family had operated a dock). She talked about all she had lost in the war, particularly her husband. Their older children were gone from home and living in the Chicago area, and she was alone. She said something about not knowing how she was going to live. She began crying.

Ellen hugged her and tried to offer comfort. Ellen en-couraged her to have faith in a divine being. She said to Mrs. Cornweller that she might talk with her preacher.

Mrs. Cornweller shrugged and muttered, "He's a damn Yankee!"

Ellen asked what she meant.

Mrs. Cornweller tried to explain about the preacher at her church. She said he was originally from the North and had protected former slaves and befriended Union troops. He once said he didn't think slavery was right, and he didn't feel that folks in Vicksburg and the South should go to war to defend it. The preacher had even provided special care for an injured Union soldier from Illinois and had him come to church when she was there. "How could he do that to me?" she exclaimed. She wondered aloud about how any preacher could aid a Union troop. She went on, "Surely, it was a great sin."

She had curiosity, though, about the Union soldier, as she'd tried to stand close enough to hear what he said. She said she had overheard him talking about his home area in Illinois—the fertile, black soil was very good for growing corn. He talked about the new equipment they now used to save labor and get more work done. Cyrus McCormick moved from Virginia to Chicago to open a machinery factory. They were able to use the machinery to produce more corn with fewer hours of labor. Mrs. Cornweller probably didn't like it that the Yankees had moved ahead of the South in farming methods. So, Mrs. Cornweller really unloaded her thoughts and prejudices on Ellen and appeared to feel better afterward.

Jasper got a job at Shawver & Pollock, a commission merchant located near the dock at the corner of Levee and Crawford Streets. He told Mr. Shawver that George W. Shepard was his father-in-law and that he needed a job. Mr. Shawver remembered George W. Shepard as a fairly regular customer. The merchant hired him to do a variety of work, such as unloading shipments, stocking goods, and loading purchases onto wagons. They paid him $1.65 a day.

Ellen helped Mrs. Cornweller straighten and clean her house and the yard around it in exchange for the cost of their room. The location was on the edge of the Vicksburg battlefield. The severe siege of Vicksburg had occurred there a few months ago. Destruction was all about, though some effort was underway to clean and reconstruct the area.

One afternoon, Ellen and Jasper took a stroll into some of the area of destruction. It was bad. Building scraps, discarded clothing, shoes, kitchenware, lead slugs from ammunition, and bones from animals or people were scattered about. A couple of obviously human skulls were evident. Parts of a tiny skeleton that appeared to be that of a young human baby were partially covered with an old cloth. Seeing all of this caused Ellen to think back on what Pa said about war. No doubt, war brought out the worst in human behavior. She thought there should be a way to avoid something like this.

After a few days, it was time for Jasper and Ellen to move on. They had to work their way to the West. In spite of their challenges, Jasper always had patience, kindness, and consideration for Ellen; he loved her. She reciprocated.

They crossed the Mississippi River on a ferry from the Vicksburg dock into Louisiana. Ellen and Jasper looked around, and the land was very flat; they liked gentle rolling hills. Fortunately, they were able to catch a ride on a wagon with a man who had brought people from

Tallulah, Louisiana, to the ferry to go into Mississippi. So the man with the wagon drove them to the train depot in Tallulah for a charge of fifty cents. They found that Union gunboats had set fire to and burned the depot for the Vicksburg, Shreveport, and Texas Railroad Company. A shack-like temporary depot was being used—not much of a place but it worked.

Ellen and Jasper caught a train for Monroe and Shreveport, Louisiana. The stop in Monroe let passengers who had reached their destinations off and new passengers on. The land still looked too flat for their liking, though there were a few hills off in the distance. It appeared that a lot of crop farming went on in the area. Lots of mules and horses and not many goats, sheep, or cattle were evident. Just maybe Ellen and Jasper would like a mix of hills and flat land.

They thought Shreveport would be their destination, but it was not to be. The Red River in Shreveport offered more flat land but not a very wide expanse compared to the Mississippi River Delta of Louisiana. More of the West was on their minds. They decided they would sleep that night on benches in the Shreveport depot before boarding an early morning train to Athens, Texas. Ellen was fearful of sleeping in a depot; there might be some "bad" people who would beat them up and rob them; also, the good-looking newly married woman might be assaulted. Jasper assured Ellen he would protect her.

They were not alone in the depot, as three other people were also staying in it that night. They seemed to be honest, law-abiding folks who did not pose threats of robbery or assault.

They had heard that the Athens area was nice hill country and a good place to put down roots. Along the way of the train as it passed through the hills, Jasper and Ellen peered out the window. They liked the lay of the land and what they saw. It wasn't flat like the Mississippi River Delta in Louisiana or steep like the Loess Hills around Vicksburg. They saw a few homes and farms with animals and fields being readied for another crop year. It appeared like an OK area to them.

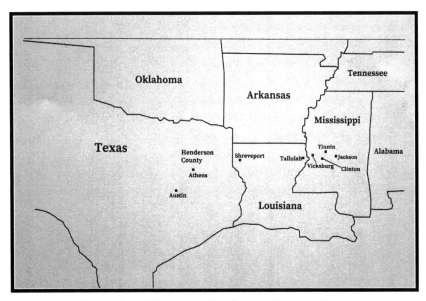

Route from Tinnin to Henderson County, Texas

About noon, the train arrived in Athens, Texas. Ellen and Jasper got off. They saw a poster that said Texas had become a state in 1845, and Henderson County had been established in 1846. The largest town around was Athens, with about three hundred people but growing fairly rapidly. The lay of the land was appealing, and the nearby Trinity River could serve as a source of water. They learned that the climate was hot and humid in the summer and mild to cool in the winter. They were excited about this being a place where they might settle down.

They walked the short streets carrying their suitcases. They looked around for a boarding house or other place to stay or to work. They didn't see much that appealed to them or that they could afford. They were getting anxious. Particularly Ellen was nervous in this new place with its strange ways of doing things. Jasper could sense that Ellen was anxious. He gave her a hug; said, "I love you"; and assured her that everything would work out.

They walked past a couple of mercantile stores, a saloon, and a couple of churches. One of the churches was a Methodist Episcopal, and the other was a Presbyterian church. The importance of the Presbyterian church in Brandon, Mississippi, in helping them get to know each other quickly came to their minds. Ellen reminded Jasper of where they had first met and began to fall in love.

Jasper was quick to respond, "Yes, that was a great place to me."

The steps of the Athens Presbyterian Church provided a place to sit briefly, rest from their walking, and contemplate.

Ellen remembered one of the sing-along songs from the evening they first met—"The Yellow Rose of Texas." She started trying to sing it, and Jasper sort of joined in. Yes, that song had helped bring them closer together now that they were in Texas. But they had not seen a yellow rose!

For the first time since marriage, Ellen began to think back to her family. She had never been away more than a night at a time. She remembered Ma and Pa. She remembered her sisters and brothers. And, don't forget, Bummer—who'd once notified Ellen that Jasper had arrived in Tinnin.

But she didn't have long to let her mind wander. They had things to do. The conversation turned to the role of church in their lives. Ellen said she and her family had sometimes gone to Mason Chapel in Tinnin. It was small and had an itinerant Methodist Episcopal preacher. Mostly, not much had gone on since Preacher Hoyle had a heart attack brought on by fright of the Union troops on Easter Sunday the previous year. She indicated that her family had a large Bible in which important dates and events were recorded. But they seldom read from it and seldom had prayer, other than a blessing before Sunday dinner. Ellen did say she had been christened as a small girl by the preacher at Mason Chapel. She continued, "I think that involved sprinkling a few drops of water on my head. How about you, Jasper?"

Jasper didn't have much to say about church. He said he had seen a few preachers. He'd once gone to a brush arbor revival and had been scared by the preacher's message about "burning in hell." He said it "sounded hot and bad" to him. He said that, when the folks were singing and the preacher was begging people to come forward and "accept Jesus Christ as savior," he went down to the front. The preacher shook his hand and said a brief prayer, adding that he would be baptized at the local creek by immersion. Jasper said, "I asked him what it was. He said dunking me under the water. That scared me." Jasper continued, saying he'd left that town before baptism. Maybe someday he would be baptized. He never learned who Jesus Christ was either. It would take some explaining to make a "believer" out of him.

But that didn't matter to Ellen. She was with the man of her dreams. She knew their love was about more than going to church and the like.

It was time to walk some more. They'd had a good conversation on the steps of the church house. It would probably serve as a foundation for future church endeavors of themselves and any children they might have. In general, they were in agreement on the role of church in their lives. They tried to accept Pa's explanation that the definition of sin varied with the situation and who was involved, but a person should always do what is right and moral. Treat others as you would like to be treated. They would affiliate in some way with a church once they had found a place for settling down. They had little idea about the church and preacher who lay ahead in their lives.

Finally, as night was approaching, they came upon the Witherspoon Hotel and Saloon. The saloon had its own name, Spoon Saloon, and was known locally as the Spoon. It wasn't new nor fancy at all, but a room was available at a rate they could possibly afford. Jasper paid $1.50 for three nights. Since Ellen and Jasper didn't drink (with their limited money, they couldn't afford to), the presence of a saloon was not important. But maybe it could be.

There was one more thing Ellen wanted to do—write a letter to Mrs. Cornweller in Vicksburg. She wanted to thank Mrs. Cornweller for befriending them by allowing them to stay in her home, but, mostly, she wanted to cheer her up. Mrs. Cornweller had seemed so down on life and her ability to survive. That night in their room at the Spoon, with the light of a flickering coal oil lamp, Ellen wrote a letter for mailing the next day. She wanted to help Mrs. Cornweller feel better and adjust to life under the flag of the United States after the Civil War. Maybe, in the back of her mind, Ellen really wanted to write her parents and tell them where she was. But she did not do so because the joining of her and Jasper had created a family divide.

They could now relax a bit after their trip from Vicksburg. Let's hope so. But serious relaxation would be a tad difficult and elusive. They had a future to plan and realize. And they had to face the challenges of getting through tomorrow, the next day, and those afterward.

6

Life with Jasper

On their first day in Athens, Ellen and Jasper found a place to stay at the Witherspoon Hotel and Saloon. It wasn't comfortable but had to do. Of course, they had never had anything in their married life but the very essentials—no luxury in their lives.

And after all, Athens was to be the place where they settled down in life. They were going to see what might be good for them and knew it would take a lot of hard work! They might have to work on shares (sharecrop) with a farmer or do other work. Then, with a little luck, they might get a few dollars and buy a horse and a few things for their needs. They could get a small farm using credit from a local merchant or bank. They were willing to work for what they got. They wanted to be honest and fair in all they did. Maybe some of their goals would take a few years. But there were more pressing needs. One was making it through their first night at the Witherspoon.

The small room they got was on the second floor and had a tiny, wood-burning fireplace. The toilet was out back. A wash pan on the floor took the place of a tub or lavatory. The bed was small for two people. It had a mattress of cotton cloth, apparently stuffed with unginned cotton. Though they couldn't see inside, it was similar to but better that the dry corn shucks in the cotton pick sack that Jasper had slept on in the closet under the steps of the Shepard home back in Tinnin. At fifty cents a night, this would have to do, and it was somewhat of an improvement over the pick sack mattress under the stairs at the Shepard home.

All seemed well when they went to bed that night. Shortly, both Ellen and Jasper had bites that itched and gave them rashes. Small bugs came out of hiding and bit them. The bite places were itchy and reddish. They were not flying bugs like mosquitoes; they were crawling under the bed sheets and in crevices. The bugs preferred darkness and tended to hide in light.

Jasper told Ellen he had seen those bugs before at a place he stayed some time ago. He said they were called bedbugs. Ellen and Jasper couldn't be choosey, as they had little money. So, they toughed it out for the three nights that had been paid in advance at the Witherspoon. They were able to mash a few of the bugs between their fingers and kill them. When mashed, the bugs let off a bad odor. Regardless, there was always time for the tender and loving touches of newlyweds!

The next day, Jasper searched around for work. He heard there was a farmer out of town a ways looking for someone to help with crops—and maybe on a sharecropper basis. He had no way to travel to the farm other than walk. It wasn't that far, just a couple or so miles. So, on the morning of the third day in Athens, he set out to walk to the farm. Ellen remained at the Witherspoon.

Ellen, being industrious, asked the barkeeper and manager in the Spoon if any jobs were available. Yes, there were. Ellen was a tad nervous; she had never been in a bar before and wanted to hear more. One opening was as a barmaid in the Spoon. With some slightly tight clothing (always long skirts) and her flirtatious good looks, she could likely make some good tips. The barkeeper said he made the drinks and that a person named Bonito could give her some tips on being a barmaid. The other job was cleaning the toilet out back and the stable area where guests who rode would keep their animals. Ellen said she would talk with her husband and come back later.

Ellen waited for Jasper to return from the farm. It seemed to be taking him a long time. When he was back, she told him what she had done and about the couple of jobs at the Spoon. He told her about his day and that a sharecropper place would be available on Smith Farm (more about Smith Farm later) on April 1, which was still nearly two weeks away. So, they decided to continue staying at the hotel for another few days. They would pay fifty cents a night and battle the bedbugs.

With Ellen's insistence and some reluctance, Jasper agreed she could be a barmaid at the Spoon. One condition was that the barkeeper permit him to sit over to one side—he could protect her from any patrons who became unruly or tried to take advantage of her. But as we know, Ellen was capable of defending herself, as she had done with Private Cason on the porch of the Shepard home when the Union troops came through.

Ellen didn't know much about being a barmaid, so she went to the Spoon the next midmorning before it opened for details. Bonito was there and told her a few things about greeting customers, taking orders, and serving liquor. She would be paid a dollar each day. Plus, she could keep any tips she made. They would provide an outfit for her to wear. She looked at it, tried it on, and thought it was a tad on the tight side. However, the skirt did go to her ankles.

Bonito also told Ellen that some customers who'd had too much to drink might try to take advantage of her. "Occasionally," she said, "one might ask if you would come to his room after closing." Bonito told her not go, though larger tips would result. Ellen knew better than to go.

Of course, Ellen was not that kind of person, anyway. She had been brought up to follow high moral standards. She was also newly married and would never betray her husband. She did have some concerns about unruly men but remembered how she' handled unwanted advances from men in the past. Ellen was comforted knowing that her man, Jasper, would be there in the Spoon to protect her if the situation was more than she could handle.

Ellen agreed to do the work. She also asked if the job for someone to clean the toilets and stable area was still available.

The answer was, "Yes."

She said, "My husband might like to take it." But she was reluctant, as she thought Jasper was qualified for a better job. They needed money, though, and this was the best job available. Maybe something better would come along in a day or so.

Jasper took the job as toilet and stable cleaner and did the cleaning early in the day before the Spoon opened. He then sat in the Spoon while Ellen greeted customers, mostly men, at the place. Ellen was really quite glamorous-looking in the outfit. She appealed to the men, particularly those who didn't know her husband was sitting over on one side.

Ellen provided table service to the seven small tables; most of the time, only four or so were occupied. The barkeeper took care of customers sitting at the counter. Some customers would first sit at the counter and then move to a table once they saw good-looking Ellen. She greeted everyone and offered light conversation. Though the job was new to her, she carefully took orders and relayed them to the barkeeper. After the drinks were ready, she would bring them to the customers. She collected money for the drinks and took it to a cash box at the bar. She tried to keep everything straight; she didn't want to make errors.

Being barmaid went well for Ellen the first three nights. She got tips of a dollar or more each night. On the fourth night, one of the customers who had drunk three whiskeys became loud. He called Ellen over and ordered another whiskey. As he did, he slapped her on the butt, and she walked away. She brought his whiskey to him and he asked her to sit with him.

She said, "No."

He grabbed her arm and pulled her onto his lap and whispered something into her ear like, "You are a hot woman."

Ellen thought she knew how to fend off men. She had done it before. This time, she flung the back of her right elbow as hard as she could into his upper gut. He turned her loose. She got up and began walking back to the bar. He coughed and quickly took a sip of whiskey and then another and another. Things could get worse the way he was behaving.

Jasper saw this indiscretion by a customer; he couldn't

accept it. He rushed to the customer and told him not to ever grab or touch Ellen and that she was his wife. He asked the man to apologize, give a nice tip, and leave the Spoon. Jasper said, "If you don't, I will drag you outside and beat the living hell out of you."

The customer complied; he could tell Jasper was upset and meant what he'd said. The few extra sips of whiskey didn't help solve the situation. A full dollar tip was left. All else was routine for Ellen that evening and for the next few nights.

The first of April was approaching. Jasper's farm sharecropping would start. He did other things besides work in sharecropping; he would be paid $1.50 a day. Both Ellen and Jasper told the barkeeper at the Spoon that their last day would be March 30 (they needed one day to get settled on the farm before Jasper's job began). And Jasper never really liked the idea of his wife being a saloon bar-maid—too many men had eyes for her. She was a mature, good-looking sixteen-going-on-seventeen-year-old bride!

So, on the morning of March 30, Jasper and Ellen placed their belongings in a couple of old suitcases and a sack, checked out of the Witherspoon, and started walk-ing to the Smith farm. They arrived midmorning and knocked on the house door. A somewhat aging, relatively heavyset woman came to the door. Jasper told her who he was and introduced Ellen. He said Mr. Smith had agreed for him to sharecrop beginning April 1. He was a day early because he wanted to get settled in and be ready when the time came.

The woman said her name was Candy. She was nice to them and said she was the wife of Mr. Smith. She also said that she served as a midwife in the local community (something Ellen and Jasper might want to know about). Candy said Mr. Smith was out on the farm and would be back by noon to work out the details with them. Compliantly, Candy always called her husband Mr. Smith.

She showed them the place where they would stay. It was a shed room attached to the main house. It had an outside door and one window with hinged shutters (no glass) that could be opened and closed. One corner of the room had a wood-burning, flat-top cast iron heater/stove that doubled as place for heating and cooking. There were a couple of straight, rough-wood chairs and a small table. A bed for two was next to one wall. The mattress was of moss or leaves—they couldn't tell with it sewn together. A couple of blankets and a deerskin were in the room. It was not a particularly appealing place but would have to do.

Candy spoke briefly about the community. She said that, according to the US Census, Willow Springs was a small place in Henderson County. It had a store that was open only a few hours a week, a church (named Flowing Waters Chapel), no doctor, no lawyer, and not a lot of anything. They would need to go into Athens for many things. But they had no extra money for making purchases.

Mr. Smith returned and greeted Jasper and met Ellen. They discussed their sharecropping. It was to be on thirds; Jasper and Ellen would get two-thirds of what was produced, and Mr. Smith would get one-third. Mr. Smith provided land, mules for plowing, and the tools needed, as well as the seed. He would also provide a wagon with a team to transport the harvested crops.

The main crop would be cotton. Some corn and vegetables would be grown. Their piece of land would stretch from the big oak tree to the cedar tree and then over the hill to the property line. The field had about twenty-seven acres divided by a small creek. They should be able to make eight to ten bales of cotton, a hundred bushels of corn, and garden vegetables without planting the full twenty-seven acres. Mr. Smith would keep an account of things they needed, including occasional cash advances, and settle up after the crops were harvested.

Jasper and Ellen would be responsible for all the work growing the crops. The cotton would be ginned in Athens, weighed, and sold. The seed removed in ginning would be exchanged for the cost of ginning.

It was time to begin getting the crops in. Ellen would work quite a bit in the field helping with the work, which was often demanding. Jasper hooked up Jonas, the mule, to the turning plow and went through several acres of field. This broke up the land but did not get it into planting condition—too many big clods. He then used a mule-pulled, single-row harrow to break and smooth the clods. Sometimes he would stop and throw old roots or limbs out of the field. After a few days, he had five acres done.

They needed more acres prepared for planting. Ellen agreed she would run the harrow behind Jasper if Mr. Smith would let them use another mule. He did. The field preparation now went about twice as fast. They soon had fourteen acres ready for cotton and turned their attention to five acres for corn, which they hand planted right off. They also prepared a couple of acres for a garden, with half an acre being planted with sweet potatoes and another half an acre with peanuts. Potatoes, beans, peas, greens, cabbage, okra, and a few other things were to be planted. Producing food was very important in their lives.

It was now time to plant the cotton (it liked warm weather and warm soil for the seed to germinate). No mechanical planters were available, so Jasper and Ellen set about planting the cotton by hand. They would make rows in the land about three feet apart. A small trench would be made in the middle of each row with a corner of the hoe blade, and four seeds would be dropped about every fifteen inches apart. The seed would then be covered about an inch deep with soil. It took a couple of weeks working hard for the fourteen acres to be planted. All was finished by May 15. Fortunately, a nice shower came, and enough of the seeds germinated to produce sufficient plants in a few days. It was certainly nice to see the plants emerge from the soil!

Commercial fertilizer was available on a limited basis but not likely to be used. Jasper and Ellen would be charged on their account for whatever they used. They decided to put a little out by hand on about five acres—the soil was fertile and had been cropped only a few years after being taken out of grass. It should produce a decent crop. After all this hard work, they were glad to hear that mechanical drills, planters, and fertilizer distributors were slowly becoming available. They hoped Mr. Smith would buy a planter and distributor when it became available—and before next year.

Most all crops came up to an OK stand; they had enough up and growing plants by the end of the first week of June to feel a little early success. But, now it was time to keep the weeds down. This was by hand pulling or cutting with a hoe. A lot of time and work went into this, particularly in a process called "chopping cotton." A hand hoe would be used to cut / dig up weeds and grass in the cotton. A mule-pulled cultivator tool could be used to remove weeds from the middles between the rows.

Farming, as Jasper well knew, was not without problems and setbacks. After the corn was about eighteen inches tall, deer got into the field one night and bit off some of the stalks. They also attacked the garden a little. Fortunately, Mr. Smith had a big dog named Pluto. He did not like deer, and they did not like him. He chased them off. In the process, some of the plants were damaged, but they survived. From now on, Pluto was allowed to run loose at night until the crops were nearly ready for harvest. There weren't any more problems with deer getting into the field.

As the summer passed, the crops grew as well as could be expected. Keeping weeds down was a never-ending job. Some cotton began to bloom about the first of July. Jasper and Ellen always enjoyed seeing cotton blooms. The blooms were formed in a bud structure called a square. Blooms were white the first day they were open in the early morning and turned to pink when aging on the second day.

Cotton bolls (the fruit structures) begin to grow after the blooms faded and shriveled. After a few weeks, the bolls were rounded and a little over an inch in diameter. Mature bolls turned brownish and began to open, exposing the white cotton fibers containing seed. Once about half of the bolls had opened, hand picking began. A second picking would be done to get the remaining cotton. Keeping fibers white (discoloring typically resulted from rain sustained over more than a few hours) and free of trash was important in having a higher-grade product that would get a better price for the harvested and ginned cotton. A cotton farmer was always excited to see the different stages of development of a cotton crop. And, fortunately, the boll weevil had not yet arrived in Texas to become a big, damaging cotton pest.

The corn began to tassel and develop immature ears with obvious silks in early July. Everyone knew two to three silk clusters on a stalk was a good sign of potential production. The silks would develop into ears of corn. The tassels produced pollen that was released into the air and came into contact with the silks, resulting in the development of corn kernels in rows on the developing cobs enclosed in green shucks. A few showers would be needed to help the ears develop.

Work began to slow a little bit after mid-July. This gave Ellen and Jasper time to experience a few things in the local area. They got to know people and went to church activities. The tiny Flowing Waters Chapel held a revival. Jasper and Ellen went. There was singing, clapping, shouting, and amens as Brother Yonah gave one of his hellfire and brimstone sermons. Some of the dozen or so people would about get into an emotional frenzy.

After the service each evening, people would socialize a bit. This helped Ellen and Jasper meet a few local citizens. One couple in particular was Bertha and Samuel Hendrick. The Hendricks were of similar age and, like Ellen and Jasper, were just getting started in farming. Having moved from the Delta area of Louisiana near Tallulah, they were accustomed to flat land. Maybe

Ellen and Jasper could help them adjust to the hills of Henderson County.

One evening after the service, Brother Yonah said he would like to come by and visit. Ellen and Jasper agreed that a visit would be fine. They would like to get better acquainted with their preacher. How about Saturday morning? Yes, they said.

Brother Yonah was there midmorning. They didn't have much but did serve him some coffee. He sat in a chair, Jasper sat in the other chair, and Ellen sat on the bed.

Brother Yonah opened with a prayer and began some guilt-making discussion about church, sin, hell, and Jesus. He wanted to know who had been saved and baptized. Ellen said she had been christened into the Methodist Episcopal Church at Mason's chapel in Tinnin, Mississippi. Jasper said he made a commitment at a brush arbor revival one time but had never gone to be baptized. Brother Yonah said he could take care of that with Jasper next Sunday morning at the special baptizing service.

Brother Yonah told Jasper to read his Bible and make a profession of faith in the Lord Jesus Christ. Jasper said he would but continued, "I don't have a Bible. Once, I looked at one and could probably read most of the words. It has some long words that I can't read, say, or understand."

The preacher told him not to worry about those long words and that he would take care of him not having a Bible; he had a New Testament in his saddle bag that he would give him. Remember, the preacher said, our slogan is "quenching the fires of hell—QFH."

Jasper wanted to know the kind or denomination of church, so he asked, "What is Flowing Waters Chapel?"

Brother Yonah said it was an independent Christian church that taught old-time Bible beliefs, such as people should love and look after each other and fear the fires of hell. Men were superior to women (their wives). Everything that happened was God's will. He said men were to father children, and women were to give birth to them. Sometimes, snakes and other animals were used to show the power of God.

Now, Ellen didn't necessarily agree with all he said but she kept quiet. After all, she had been taught to respect preachers and trust what they said and did. But should she with Brother Yonah? Something in her mind raised a red flag.

Ellen said, "Brother Yonah, tell us about yourself."

He spoke. He told them he'd begun his preaching in the Blue Ridge Mountains of northeast Georgia in the late 1840s. He stated that this was not long after the Cherokee Indians had been chased out to the Cherokee Nation area of the Louisiana Purchase for the benefit of the white folks. He talked about burying slaves in graves that were not marked so they wouldn't create a problem. He further talked about slaves buried separately from whites and outside cemetery fences.

The preacher said a lot of people of Scotland ancestry lived in this area of Georgia, and they liked to make whiskey. He said that whiskey was the downfall of some people who drank too much. He went on to say that, before he came to Texas, he would occasionally sample some of it and sometimes drink way too much and pass out. Those folks knew how to make moonshine! He said that, when he became a preacher, he quit most of his drinking, adding, "A preacher needs to know how drinking affects church members."

Brother Yonah also indicated that money from whiskey was often used in doing good church work. Bad money sometimes resulted in good work and paid a preacher. Gold mining and timber harvest were also ways folks worked, and a few got wealthy. He described how the town of Helen, Georgia, had been stripped of nearly all harvestable wood by greedy loggers. He told them about Hardman Farm and that it was particularly identified with the wealth of influential Southerners with connections to the old South in Milledgeville. Things went on there that weren't even of the old South. The owner sometimes tethered his wife on hooks in their bedroom, deemed her insane, and went to another room to carry on with her attractive nurse. (The Hardman Farm house stands to this day with the tethers on the wall. Interestingly, word is that it has apparently been more than a century since the tethers were used.)

Brother Yonah told Ellen and Jasper that he needed something new after time in the mountains. He needed to get away from slave brutality in the Piedmont area and the crushing of the Cherokee Indians by the US government. Most of all (though he didn't say so), he wanted to get away from his wife of nineteen years and five children. She had worked some in the little mountain town of Helen in a café and boarding house. She had met and entertained men and had opportunities to meet many others. In a frank statement, Brother Yonah said he wasn't sure if he was the father of all of the children that he was responsible for feeding and clothing, but he'd tried to accept them as his own. After all, what else could he do as a preacher?

Helen was an early gold mine and timber town. Many men came to the town for work. Some of the men had become very close friends with Brother Yonah's wife. He did not like what was going on. Divorces were about impossible. So, he'd deserted her and moved to Texas in 1862 and formed Flowing Waters Chapel. He made no attempt to keep in contact with any of his children. It seemed he had made a move to escape responsibility. But neither Ellen nor Jasper would ask about that. Brother Yonah indicated he had prayed to God for forgiveness of his past sins and that he felt forgiven.

By then, it was time for Brother Yonah to go. He said a goodbye prayer and told Jasper he would baptize him next

Sunday at Watson Creek. No more than a hundred yards from the church house, a small pool in the creek was often used for baptizing. He also asked them if they would keep the private matters he'd discussed to themselves; it would be embarrassing if the information got out in the community. Brother Yonah rode off on a fine horse.

After the preacher left, Jasper and Ellen talked a bit. Jasper decided he would go to be baptized. He didn't want a big deal made out of it. He told Ellen about a person who was baptized, got into some home brew afterward, and went home drunk and beat his wife. "You know," he said, "churches are not always what they are supposed to be. They may be more about taking up collection than anything else."

Jasper also did not think that the preacher should have deserted his wife and five children. But—um!—had Jasper ever heard of such before? It sometimes happened, but no decent man would desert a family.

The summer moved on. Ellen and Jasper continued with Sunday services at Flowing Waters Chapel. Crops were maturing. Some vegetables had been harvested, including potatoes and squash. Time was needed for harvesting cotton and corn. So, by early September, it was time to pick cotton. The fluffy seed cotton was plucked from the open boles and put in a pick sack. Both Jasper and Ellen worked long days and picked as fast as they could. When the amount weighed about 1,200 pounds, a bale was taken on a wagon to the gin in Athens. After ginning, average weight of bales was a little over five hundred pounds.

After a couple of weeks, three bales had been ginned, and the picking was continuing. Both Ellen and Jasper were working as hard and as fast as they could. But Ellen, for some reason, started not to feel well in a way she had never felt before. She told Jasper that her bleed time did not happen on schedule; it was at least three weeks late. She said she felt puffy and kind of big-bellied. Maybe she was going to have a baby. But she kept picking; they couldn't waste time.

The next morning, she told Jasper she was beginning to bleed in a way she didn't know about—the bleeding was very heavy. After a couple of days, Jasper asked Candy, as a midwife, to come by the room to see Ellen. She did. After a brief conversation, she said that Ellen was likely having a miscarriage, or, as she also said, a "spontaneous abortion." She recommended that Ellen rest in bed for a couple more days and see how she felt. Candy did mention the name of a doctor in Athens. Jasper had to pick cotton by himself. And in a couple more days Ellen was beginning to feel almost back to her usual self, though she was a tad weak and downhearted. No doubt, she'd had a miscarriage. After about a week, Ellen returned to picking. She suffered mild depression for a few days—something they didn't know much about in 1864.

During all of this, Ellen had a birthday. On September 7, she turned seventeen years of age. It was different this year. She was not with Pa or Ma or her siblings. Jasper didn't realize it was her birthday until she told him. He told her, "Happy birthday," and gave her tender kisses. He found a gardenia shrub blooming near the front of the house and picked a bouquet of three blossoms. They had such a sweet fragrance; this helped Ellen adjust to being away from her family, and she was improving from the miscarriage.

The cotton and corn harvest progressed. They wound up with eleven bales of cotton or about 5,526 pounds of lint cotton. Of everything harvested, Mr. Smith got a third. At $0.08 a pound, the value of the cotton was $442.72, of which $148 went to Mr. Smith. Out of the two-thirds for Jasper and Ellen, Mr. Smith deducted the costs of furnishings charged to their account since April 1. Ellen and Jasper had lived frugally to keep the costs down. The amount owed was $98, which left them about $195—not much considering all the work they had done but in line with other farms.

They harvested 110 bushels of corn, with a third going to Mr. Smith. The corn was stored in a space Mr. Smith let them use adjacent to the corncrib. It would be used for making corn meal and hominy and as animal feed. Having corn helped Ellen and Jasper have food for several months.

Mr. Smith asked Jasper to speak with him. He wanted to know if Jasper and Ellen would be there next year. Jasper said they would if the sharecropper arrangements were the same. They would be. Mr. Smith also said there would be a little day work during the winter, for which Jasper would be paid. Jasper told him he really needed the work, and if the job was right, Ellen would also work.

They found Mr. Smith to be a nice, honest farm man. Some paid day work helped the couple have money for clothing and food. Spring was approaching; Jasper and Ellen began cleaning the fields. This year Mr. Smith let them have four additional acres. So, Ellen and Jasper slightly expanded their farming, particularly their cash crop—cotton.

The next couple of years went routinely. They saved what money they could and began to look for farm acreage they might buy. They wanted a place with a small house and stable or barn. They found it and took out a mortgage.

In the summer of their fourth year in Henderson County, Ellen was pregnant. She spoke with Candy and got suggestions to help avoid another miscarriage. Candy was helpful in many ways. She talked to her about exercise, well-balanced meals, weight management, and avoiding stress. She talked about trimesters (something new to Ellen) and preparing for the birth of a baby.

Candy explained that the baby would be due 280 days

from the first day of her last period. She said she would help with the birth process and cutting the cord. She would support the baby's head as it emerged and hold the baby so any fluids in its mouth and nose would drain away. She would make sure the baby was breathing. The baby would be placed on the mother's chest with the cord connected. Candy explained how the cord would not be cut as long as it was pulsating—a sign that the embryonic sac (*placenta*, which was a fancy word to Ellen) had not separated. Separation of the placenta (they called it after-birth in Tinnin) was usually within ten minutes after a birth. Candy talked about how she would tie the cord and cover the baby to keep it warm. She also talked to Ellen about how to breastfeed the baby.

The big day arrived. Ellen went into labor. Jasper went next door and got Candy. Ellen delivered the baby with Candy's help on February 3, 1868. Candy announced that it was a boy. Ellen and Jasper had decided, if the baby was a boy, they would name him Ira Jasper Lee. Both parents were very happy with the new baby son.

Being a mother was something new to Ellen. Providing for a newborn was not new. Ellen, as the oldest child in her family, had helped her mother with her younger siblings. She had made a few items of clothing, diapers, and blankets. Fortunately, there were no problems with the baby or its mother. Ira was healthy and grew well. Both Jasper and Ellen adored him.

But Ellen had an emptiness. She had not informed her Ma and Pa Shepard in Tinnin, Mississippi, about the birth of their firstborn grandchild. In fact, she had not had any contact with them since March 1864. No contact was planned. Situations sometimes change, just as they would several years later.

Ellen had additional responsibilities with home, baby, and farmwork. Ira was about six weeks of age when the time for major fieldwork arrived. Jasper prepared a small wooden box with a blanket so Ellen could have baby Ira near her in the field for nursing, comfort, and care. After all, they didn't own a cow, and milk was not available at a store; Ellen had to produce the milk for Ira!

Jasper and Ellen had begun to develop a good reputation in the Henderson County community where they lived. They had an open account at Morrison and Greenwood Mercantile. This allowed them to get things for their home and farm and pay for them when the crops were harvested at the end of the season. The year 1868 was a good example. Beginning February 21, 1868, they got a number of things for farming and living on account throughout the spring and summer. Examples include two pecks of potatoes, twenty-two yards of cotton cloth and four yards of linen, a wood chisel, a looking glass, a pottery dish, and a twelve-pound smoothing iron. The last charge was ten cents for turnip seed made on August 31. This open account was paid off in the fall with the sale of the harvested cotton. Ellen and Jasper had figured out how to live and farm without having cash on hand.

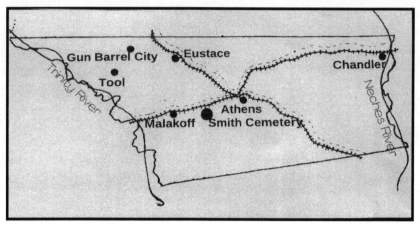

A map of Henderson County, Texas, shows that Athens was the railroad crossroads of East Texas in 1865. Note that Smith Cemetery is a short distance west of Athens.

Ellen and Jasper continued to pursue their goals of owning a farm. They located a good-sized piece of property that seemed right for them. They spoke with Landlord Smith about it and their goals. He said that, for their long-term benefit, they needed to find a way to buy it. He would understand if they no longer sharecropped.

In October 1869, Jasper entered into a promissory note agreement with a Randall Odom to buy two hundred acres of land. The note was payable in full on January 1, 1871. The approval of Ellen as Jasper's wife was not needed for him to enter into such an agreement. The property included a residence where they would live. The farm property was in the same community where they had been living. The location was good, as was the acreage for row cropping. They used savings to get a couple of mules, plows, and hand tools. A line of credit was arranged from a local merchant until crop harvest in the fall. Getting new land into production required extra effort. Some of it had not been row cropped before and grew scattered trees and grasses and broadleaf plants. The soil was rough for planting and tillage.

A small house on the land became home for Ellen, Jasper, and Ira when they moved in January 1870. The day they moved into their house, the home of a neighbor burned in the night. All died in the fire except a fourteen-year-old girl named Mary. They had her move in with them. In exchange for room and board, she could help care for Ira, who was now approaching two years of age. Ellen could now have a little more flexibility with farmwork.

Farm life and work progressed as well as could be expected for Ellen and Jasper. They lived frugally and saved as they could toward a farm of their own. Jasper became more concerned with civic responsibility and was a property owner. He registered to vote in November 1869. Ellen couldn't register because she was a female. That slight always concerned her—she felt she was equal in most regards to Jasper and other men. (The right for white women to vote came in the United States on August

18, 1920, when the Nineteenth Amendment to the US Constitution was passed. Ellen had died in 1918.)

The crops did well in 1870, considering the nature of the land. Jasper and Ellen got in twenty acres of cotton; fifteen acres of corn; and a couple of acres of vegetables, including sweet potatoes. All of these crops required a great deal of hand labor. Not much animal-powered equipment was available, except for basic plows and cultivators. Fortunately, adequate rainfall promoted growth and productivity.

In July of that year, an unknown person on a horse came onto the property. Jasper investigated. He learned that the man was a US Federal Census enumerator. Jasper cooperated as the head of household. He described his four-person household—himself, Ellen, baby Ira, and the young female live-in worker named Mary. The information was recorded by the enumerator.

Crops matured. Harvest began in late summer. Jasper worked as hard as he could; he had a mortgage payment staring him in the face. Some cotton was out and ginned, but a few bales remained in the field. Maybe he was under more than usual stress.

And, then tragedy! How would Ellen carry on? She had no contact with family. She was all alone.

7

Catastrophe

Tragedy struck, and many of Ellen's hopes and aspirations came to an end in November 1870. Or maybe this was a tragic time of reorientation.

Ellen was awakened in the early morning of November 15 by sounds of Jasper gasping for breath and unable to speak well. She talked to him about his feelings; he only made a few sounds, but she did understand that he had a bad chest pain. She held his hands and kissed him on the forehead.

Ellen ran to the next house about a quarter of a mile away. A young family lived there named Eudy. She alerted the man, Jay, to Jasper's situation and asked if he could quickly summon a nearby doctor. It was some three miles to Athens and the nearest doctor. Eudy saddled his horse and rode off at a great speed. In town, he went to the doctor's home and told him.

Dr. Pierpont Ponder immediately came in his horse and buggy (typical travel mode for a physician in those days making house calls, the buggy had one seat for two people and a folding cover). Dr. Ponder was an experienced physician. He had administered to a wide range of health conditions over the years. He had sometimes brought good news and, other times, bad news. Regardless, he was held in high regards for his care and consideration of all patients regardless of income and social status.

Everything happened quickly. In about thirty minutes, Dr. Ponder was attending to Jasper. He checked for breathing, pulse, skin color, and eye condition. Jasper was breathing irregularly with effort to get his breath. He couldn't talk coherently and appeared to be fading in and out of consciousness. Dr. Ponder gave him a small dose of paregoric by mouth. He told Ellen what it was and that it contained, among other things, opium. It would relax the body and help relieve pain. It might aid the body in restoring certain functions such as breathing and heartbeat. He told Ellen she could watch chest movement and check for a pulse (heartbeat) on the vein in Jasper's wrist.

Dr. Ponder spent some time with Jasper; he seemed to be stabilizing, and his vital signs were a tad stronger. Then he had to go. He asked Ellen if she had any whiskey she might give Jasper as a medicinal. She answered, "No."

Dr. Ponder said he would come back late that afternoon to check on Jasper and bring a small bottle of whiskey. He ask if Old Dexter bourbon would be OK; Ellen said it would (She remembered this label as the kind of bourbon her father bought in half-barrel amounts in Vicksburg at Duff Green Mercantile.) As the doctor was leaving, he handed Ellen a small bottle of paregoric and said that, if Jasper appeared to be in major pain, she was to give him half a teaspoon by mouth. Interestingly, Dr. Ponder was a physician who cared more about his patients than he did about the money he made in practicing medicine.

Ellen spent the day caring for Jasper. She bathed his face and hands in slightly warm water. She brushed his hair. She tried to give him a little food and began with molasses on a small piece of cornpone—something he normally really liked. He ate a little and refused more. He drank a couple of swallows of water. At midday, he got a little better, and she was able to help him to go pee; at least his kidneys were functioning. Afterward, Jasper fell back asleep on the bed; Ellen was at his side all of the time (except when little Ira needed attention).

Midafternoon, Ellen went out to check on animals and things around the barn. All appeared in good order. She fed corn to the horses, mules, oxen, and pigs. As she was outside, Brother Yonah was riding by in his wagon. He had no idea that Jasper was gravely ill. He stopped and said hello to Ellen; she told him about Jasper. Brother Yonah asked if he could see Jasper and offer a prayer. Though she wasn't too keen on the idea, she was courteous and invited Brother Yonah to go inside. He greeted Jasper, who made no response, though there was slight facial recognition. He held Jasper's hand and offered a prayer of healing for him. He said he was glad he had baptized Jasper. Then the preacher left; he said a few words and, honestly, wasn't all that sincere about the well-being of Jasper but seemed more caring for Ellen.

It was now getting late in the afternoon. Dr. Ponder was due back at any time to check on the condition of Jasper. He arrived before dark and checked his vital signs. Overall, he noticed little change since morning. He asked if another dose of paregoric had been given; the answer was no. Dr. Ponder told Ellen to keep Jasper comfortable. Occasionally, she should offer him a little water with a bit of honey in it. He handed Ellen the bottle of Old Dexter Bourbon and said she could give him one or two teaspoons a couple of times through the night. It might be best to mix the bourbon in water and have him drink it. Of course, she could give him anything he would eat, but she wasn't to try and force liquids or solids into him if he didn't swallow; it might be pulled into his lungs, resulting in pneumonia.

Dr. Ponder now had to go. He said he'd be back in the morning just after sunrise. Of course, in the back of his mind, he didn't think Jasper would make it through the night. But he didn't say so.

Knowing Dr. Ponder would be back helped Ellen feel a tad better, though she was very concerned about getting through the night. Ellen cared for Ira and got him to sleep. She couldn't sleep. All she could do was think about Jasper, check on him, and wonder about what might happen in the future.

About a half hour after Dr. Ponder left, Ellen sensed that Jasper was in pain and needed fluids and relief. She fixed a half cup of water with honey and a teaspoon of bourbon. She was able to get Jasper to drink about half of it before he couldn't swallow. It appeared he was now sucking the fluid into his lungs. He wheezed, coughed, slobbered, and spit. Things didn't look good. The little bit of bourbon resulted in his going to sleep; Ellen would try to get some rest as well.

The next morning, Jasper had little chest movement. His eyes were mostly closed. He did not respond to questions. His body was still warm, so Ellen rubbed his head and held his hands. She knew Dr. Ponder would be there soon.

Conditions had deteriorated by the time of Dr. Ponder's arrival.

Jasper was not breathing and had no pulse, his skin color was fading skin, and his eyes were glazed. His body was cooling. He was dead. Dr. Ponder told Ellen that Jasper did not live. He covered Jasper's body with a blanket. It was November 16, 1870. Dr. Ponder told Ellen he was sorry for her loss and wished her well. Ellen told him she would come by his office in a few days to pay the account. He said not to worry.

Tears came to Ellen's eyes. She pulled the blanket back and kissed Jasper's forehead again; she stroked the hair on his head. She asked if there was anything she could have done to save his life. And, then she asked what had caused his death.

Dr. Ponder said, "Probably heart failure or maybe a stroke. How was his diet? Had he had chest pains, shortness of breath, or anything like that?"

Ellen wasn't sure. She said, "Jasper was not a man to complain and be sickly. He kept working all the time—seven days a week. He had a lot on his mind, such as the mortgage that is due and getting the last of the crops harvested."

Dr. Ponder then said something about stress.

As he was leaving, Dr. Ponder indicated he would tell the county coroner, Mr. Medford, who was also the local funeral director, when he got back to Athens. Dr. Ponder further stated that Mr. Medford would probably be out to the house in an hour or so. He would discuss funeral arrangements and talk about what Ellen wanted. Dr. Ponder said to leave the body covered as it was until Mr. Medford arrived.

Jasper had died. Suddenly. Ellen was twenty-three years of age with a two-going-on-three-year-old son. She had to make decisions and act quickly. What was she to do? The decisions had to be ones she could live with the rest of her life. She had few people she could turn to for suggestions or help as she faced burying her husband.

On this tragic day, Ellen was alone with a small son. She had shared life with Jasper for six years and eight months. They had many hopes and goals that would have carried them for years to come. What was she to do? How was she to provide for herself and her son? How was she to settle the estate of her husband? How would she relate to the advances of adoring men who had ambitions with her? After all, she was a good-looking woman only twenty-three years of age.

The love of her life was gone. Her hopes for the future were dashed. She thought she might never love again. How would Ellen move forward with life? She had no contact with family. She was all alone.

Though it was something she had never done before, Ellen began to think about the burial of Jasper. Above all, Ellen wanted a proper burial for her beloved husband. But she had other things to think about and do. Animals on the farm had to be fed and otherwise cared for. Harvested and yet-to-be harvested crops had to be managed.

Ellen, first of all, wanted to memorialize Jasper to the extent her means would allow. Mr. Medford, the funeral director, arrived and talked about a range of things. Many required a good bit of money, which Ellen didn't have. She had to economize in arranging for Jasper's funeral. She was glad that Dr. Ponder had informed an experienced funeral director. Ellen did what she could for a proper burial for Jasper that she could afford. She soon became comfortable with this funeral director; he appeared honest and of high integrity. She needed help in arranging a burial plot in Smith Cemetery.

Overall, Ellen found Mr. Medford to be sympathetic and understanding of her situation. Together, they worked out the details of an order of service:

Memorial Service
Flowing Waters Church
Brother Yonah, in charge

Jasper H. Lee (born on March 27, 1827, died on November 16, 1870, age forty-three years and seven months)

Service:

- Purpose of gathering and brief summary of the life of Jasper by Brother Yonah
- Short prayer by Brother Yonah
- Song by those gathered: "What a Friend We Have in Jesus"
- Scripture reading: Psalm 23

- Short message by Brother Yonah
- Song by those gathered: "Amazing Grace"
- Ending prayer by Brother Yonah

Interment in Smith Cemetery.

Casual covered-dish dinner by members of Flowing Waters Church

Now all Ellen needed to do was work out the details with Brother Yonah. She needed Brother Yonah to deliver a short eulogy at a memorial service in tiny Flowing Waters Chapel. She would ask him about the order of service that she and Mr. Medford had prepared. She hoped the preacher would accept it.

Mr. Medford placed a velvet-lined pine casket he had brought with him beside Jasper's body on the bed. He was going to take the body back to the funeral home for preparation and then bring it to Flowing Waters Church, but Ellen had other ideas. She wanted to bathe, dress, and groom the body in their home. She had a new black jacket, as well as pants and shirt for dressing the body. She wanted Jasper to lie in repose in the house where he had lived for about a year. It is also the house that involved a lot of dreams about their future together.

On his way back to Athens, Mr. Medford stopped by Flowing Waters Church and told Brother Yonah what had happened. Brother Yonah quickly went to see Ellen; they talked. He hugged Ellen and Ira. Ellen asked him to deliver the memorial service. He was asked to keep it simple and sophisticated and not to make a "come-to-Jesus" sermon. A burial site was arranged in Smith Cemetery through one of the members of Flowing Waters Church. This cemetery was just across the road from the church and conveniently located in the community for those who wished to pay their respects at a memorial service. Two church members volunteered to dig the grave.

Ellen was surprised at the comfort and support Brother Yonah gave her. Was it sincere? He was normally self-centered and ready to condemn the "sinners" around him in the world. She likely had some sort of thoughts about a few dollars being passed to the preacher for doing the eulogy. Was he promoting his own financial well-being at the expense of a newly widowed young mother and son? Or, since he was living as a single person, was he viewing Ellen as a potential preacher's wife? Those questions were never uttered aloud.

The time for the funeral was two days after Jasper died. Ellen asked the funeral director to assist in managing the casket for viewing the body in her home. They placed the casket in the front room of the house. It was located with one end on a homemade pine table and the other end on another homemade oak table. Both tables had been built by Jasper from local wood. People could enter from the porch. He looked good in the casket (or at least as good as a dead man could). She and Ira were very sad. They kissed the body's cold forehead and said goodbye in a way only a loving wife and son could do.

Ellen prepared a casket bouquet of a dozen wild red roses that she and Ira picked from a rambling rose vine on the bank at the entrance to the barn on the farm. Several people came by to pay their respects to Jasper. Each would linger a bit, view Jasper's body, and offer condolences. Most offered assistance to Ellen. But she, being an independent person, was reluctant to ask for help. A few people brought dishes of prepared food for Ellen and Ira. Brother Yonah came by four times; he wanted to be sure to provide "comfort" in this time of loss. He also was quite willing to eat some of the food that had been brought.

The casket was moved from the home by Mr. Medford in the back of a horse-drawn wagon and relocated to Flowing Waters Church. It was taken inside and placed at the front of the church sanctuary by the pallbearers. Six local men from Flowing Waters Church served as pallbearers. Ellen was very grateful for their help.

A few local neighbors attended the service—no family members were in attendance, as they had no family in the area. Some brought small bouquets of flowers picked from their yards. Sweetest of all was a bouquet of gardenias, which reminded Ellen of the bouquet Jasper had brought her years ago in Tinnin. Brother Yonah delivered the eulogy much as the service had been planned. Burial was in Smith Cemetery. Ellen gave Brother Yonah two dollars afterward in appreciation for his help.

An engraved stone marker was installed by Mr. Medford a couple of weeks later. It had the inscription, "Jasper Henry Lee, Born March 27, 1827, Died November 16, 1870. Father of Ira Jasper Lee." (The marker with that inscription stands to this day in a somewhat remote location in Henderson County, Texas.) After the marker was up, Ellen and Ira rode in their horse-drawn wagon into Athens and went by the funeral director's office to pay the changes. Mr. Medford kept costs to a minimum, and Ellen was able to use grocery money to pay. Some folks viewed it a bit out of the ordinary for Ellen's name to be left off the grave marker.

One family provided particular support. The Bell family had moved to Henderson County from Mississippi a few years earlier. The family had several children and had settled near where Ellen and Jasper had bought the farm land. A young man named Walter Nelson Bell was quite helpful. He was about two or so years younger than Ellen and was able to sense some of the difficulty she was having. He knew Ellen and Ira would have to move from the farmhouse they had lived in by the last of December or, at the latest, early January. The mortgage was due January 1, and money to pay was not available. Maybe she could have a little grace time in paying, but that didn't fit the reputation of the man who held the mortgage. Nelson and his aging parents agreed to provide a place for Ellen and Ira to sleep in exchange for her work in the home and on the farm. Food was provided with the regular family meals.

Other things were already happening that tended to fail to recognize the memory of Jasper. Men appeared to come from out of nowhere. They wanted to take advantage of good-looking, twenty-three year-old Ellen. But, Ellen was strong; she knew right from wrong, and she would speak up for herself and her son, Ira. Some wanted various things from Jasper's estate; others wanted Ellen!

After a proper burial in Smith Cemetery, settling the estate was of first order. She asked Mr. Medford for guidance. How would the estate be settled? What would be the outcome? Ellen and Ira had little to nothing to live on. How would they have food? Clothing? Shelter?

Answers were not easy. Many challenges lay ahead.

The mortgage was due. The house they lived in was included in the mortgage agreement. The court needed to settle the estate of Jasper Henry Lee. Ellen, as a female, had few if any rights. Harvest of crops had not been completed at the time of Jasper's death. It wouldn't be easy.

Ellen could not turn to her parents in Tinnin, Mississippi. They had pretty much cast her away; she had pretty much cast them away. But love is greater than relationships in human life. She had married outside the approval of her family. What would be the result? Now, the love of Ellen's life was dead. What would happen?

Where was the good work of Flowing Waters Chapel during difficult times? Most of the time, Brother Yonah was not to be seen. Some church members jokingly said he was probably preparing frightening sermons. As a preacher, he could be counted on to baptize, preach fire and brimstone sermons, and do funerals. But when needs arose, he didn't seem to be around. When he was around, he did not appear very sincere. Supposedly he was in hopes that members would provide support to those in need. Maybe some of the trusted members of the church were also individuals who tried to "beat" Ellen out of the proceeds of Jasper's estate. After all, Brother Yonah had earlier lived with a wife, children, and church congregation in the mountains of Georgia. He had observed great cruelty to slaves and native Americans. He'd deserted all of this for a new life in Henderson County. But was he still married to the mother of his children (the wife who worked for gold miners and loggers in bars and cheap rental rooms)?

Brother Yonah appeared to give Ellen and Jasper special attention. Maybe he suspected some vulnerability. He visited Ellen at her home shortly after the funeral; he was always very nice, willing to eat, and appeared sincere in expressing sorrow and offering support. He reminded Ellen that the church Thanksgiving meal was coming up and invited her and Ira to attend. Maybe she could bring a dish of some type if she could afford it. Ellen and Ira did go. She prepared and took sweet potato casserole using sweet potatoes she and Jasper had grown. It was a nice group that offered support to Ellen as they could.

In early December, Brother Yonah went by to see Ellen and Ira. He offered help as needed. He said he could get church members involved in helping her. He asked her to come see him if she got lonely. Nice, but not the kind of help she wanted. She wanted sincere interest and help.

The next week, Brother Yonah again visited. He told her of the Christmas program and dinner coming up at the church and invited Ellen and Ira to attend. He said he would come in his wagon and transport them to the church. They went along. It was good to get better acquainted with people in the community. Brother Yonah arranged the Christmas dinner seating so he would be next to Ellen. Was he trying to "make a move" on Ellen and doing so too quickly? He appeared to be after friendship beyond routine for an older and most likely married preacher who was attempting to help a grieving young woman and her young son.

Ellen made one of her special dishes—Mama Tinnin's apple and cheese casserole. She was able to get red wax, yellow hoop cheese and other needed ingredients at the mercantile store in Athens—a special and extravagant thing for her to do. Ellen had picked the apples from a wild tree on their farm and had stored them for about a month. Brother Yonah bragged on how good the casserole was and went back for a second serving. Other people liked it too; the dish was scraped clean.

After the meal, there was a short program. Brother Yonah made himself to be Santa and gave all the little children (only six were there) a small candy treat. He hugged each child and offered admonishment to behave or there would be no gifts on Christmas Eve. The program ended with the reading of selected verses from Luke 2 in the Bible and a short prayer. Somehow, Ira wound up with two pieces of candy—probably the doings of the preacher to gain favor.

Brother Yonah would sometimes come by and help with light farmwork, such as tending animals and cutting a few pieces of firewood. He now usually chose not to eat with Ellen and Ira. Ellen shared her mortgage situation and that she would have to move out before the end of December. She shared that the Bell family had invited her and Ira to stay at their home until they got their situation worked out. On moving day, Brother Yonah helped Ellen and Ira pack. He brought his wagon to help move the few things that were to go.

Ellen left some big things in the house and on the farm. The place was being foreclosed. The mortgage payment could not be made on January 1. She did take a few household items, a horse, a light one-horse wagon, and some corn for feed and grinding.

One day, Brother Yonah told Ellen that, if it didn't work out to live at the Bell home, she and Ira could live at his home. That statement was a surprise to Ellen. She wasn't ready for anything other than security and safety. She was still grieving for Jasper. Fortunately, she was able to make it work to live with the Bell family.

Ellen and Ira went to Sunday services at the Flowing Waters Chapel. The congregation sang hymns and listened to the sermons by Brother Yonah. Each Sunday, he would give Ellen a special goodbye hug and say that he would be by to see them during the week. Attending the services allowed Ellen to meet and talk with people, and it allowed Ira to have a few friends for playing. But something seemed out of place about the relationship the preacher was trying to develop.

Ellen talked quietly to one of the church members about the nature of Brother Yonah. That individual didn't know much about his past; she didn't think any church member would know. She learned that Brother Yonah had shown up one day and gotten access to an old out-of-service church house and started Flowing Waters Chapel. He'd cleaned and fixed up the place a bit. He'd visited families, asking them to come to the new church he was leading. He always had prayers about the church and God. He developed a slogan for the church—"Opening

Heaven." He could use that slogan in a sermon to strike fear in members of the congregation and offer them hope if they did what *he* said. He had a second slogan that he sometimes used, "Quenching the Fires of Hell" (QFH). If he was preaching loud and fast and had a lapse in thought, he would say QFH once, twice, or however many times he needed until he regained his thoughts. Every time Brother Yonah got into a heated sermon on sin, guilt, and QFH, Ellen would think back to the delightful Presbyterian church in Brandon, Mississippi, where she'd met Jasper. It was a calm and loving kind of place.

Though he had once shared some of his past with Jasper and Ellen, Brother Yonah never told the church folks much about himself other than that he was from the mountains of northern Georgia. In fact, he never told them if he was using his real name, his age (he appeared to be in his late fifties or early sixties), or about his education or lack thereof. He never told them about his wife and several children. He just pretended he had never been married or fathered children.

Brother Yonah owned the church property and marketed his services well. He was able to attract enough people to come to the church to make it successful. He could get the people who came to give money from their meager amounts. Most of the contributions went straight into his pockets. He had the ability to strike fear in those who came to church by creating guilt in a person who did not show up on Sunday. He did so by frequently preaching about sinning and the fires in hell. He often invoked how Flowing Waters Chapel was quenching the fires of hell. It probably helped that there were no other churches in the community. The church house doubled as a community center for selected social events, including weddings and seasonal dinners.

So, was Brother Yonah a true believer?(Some might ask, "What is a true believer?" Your best answer might come from checking with a minister of a local Protestant faith.) Was he sending a little money back to northeast Georgia for the family he had apparently deserted? Was he investing money in a business enterprise he might one day go into on a full-time basis? One time, in the passion of a fiery sermon, the mention of a tiny desert town known as Las Vegas slipped out of his mouth. He quickly refocused and never mentioned Las Vegas again.

Brother Yonah was by to visit Ellen like clockwork. He didn't miss; nor was he late. The Bells were kind of amazed at the goings-on. One day, he asked if Mrs. Bell would keep Ira while he and Ellen went for a walk in the woods. Ellen heard the question and refused to go walking. She simply could not assess all that was on Brother Yonah's mind. His intentions might have been something that would compromise the lifelong love and commitment Ellen had made to Jasper.

This day in mid-January was no different from recent

visits; he'd brought a small bouquet of early-blooming daffodil flowers. He reached and grabbed Ellen's hand and raised it to give it a kiss. Another time he reached and held her hand and pulled her toward him for an embrace. The preacher was being open about the desire to build a romantic relationship, even considering the nature of his job as a minister. He also did not know about past times when Ellen had extricated herself from embraces of men, as with the powerful right forearm to Private Cason on the porch of the Shepard home or the sharp elbow to the midsection of the boozing customer at the Spoon in Athens. Preachers (and all men) should beware of Ellen. (Further, they should never make unwanted advances toward any woman.)

Brother Yonah returned a couple of days later. Ira was taking a nap. Mrs. Bell was home and everyone else was out working, getting the fields ready for spring plowing and planting. He calculated that this would be a good time to try to "connect" with Ellen. He told her he needed her help at Flowing Waters Chapel in arranging the pulpit for a special service that was to be held on Sunday. He quickly seized on a weak moment in Ellen's defense against his advances—maybe what he had in mind didn't register with her.

They rode to the church in the horse-pulled wagon. When they arrived, he jumped out and went around to Ellen's side and lifted her out of the wagon and to the ground. He said, "See, I am strong. My strength is greater when I am around you. I think you are a beautiful woman of God. As a man of God, I need your help arranging chairs around the pulpit and with other matters we will talk about later."

They went inside the church and walked to the pulpit. Ellen noted that there were no chairs to arrange.

They got to the pulpit and sat down on the edge. She said nothing. He reached over and grabbed her around the body and whispered, "Praise the Lord."

By then, Ellen had had enough. She wanted no more advances from a preacher—a fake preacher at that. She remembered the success of elbow throws and promptly delivered one into the preachers midgut with such power that he fell over onto the pulpit.

He gasped and shouted, "Holy crap, what have you done?"

Ellen dashed out of the church and jumped into the wagon, grabbed the reins, and rapidly drove the horse and wagon back to the Bell house. The preacher, once he got over the blow and fall onto the pulpit, would have to walk back to retrieve his horse and wagon.

Brother Yonah made no more advances toward Ellen. He became somewhat of a recluse around her, even though Ellen and Ira still went to Flowing Waters Chapel occasionally. Obviously, his niceness to Ellen had little to do with sincerity toward her in her time of grieving.

Ellen was a good mother and tried to continue raising their son just as Jasper would have wished. She continued to nurse him well past two years of age. Following Jasper's death, nursing providing some security and bonding for both Ellen and Ira. Of course, he was eating some chewed solid foods from the table (Ellen chewed and spit out the food for feeding with a spoon).

Ellen was appealing and, some men figured, available. Men tried to take advantage of Ellen. She was smart. She was defensive. Was she flirtatious or just personable? Maybe she was not sufficiently appreciated. We shall see.

Just as bad things can happen to people who do good, good things happen to people who do evil. Such was the case with Ellen. Though there were men who stole from the estate and otherwise tried to take advantage of her, there were also people who reached out to Ellen and helped her in this difficult time.

Ellen and Ira managed with life in the Bell home. They certainly appreciated the Bell's generosity; they were nice folks. All of the Bell's children were gone from home except Nelson. This made a little more space. But Ellen did not know how long they could stay. Ellen would frequently mention to Mr. and Mrs. Bell how much she appreciated staying there, assuring them that, when they could, they would move out. She tentatively set moving out as being the time when Jasper's estate settled.

Unfortunately, Mrs. Bell became quite ill in late January and died after a couple of weeks. No one knew much about her illness. She had appeared to be in declining health for a while; maybe it was breast cancer. She was in pain quite a bit. So, Ellen was in just the right place to help a grieving family. She could help maintain the household.

Just how "things" developed between Ellen and Nelson is unknown—nothing more than friendship. She probably supported his grieving in the death of his mother. She probably also confided in him and told him the story of her love, marriage, and life with Jasper and about his demise. She, no doubt, told him about her family back in Mississippi, who she hadn't seen or heard from since March 1864. And she made no effort to contact them, though she needed support in coping with life.

Here was single Ellen—a smart, good-looking woman in her midtwenties. She was temporarily living in the same house as a single young man. Several men in the community eyed her. Maybe she stayed in Texas because of a possible romance with one or more of them. But at least until 1875, she stayed to honorably probate the estate of her deceased husband. During this time, she kept thinking to herself, *Where did all of the men come from after Jasper died?*

8

Theft and Integrity: Estate Action

Tragic!

Yes, it was a tragic day in 1870 when Jasper suddenly died. Ellen was now to live alone with a small son. She had shared life with Jasper for six years and eight months. Together, they had experienced much happiness and set many hopes and goals. The time was cut short—way too short, in her opinion.

After a proper and affordable burial in Smith Cemetery, settling the estate was of first order. How? What would be the outcome? How was Ellen to provide for herself and her son, Ira? They had little-to-nothing to live on. How would they have food? Clothing? Shelter? How would she relate to the advances of adoring men who had ambitions with her? It wouldn't be easy to take care of matters without unwanted attention. After all, she was a smart woman and only twenty-three years of age. But she was still grieving from the loss of her Jasper.

Men appeared to come for Ellen out of nowhere. Some might have lusted after her. Others wanted to take advantage of the estate Jasper left. Yes, they planned to steal from a widow with a small son! But Ellen was strong; she knew right from wrong and she would speak up for herself and her son. Among the first repeated advances she had to fight off her those of the preacher of the church she attended, Flowing Waters. Can you believe a preacher would take advantage of a young widow? Yes, it was kind of like Jasper had said. "The bigger they come the harder they fall!"

Ellen was not ready to begin thinking about another man in her life. After all, she had made a lifelong commitment to Jasper. Maybe she really didn't want another man.

After the last defense of her very being, the preacher left her alone and seemed to become sullen if anywhere near her. It seemed that, if the preacher couldn't have her, he was not going to make life any easier for her. There would be numerous other times when she needed to defend herself and her son from other men. She was smart, but she didn't know all of the 1870s estate laws and situations that would arise. She could also be defensive and protective of what was hers. She was a good mother and wanted to be an even better one. Maybe she was not sufficiently appreciated by the people in the community where she lived. We shall see.

Answers were not easy. Many challenges lay ahead. Ellen made up her mind that she was going to be up to the task. She recalled something said by one of her past preachers—something to the effect of the Lord would give her no more than she could handle. Sometimes, she wondered why she had been given so much. She was quite capable, but she needed a lot of time to think—to meditate. In addition to a concerted effort to properly settle the estate, a little luck would certainly be useful.

Ellen, as a female, had few if any government-granted rights. She owned no property and, though she worked on the land, she hadn't had much of a role in the management of the farm. The animals needed care until they could be properly under the care of the next owner. Harvest of crops had not been completed at the time of Jasper's death.

The mortgage was due on January 1. Jasper had all the plans in place to pay the mortgage. But just as human life is frail, he had not finalized these plans with the mortgage holder before his death. Many situations were in play. The house they lived in was included in the mortgage agreement. The estate of Jasper Henry Lee needed to be settled in a timely, honest, and legal manner.

Fortunately, the Bell family had invited Ellen and Ira

to live with them until she could get her situation worked out. They moved in before January 1, 1871. Ellen thought probating of the estate would go quickly, but she had no experience with such matters. She thought she could move on with her life once that was done but the process went slowly. As was sometimes said where she grew up, it moved at a snail's pace.

Ellen could not turn to her parents in Tinnin, Mississippi. She had pretty much cast them away; they had moved on, realizing that the choice she made for a man was now beyond something they could do anything about. At the time of her marriage to Jasper, Ellen had wanted to move ahead with her life with the man she loved. But parental love is often greater than most other relationships of love in human life. She had married outside the approval of her family. What would be the reaction of her parents now that the love of Ellen's life was dead? How would Ellen and Ira live the rest of their lives? Of course, Ma and Pa Shepard did not know that Jasper was dead.

The estate settlement was not going to be easy. Texas laws granted to a husband certain rights relating to his wife's separate property as well as their community property. Women had few legal rights in 1870. Mostly, women couldn't own property; nor could they make many decisions on their own. Jasper did not have a will—a big disadvantage. So, Ellen had to defend Jasper's estate against theft and other bad actions. Settling was going to be challenging, to say the least. Fortunately, she could quickly assess human behavior. She would take steps to defend the proceeds of the estate as best she could under the laws at that time. She also wanted to move ahead quickly and fairly to settle the estate soon.

Ellen needed an administrator to handle the matters related to the estate. She knew she did not want the attorney who had been involved in drafting papers related to the property they'd bought and their mortgage. She asked around in the community about the probate process. She particularly asked the people who she knew and trusted at church. (Brother Yonah was not one of them.) Rural Henderson County did not have many attorneys or professional people.

The major recommendation was that she should become informed about the process. She decided to begin by going to the county clerk's office. So, in early December, Ellen harnessed her horse to the wagon, took Ira with her, and drove into Athens to the clerk's office. She learned that an estate was comprised of the assets and liabilities the person had at the time of death. Probating was the legal process used to settle an estate and included the business affairs of a person who has died. The dead person was sometimes referred to as "the decedent" or "the testator." Legal notification of the death of an individual was needed to assure that all people with claims had the opportunity to get what was due them. Notifications were posted on courthouse walls; published in the weekly newspaper (for three consecutive weeks); and announced at public gatherings, such as a meeting of the county commission.

Jasper did not have a will. Regardless, creditors and others with interest in the estate would be paid first. Heirs would receive any assets that remained. These assets would be divided among heirs based on legal rights to them. Ellen learned that she, as the surviving widow, was the heir to Jasper's estate. She was told in the clerk's office that the process for her would require an administrator. Someone was needed to accurately identify and collect the property, pay all debts and other claims such as taxes, and transfer the remaining property to the heirs. She learned that the property might be sold by the administrator, costs of doing the administrator work deducted, and the balance would be given to the heir.

The clerk's office suggested W. G. Price as administrator. The clerk noted he was experienced in probating estates. She was told that, in addition to being a lawyer, Price ran a small store across from the courthouse, so it was fairly easy to find him. She wanted to talk with him and assess how well he could relate to her and represent her in settling Jasper's estate. After arrival at the store, she introduced herself and told him her purpose. Mr. Price readily indicated that he could possibly help. He mentioned other estates he had done. He and Ellen, along with Ira, went into a small back room (which kind of doubled as an office) for discussion. Ellen was businesslike about her purpose. She concluded that Mr. Price would be a good administrator for Jasper's estate. Overall, he appeared to have high integrity and be someone she could trust. She felt he might be able to offer suggestions and be a person who would listen to her concerns as a woman and mother. Did she misjudge him? She also thought in the back of her mind that she might later need an attorney.

Discussion of the procedures in settling an estate intimidated Ellen a bit. She realized she needed help. Ellen and Price discussed, in general, contents of the estate, family and heirs, general procedures in Texas, and costs. Ellen indicated that she wanted Price to come to the farm, and she would help him develop an inventory of the contents of the estate. It was agreed that Mr. Price would be the administrator. She wanted to be sure Mr. Price knew she wanted to move ahead expeditiously. She did not have the money to post the needed bond with the clerk's office, so Mr. Price did it. Ellen would eventually give Price a power of attorney in probating the estate.

On December 10, 1870, the Texas District Court for Henderson County, with Jeff E. Thompson as clerk, recorded the following document:

> Now comes W. G. Price, a person of
> good character residing in the County

of Henderson and State of Texas, and respectfully applies for letters of temporary
administration pro tem upon the Estate of
Jasper H. Lee, dec'd late of said county, and
respectfully states that Jasper H Lee of the
County of Henderson and State of Texas
and domiciled therein died on the 16th day
of November AD 1870 and leaving no will to
the knowledge of this applicant and leaving
a surviving wife, Ellen Lee, and one child,
Ira Lee about 3 years of age, and a personal estate of the value of seven hundred,
thirty-two dollars as estimated according to
law and which needs immediate attention ...
I do solemnly swear that I will well and truly
perform the duties of temporary administrator of the Estate of Jasper H. Lee, deceased,
subscribed and sworn to before me this 10th
day of December AD 1870

Signed W.G. Price.
Jeff E. Thompson, clk, District Court
Henderson County

Shortly after this sworn oath, Price was out in the
community talking about his role as temporary administrator of Jasper's estate. Ethically, this was not the thing he

should do. He was overheard telling a couple of men at his store about some of the contents of the estate—excellent oxen, horses, and a mule and an assortment of well-kept tools. He went on to talk about the young, good-looking surviving wife of Jasper. He said she might soon be looking around for another man and that she probably would be a pushover when it came to the estate. (He didn't know Ellen!) Items could be bought at low prices; just see him. As people recounted Price's story, the notions of deals probably got bigger and bigger.

If Ellen had heard this, she would have let him have it! Not only was it disrespectful of her, but it encouraged dishonesty regarding the items in Jasper's estate. Ellen had grown up in a family with a "good farm business sense" in Mississippi. She knew a lot about the values of farmland, crops, and animals. She was not going to be a pushover!

The first filing of estate matters in the Texas District Court was on December 17, 1870. Clerk Jeff E. Thompson, District Court Henderson County, Texas, prepared the filing documents on behalf of the heirs of Jasper H. Lee. Attorney W. G. Price was earlier appointed to serve as temporary probate administrator. Price made a bond and an oath related to fulfilling the probate of the estate as per Texas laws. Clerk Thompson filed the necessary papers.

On the occasions when Price saw friends and acquaintances after he made his bond and was sworn to the duties of probate administration of the estate of Jasper H. Lee, he would talk about good deals with estate items. Just see him. He would tell them about the death of Jasper and a little about the contents of the estate. Some of the individuals were W. L. Crowson, J. T. Straite, and J. V. Sheldon. He implied that some of the items could be had as "deals."

Through a friend at Flowing Waters Chapel, Ellen got wind of what was being discussed. It seemed to her that she was going to be cheated if she didn't stand up for herself. So maybe something good had come out of getting involved with the church. To prove that cheating was going on would take some time.

Price made attempts in December to move ahead with some of the estate. He had some success in getting the remaining cotton picked.

Cotton had value only when harvested! As a cash crop, it was important to the value of the estate, particularly one such as this that was small. Price kept some receipts and records. Evidently, some of the cotton "got lost" after harvest and ginning. Some items of farm equipment and tools kind of went missing in the vouchers filed with the court.

Progress was slow. Some of the animals were being sold at very low prices. These low amounts did not reflect well on the overall value of the estate. Records and receipts were supposedly being kept. Unharvested cotton would have been a loss. Fortunately, people were found to pick it this late in the year. Ellen got to keep one of the horses and a single-horse wagon for her personal use. She was able to use a stable at the Bell's farm after she had to move.

Ellen wanted faster progress. Every week or so she harnessed her horse and wagon and headed into Athens to meet with Mr. Price or to go by the courthouse. Sometimes Ira would ride with her; other times Nelson Bell might keep him. While there, she would sometimes go by the mercantile store to pick up a thing or two.

In March, 1871, additional papers were filed in the District Court. The result was to remove the word "temporary" from Price as estate administrator. Part of the document read as follows:

The State of Texas, County of Henderson,

Know all men by the presents that I, Ellen S. Lee, of said County and State as such surviving wife do hereby authorize, appoint, and constitute W. G. Price of said County my attorney in fact and in my stead (hereby waiving my privileges) to apply for and obtain letters of administration upon the estate of my late deceased husband hereby certifying his action in the premises as witness my hand this 6th day of March AD 1871.

Signed Ellen S. Lee

Ellen's signature was witnessed by Clerk Thompson. Stamps were added to show this was an official, legal document. W. G. Price was no longer the temporary administrator.

Ellen soon observed that Mr. Price was not able to gain a quick, forthright settlement. Some items in the estate vanished or were sold by the administrator at ridiculously low prices to friends and relatives. The administrator made a number of questionable charges, such as the daily charges for collecting property, hiring hands to pick cotton, and advertising property for sale. Daily charges were made for weighing the cotton into as late as March 10, 1871. Cotton harvest is normally completed by the end of November, but circumstances that extended the harvest a bit were involved. The court, as an interim step, provided Ellen with a little money such as a one-time amount of $10.93 to buy coffee and salt. It was a good thing she had a little money that she'd saved. She was frugal with what she had.

Progress moved at a snail's pace. Were flagrant attempts being made to cheat Ellen and Ira? Most likely. She began to think that something wasn't going as it should have gone. So, not being a person to roll over and allow others to take advantage of her, Ellen went to court against the administrator of the estate. Price now had an attorney, P. T. Tannehill, to help him defend himself against charges of improper conduct. Ellen had to get the services of a legal firm to represent her interests.

In the March 1871 term of the district court, papers were filed to gain payment for Dr. Pierpont Ponder. Ellen had told him in November 1870 that she would come into Athens to his office and make the payment, but Dr. Ponder seemed to indicate there was no rush. On March 13, 1871, Judge J. H. Skinner, awarded Dr. Ponder the sum of $11.65 from Jasper's estate. This was for visits to Jasper when sick and medications, including quinine, paregoric, and medicinal bourbon. Administrator Price was the intermediary in gaining payment for Dr. Ponder.

Now, this seemed reasonable to Ellen, but her feelings were hurt. She was going to pay the amount, but Dr. Ponder had discouraged her. Ellen began to think, *Just about everything is stacked against women. If I were a man, it wouldn't be this way—not even in Texas.* (Maybe she was beginning to have questions in her mind about continuing to live in the state.)

More action occurred at the July 1871 term of court. The presiding judge was the Honorable G. Scott of the Texas District Court serving Henderson County, Texas. Ellen was present to observe progress. Her attorney was there to represent her best interests in court proceedings. Estate Administrator Price presented the court with a partial listing of items and values in the estate of Jasper H. Lee. He also petitioned the court to reimburse him certain expenses he had incurred as administrator of the estate. Price requested $17.88 he'd paid for taxes on the land for the 1870 tax year, and he had a receipt. He then submitted receipts from two individuals for a total of $15 for hauling a total of six bales of cotton to the gin. He also had a receipt for $19 that had been provided to Ellen S. Lee. He requested $2 as a reimbursement for two bushels of corn fed to the team that pulled the wagon loaded with cotton. He requested permission of the court to sell three bales of cotton for supplies for the surviving wife and child. Overall, property valued at $730 had been sold; numerous charges were made against the income. One charge of particular interest was a payment of $10.65 to the doctor for attending to Jasper in his final two days. To Ellen, this was an appropriate payment.

Price sought approval by the court for himself to receive several payments. Ellen wondered if these were honest and fair, but she stayed quiet for now.

Among estate items, there were two horses valued at $75 each, two yoke of oxen valued at $40, twenty head of hogs valued at $40, one mule valued at $100, and one double-barrel shotgun valued at $8. Many other miscellaneous farm tools were included, such as saddles and saddlebags, carpentry tools, and hoes and shovels. Most importantly, animals required care. They needed feeding and watering. This meant Ellen had to have feed available and tend to them each and every day until they had new owners or, at least, someone to take care of them. Ellen appreciated animals too much for there to be any mistreatment or failing to provide for the needs of the animals. The feed was corn grain and some fodder that had been harvested on the farm.

Judge Scott made some important findings. He found the said estate was worth about $4,000. Encumbrances and liens amounted to $2,200. The husband had left no homestead for his surviving wife and son. He ruled the estate was not of sufficient wealth to be subject to administration. He ruled on errors in submissions by the individual who had earlier and in error been appointed administrator, W. G. Price. Some of these had been the subject of earlier court action.

Price attempted to justify the work he had done. The situation was now quite entangled with court activity, administrator "doings," and the surviving wife's needs. Price had made regular but sometimes half-hearted attempts to move ahead with his role as administrator of the estate. Some work was sloppy to the extent it might have purposefully been done in such a manner so as to defraud the estate. At one point, the judge of the court decried the sloppy writing used to record estate items and disposals. The indication was that some written names and descriptions were not decipherable. The judge admonished that records be kept with neater penmanship. Further, the judge specified that accuracy and fairness were extremely important.

Court action was continued far beyond what Ellen

thought necessary. The longer it went on, the better she understood why. Sometimes, it seemed things repeated themselves.

Ellen Lee was issued a subpoena to appear in court on of November 4, 1872. In court action that day, Ellen Lee became a plaintiff against W. G. Price, defendant. Three other individuals were also named as defendants—W. S. Crowson, J. T. Straite, and J. V. Sheldon. It appeared to Ellen that some things were repeated in court; maybe that was the way it should be.

Ellen could sense she was continuing to be short-changed. She was a gutsy woman to take on the court-appointed probate administrator. But she did. Her attorney (the firm of Farrell, Eaves, and Keith) was quite helpful in this regard. In short, the administrator was making false claims and not offering full accounting of the items in the estate. Maybe his vouchers reflected what was good for him and his buddies.

About two years had passed since Jasper's death. The estate wasn't settled. Ellen made up her mind; she wasn't going to roll over and be swindled. Her new attorney helped her file court challenges. On November 7, 1872, court action was initiated to challenge the financial records and proposed settlement previously filed by W. G. Price.

In that same term of the Court, Ellen's attorney presented a compelling case about the estate administrator's flagrant disregard of honesty and integrity. After all evidence was presented, the attorney asked that "the said administrator, W. G. Price, be held in contempt of your honor and the Court for failing to file receipts and vouchers as required."

The judge delayed any action until later in November. It seemed court hearings sometimes resulted in very little progress.

Four major challenges were introduced into the court. In summary, these were, (1) Price did not turn over money from the sale of cotton, (2) records could not be comprehended because they were so poorly written and kept, (3) Price paid himself without filing vouchers, and (4) Price said the estate still owed him money. In all, fourteen bales of cotton were included. Court documents showed that the bales were valued at well over $100 each. Additional court documents showed that Price took possession of farming tools. Court records also showed that some items were sold far below value, such as two yoke of oxen for $25, when, according to court documents, they would have been worth at least $80. The same situation existed with two horses, forty head of hogs, 150 bushels of corn, and many other items; among those were a shotgun, a pistol, and saddles and saddlebags. Ellen was fuming over the treatment she had received at the hands of the estate administrator.

Court action continued on November 23, 1872, with

the filing of papers in the case of Ellen Lee, surviving wife of Jasper H. Lee, deceased, vs. W. G. Price, administrator. One claim in court was that of Dr. Ponder for services and medicines for Jasper H. Lee shortly before his death. The total amount billed was $11.65. A receipt signed by Dr. Ponder in July 1871 was presented as evidence in court proceedings that this had been properly handled. Price defended his other actions in administering the estate and promised to move ahead honestly and fairly. Further decisions were delayed until the March 1873 term of the court.

This estate administration had taken so long and wasn't over yet. Ellen was becoming disillusioned with the process. She was concerned whether, in death, her Jasper would ever receive justice. But more was on the way—some through court action and some through confidential conversations with friends.

Friends continued to tell her of the "good deals" people in the community got when they dealt with Administrator Price to acquire items in Jasper's estate. In some cases, they insinuated that Price would cut a price far below true value if he was given the equivalent of a bribe by the buyer. Others had different experiences. All of this broke Ellen's sense of the decency of human beings. She and Jasper had lived in poverty, worked hard, and been smart in order to acquire what little they had. Ellen found what was now happening sad.

It would soon be time for the March 1873 term of

court. Summons were issued to certain individuals, one being W. S. Crowson. The court date was set for Monday, March 2, 1873. Court records include the following:

> The State of Texas
> County of Henderson
> Ellen Lee surviving wife of Jasper H. Lee deceased
> vs
> Wm. G. Price, Administrator
>
> Now at this term of the Court comes Wm. G. Price administrator pro tem of the Estate of Jasper H. Lee deceased by his attorney and the attorney for said Estate leave of the Court being first had and obtained and amends his answers and reports in answer to the execution filed … the cotton has been sold and thus he is ready to verify …denies exception …is ready to prove the facts alleged … and that he has complied with the requirements except for receipts … That on or about July 1871 that he delivered all property of said Estate then in his possession or under his control to said surviving wife and that she willingly signed a receipt for it … all property in his possession as administrator

has been delivered to said surviving wife ... all property not sold remained in the actual possession of said surviving wife and family for their use and benefit and was exempt from forced sale.

Other Court hearings were needed to get at the full and accurate truth of the estate of Jasper H. Lee. Ellen was always present—always thinking and always defending herself and her son, Ira.

Finally, the probate of the estate was completed on February 25, 1875. From the original honest itemization of the estate value at about $4,200, only a few hundred dollars were left. What happened to the value and why had the process taken so long? How did Ellen and Ira survive? Fortunately, twenty-three-year-old Ellen (she was about twenty-eight years of age at settlement) stood up for herself and Ira and demanded fairness. She was able to keep the horse and wagon she had used since Jasper's death in November 1870; that was her transportation. Court records show the full and complete transcript of orders was issued on July 17, 1876—nearly six and a half years after Jasper's death. Some of the delay was attributed to lax efforts by court employees to see that what was needed to be done was done in a timely manner. Not moving ahead certainly delayed any plans Ellen might make for her "life after Jasper."

By the time the estate was settled, little of value was left. Some had been granted to Ellen for living. Other was taken by creditors, such as the holder of the mortgage on the farm. Loss occurred through undervaluing items sold, including animals, equipment, and tools. And, it was reported, some items were taken by the administrator. Ellen sometimes wondered why people were so corrupt and dishonest. Why couldn't people be honest and fair in life? Why couldn't people treat others as they would like to be treated? This was especially true when grieving over the loss of a loved one when other sorrows and challenges had to be dealt with.

Ellen continued to focus on raising her son and on reacquainting herself with her family in Mississippi. And getting reacquainted with her family was another story that was playing out during some of the court actions to settle Jasper's estate. She and Ira continued to live in the Bell house. Both Mr. and Mrs. Bell were now deceased.

An observation of Ira's development by Ellen was that he needed a man to teach him about manly things—not just how to be personable, courteous, and genuine but how to groom, dress, and not have body odor. Ellen worked on this a little; so did Nelson. She also noted that Ira needed to be taught skills associated with life on a farm, particularly as he got a little older. She thought he needed to know how to lay out straight rows in a field, plant sweet potato slips and harvest sweet potatoes with a plow, and butcher a pig. Other areas in which she thought he needed to develop skills in included gathering honey, sharpening a plow point, and operating a smokehouse to assure that meat was properly preserved and seasoned. For each of these, an experienced person would be the best teacher. She felt that neither Nelson nor herself were qualified. She felt Ira needed a stronger, more credible teacher. And that teacher should be Pa!

What other things had been underway in Ellen's life? Jasper was gone and couldn't be brought back. Ellen wanted to move on.

9

Sister Reunion

Do the right thing, and situations will turn out to the good. Such was the case with Ellen. Though there were men who tried to steal from the estate and otherwise take advantage of her, there were also people who reached out to help her in this difficult time. You would think those who reached out would have been part of the Flowing Waters church community. Not so.

Ellen never thought of herself as a widow, much less as a widow with a child. She was still young enough to think of herself as a young woman with intelligence and energy to become whatever she wished, though she might have to overcome obstacles. She also realized she might need support from others along the way.

Most places have families with the extraordinary

ability to reach out and help others. One such family was of particular support for Ellen. The Bell family had moved to Henderson County from Mississippi a few years earlier. They were from the southern part of Mississippi and not near Tinnin. The family had several young adult children and settled near where Ellen and Jasper had bought the farmland. A son named Walter Nelson Bell (called Nelson) was particularly helpful. He was about two years younger than Ellen and could sense some of the difficulty she was having. He and his family provided a place for Ellen and Ira to sleep until the estate was settled and they could move on with life. In exchange for work in the home and on the farm, food was provided. It wasn't long before Mrs. Bell and then Mr. Bell died. This left Ellen with an important role in the home, where Nelson had become the head of household.

Just how "things" developed between Ellen and Nelson is unknown; nothing more than supportive friendship was between them. She probably confided in him as the estate probate drug on. She told him the story of her love, marriage, and life with Jasper and about her experience of his death. She, no doubt, told him about her family back in Mississippi and how she hadn't seen or heard from them since March 1864. She made no known effort to contact them, though she needed support in coping with life. Not making contact was not like Ellen; she loved people and valued family.

Nelson decided he would try to build a bridge to connect Ellen with her family. He needed permission from Ellen to do so. He also knew Ellen had younger sisters who were about ready for taking by a man; maybe he might be such a man. He certainly knew Ellen had a lot of desirable qualities, and her sisters were probably much like her. Nelson did not know that those young women were searching for romance and a good man.

Nelson asked Ellen if he could write to her parents with information about her—telling them where she was and about her situation in life. Ellen agreed, though she did not know how the letter might be received. Ellen provided the mailing address; Nelson wrote the letter in 1872—during major probate hearings. George and Sarah Shepard (Pa and Ma) in Clinton (Tinnin), Mississippi, received the letter in a few days.

In the letter, Nelson introduced himself and told of Ellen's whereabouts in Henderson County, Texas. He informed her parents of the birth of Ellen's son, Ira Jasper, in 1868 and that Jasper had died in 1870. He described the efforts to settle the estate and of the loss of income, home, and farm upon Jasper's death. He also said that Ellen and Ira had a place to live and that they were doing OK.

Receiving word about the death of Jasper probably created at least a little sympathy with Pa and Ma, particularly Pa. Though he did not like Jasper, he had immense love for his oldest daughter. He wanted a good life for her.

Upon getting the letter, Ma immediately wrote back. They were sympathetic to their daughter Ellen. She wrote of events in the family in the eight years since the then newly married Ellen had left with Jasper. She wanted to see Ira Jasper, their four-year-old grandson who they hadn't known existed until Nelson wrote. Ellen's sisters also wrote back. They had missed Ellen as the leader of the siblings. She was the older sister who all of them looked up to.

Ellen continued focus on raising her son, living in the Bell home, and communicating with her family in Mississippi. It was hard for Ellen to get her thoughts organized around her family and a return to Tinnin.

After a couple of exchanges of letters with family, her sister Georgia Ann Shepard wrote and asked about her coming to visit. Ellen responded positively. Georgia Ann began planning to travel to Henderson County. For a young woman (age twenty) who hadn't been much of any place, this would be quite a trip. Maybe she had thought about the potential of marrying Nelson. It seems the sisters always placed finding a man as a high priority.

In April 1874, Georgia Ann and Pa, along with two of her sisters, Rachel and Mag, traveled to Vicksburg on the train. Her plans were to cross the river on a ferry and get another train from Tallulah, Louisiana, on to Shreveport and Athens.

A big problem presented itself. The Mississippi River

at Vicksburg had flooded extensively out over the delta area for miles. The flooding stopped train traffic from originating at a nearby depot in Tallulah, Louisiana. Such floods usually resulted from heavy snow melts in the upper Midwest and rain along the river. Levees and other flood control structures had not been constructed.

Plans had to be altered. Georgia Ann asked and found that she could travel much of the trip by boat, but this would take two or more weeks. The travel involved going south on the Mississippi River and back to the northwest on the Red River to Shreveport, where she would catch a train. She was told that the operator of the boat would assure her safety—no men would be harassing her (like her sister Ellen, she was good-looking). The cost would be eighteen dollars, and she had the money to pay. Georgia Ann went. Pa and her sisters returned to Tinnin. But they feared for Georgia Ann. What if there was a problem?

Here is an excerpt from a letter written April 12, 1874, to Ellen in Texas by her sister Mag

My dear and affectionate sister,

I this cloudy evening take the pleasure to write you a few lines. We are all well at present. Sister Ellen, Georgia Ann has started to Texas. Pa, Rachel, and myself went with her as far as Vicksburg on April 6. We went with the intention of going across the Mississippi River with her and seeing her on the cars but the river was too high. The cars could not run any ways close to the river so there was no chance for her to cross unless she had gone a long ways in a skiff and there was several told us that it would be dangerous to cross that way. I never saw so much water in all of my life.

The letter continued. It explained that Georgia Ann had very nearly backed out on the trip. But with her spunk and high energy, she'd worked out the trip to go see her sister in Texas.

More from the letter of April 12, explains:

Georgia Ann came very near coming home and waiting for the river to run down. Mr. Green, the gentleman who sells tickets, persuaded her that if she wanted to go to Texas to go on a boat by all means. He said that the next boat would be on Wednesday, April 8, going to Shreveport. He explained the route was to travel down the Mississippi and back up the Red River. He told her that she could get on it at Vicksburg and wouldn't have to change at all until she got to Shreveport. She would then get the train (car) in Shreveport to complete the trip.

Amazing! Georgia Ann was a brave twenty-year-old woman! With virtually no travel experience, she had little reluctance to change travel plans because she was dealing with people she trusted. Trust was based on how the people presented themselves to her. Personal relationships were very important. Getting to know ticket agents and others involved with travel helped her have a feeling of confidence.

The sisters immediately wrote and mailed letters to Ellen alerting her of Georgia Ann's plans.

The letter of April 12 continued:

> There was a lady who also persuaded her to go on a boat. She concluded that she had better go on a boat. We left her in Vicksburg in care of Mr. Green and Mrs. Burgess. Mr. Green said he was well acquainted with the captain and he was a perfect gentleman. He said he would put her in the care of the captain. He said he would sell her a ticket to Shreveport for 18 dollars. Ma received a letter from Georgia Ann written Wednesday morning indicating that she expected to start that evening if the boat came, and I

guess it came for she said if it didn't she would come home. She hasn't come and we know by that she must be gone. Georgia Ann wrote in that letter to Ma that there was a gentleman staying at the same place where she was staying and going on the same boat ride to Shreveport. He said he would assist her all he could. There was some lady expected to take the same boat so I recon she will have plenty of company.

Sister Rachel immediately wrote and mailed a letter to Ellen, alerting her of Georgia Ann's plans. Ellen received the letter two days before Georgia Ann was due to arrive. This allowed Ellen to plan and be at the depot in Athens when the train carrying her sister was scheduled to arrive.

Ellen received a letter from Georgia Ann one day before she was to arrive. This alerted Ellen as to when to be at the depot in Athens. Now, if the train carrying her sister would just arrive on time, Ellen would be fine.

After a few days of travel, Georgia Ann made it to Athens. She was met at the depot by Ellen and Ira (now six years of age). What a glorious reunion of sisters! For Ira, what an introduction to his Aunt Georgia Ann!

There were many things to talk about. Ellen told Georgia Ann about Henderson County and the family with whom she was staying. She talked about all the efforts in settling deceased Jasper's estate, explaining that the effort was still underway. Ellen didn't say much about the administrator trying to steal everything of value from the estate.

Georgia Ann told Ellen about some things and people in the Tinnin, Mississippi, vicinity. The farm continued with Ma and Pa and the children adjusting to doing more work now that the slaves had been freed. Crops had been doing well, but acreage was reduced; they no longer had to produce foods for the slaves, particularly the pinda (aka peanut). Ellen asked especially about the two dogs—Bummer and Ritz. Georgia Ann said that Bummer was still his usual loud-barking, one-eyed watch dog self and that Ritz had died when he'd nipped at a mule's heels—the mule having subsequently kicked him in the head. Ma and Pa had discussed getting another dog but had not yet done so. They thought Bummer might not be around much longer either. Maybe a nearby farm would have a litter of puppies and give them a weanling to raise and train to guard the property.

She said that some of the now free slaves had stayed close around. Others worked as sharecroppers. Most had left for places unknown but likely big cities in the North, such as Chicago and Detroit. Ellen interjected that Pa was kind to his slaves and had never mistreated them. Georgia Ann said that, once freed, they had good regards for him. They never did harm to him, his family, or his property. But that was not so out in the community. Sometimes fearful and dreadful things happened in the community and the nearby towns of Clinton, Jackson, and Bolton.

Georgia Ann talked of relationship issues between the white and black (freed slaves) people in Hinds County. Black males had joined the Republican party and began voting in 1867 (females couldn't vote for over another half century). Black and white Republican organizers would come through the community and promote registration and voting. Black officials were elected to several offices at state and local levels. She said Pa had told her skin color didn't matter as long as the elected officials did their jobs properly.

Occasionally the activities of the organizers promoted unrest. Georgia Ann said she and family didn't go out much and sought to avoid public areas. Probably more than anything, some of the whites knew their Pa George, had voted the Union ticket before the Civil War, and they didn't like it. Some white people feared the rising power of black men. A few whites formed marauding vigilante groups that went around the countryside shooting, hanging, and otherwise being violent in the mistreatment of black people. The riot/massacre situation in Clinton was a particular issue.

Georgia Ann said Pa did not like what was going on among people. He wanted people to get along and live in harmony. He was also fearful and did not like violence. A few times he said he regretted moving to Tinnin from Indiana. But when pressed, he would say that, overall, things had worked out for the good.

Ellen drove the horse-pulled wagon out to the Willow Springs community. They went to the Bell home, where Georgia Ann was introduced to Nelson Bell; Mr. and Mrs. Bell had died, and the other children had left home. Nelson agreed Georgia Ann could stay temporarily—as long as Ellen and Ira were there. Space was available because the older children had moved out of the house. No one knew how long Georgia Ann would be there. She had no return travel plans; nor did she have money to pay for travel back to Tinnin.

The first order was to get Georgia Ann settled in a living area. She got a small room not far from Ellen's. It had a few things in it—about like what she had back home—including a small bed with a mattress stuffed with cotton, a stool, and couple of shelves on the wall. A small looking glass was on one wall. A medium-sized shuttered window with hinges and a latch was on an exterior wall. It could be opened as desired to let light in and control entry of outside air. A slop jar was under the edge of the bed. It was for night or bad day use and had to be emptied each day. If not emptied regularly, it could develop a bad odor. Ellen told Georgia Ann that nothing smelled worse than an unemptied slop jar! Ellen and Nelson showed her a two-holer outback. Water was brought in a cedar bucket from a nearby spring.

At the Nelson home, Georgia Ann was also introduced to the guard dog named Bite and the gentle milk cow named Three Teats (a quarter of her udder had been injured; the teat had shrunk and did not produce milk). Bite was to be respected. The dog more often growled than barked. But it was large enough to attack about anything that appeared on the farm that it didn't know or like. It had been known to destroy animals that ventured too close to the house, including a skunk a few months ago. Three Teats was a calm and easy-to-milk cow; she was aging and probably would soon be replaced, particularly if more milk was needed.

Next would be to find some kind of work she could do. She and Ellen could work together around the Bell house and on their farm. Georgia Ann was good with animals. She liked caring for them. She would help with the birth of babies and get a newborn to nurse. She would also provide care for an injured or sick animal. (Her reputation for this soon spread to other animal owners in the community.)

The sisters were happy to have a reunion. Ellen found it nice to have a sister to talk to and get news from back home. It took a while to make up for eight years. They were careful not to get into controversial subjects, where differences of opinion could create friction.

Georgia Ann, now barely twenty-one years of age, was born to George and Sarah Shepard five years after Ellen. There were two sisters in the family between Ellen and Georgia Ann, who were still single. Their parents generally opposed every man their daughters brought around. But, by age twenty-one in the 1870s, most young women were beginning to seek out a husband in desperation, for fear of not finding a man who had desirable qualities. No woman wanted to be designated an "old maid." But that might not have been so bad if a desirable man wasn't around. After all, what is so wonderful about living around a cranky, abusive, and disagreeable old man who is not a good provider?

And now, Georgia Ann, like some of the other sisters, wanted Ellen to help her find romance. She didn't have to go far. Nelson and Georgia Ann connected eyes when they were first introduced. Romance began to sparkle. Nelson and Georgia Ann seemed a good fit. Nelson was always very gentlemanly toward Georgia Ann. Of course, she wrote back to family in Mississippi that she had found this really nice man. Maybe she called him sweetheart and hinted of marriage in letters sent in late 1875. This probably puzzled Pa, as he wasn't around to make an assessment and offer his opinion on this particular man.

Nelson and Georgia Ann were married in early 1876. They got a marriage license from the clerk's office at the courthouse in Athens. The wedding at Flowing Waters

Church was quite simple. Only a few people were there. Brother Yonah performed the ceremony. He was very traditional and preachy. After the ceremony, he approached Ellen as if nothing had ever happened between the two of them. He seemingly wanted to patch up their relationship. He said he wanted to offer the church's special blessing privately to her sometime. What did he have in mind? Ellen was cordial but cool; she didn't want anything to do with this creepy preacher.

When the new Mr. and Mrs. Bell got back to the house, Georgia moved her limited possessions into Nelson's— and now their—bedroom. They appeared very happy together and seemed to be a nearly perfect couple. They continued to live in the Bell house (as did Ellen and Ira). The marriage, however, did somewhat limit the relationship of Ellen and her sister. They talked less and spent less time together. Georgia Ann was now committed to Nelson. Just as Ellen had had a strong commitment to her man, Jasper, Georgia Ann had a strong commitment to her man, Nelson. Anyway, Ellen had her eight-year old son, Ira, as a source of energy and joy.

Nelson was somewhat of a local game hunter. He was a top marksman (different from anything in the Shepard family in Mississippi). He could harvest the smallest bird, rabbit, or squirrel. Game meat was about the only meat they had to eat much of the time. Ellen used these as she prepared a meal for the wedding night. The menu did not include only foods she and Georgia Ann had grown up with in Mississippi. She fixed a couple of new preparations, including buttermilk corn bread and quail with pepper stuffing. Among the dishes were squirrel dumplings, roasted sweet potatoes, and apple cobbler. They had a little cider to drink, which Nelson made from apples that grew on the farm. Overall, it was a nice dinner within budgetary and customary confines.

Ellen sent a letter to Ma and Pa and told them about the wedding. She said Nelson was a nice-looking and considerate young man and that he owned a farm in Henderson County. Ellen was certain Nelson would be a kind, loving husband for Georgia Ann. She wrote about the wedding and the dinner. She said Brother Yonah had conducted the ceremony. A few people were there. She wrote about the dinner she'd prepared and how everyone had seemed to enjoy it. Of course, Pa and Ma viewed the marriage as another daughter lost to some man they didn't know much about and had never met. At least, he was about Georgia Ann's age and did not have the questionable background of coming from "back east someplace." Maybe Pa and Ma would have been happier about their daughters marrying if they had shown a little more interest in the beaus and sweethearts their daughters brought around.

As was often the case in the 1870s, pregnancy didn't wait long after marriage. So, Georgia Ann was soon expecting their first child; Nelson was happy, as having fathered a child boosted his perceived manliness. The pregnancy progressed without complications. Ellen introduced her sister to midwife Candy Smith, who had helped with the delivery of Ira.

Early on February 1, Georgia Ann thought she was going into labor. She sent Nelson to get Candy, who came quickly and confirmed the birth was likely an hour or so away. All went well that day (February 1, 1877), and Nelson and Georgia Ann became the parents of a healthy baby daughter, who they named Sarah Ellen Bell. They chose a name that recognized Georgia Ann's mother, Sarah, and older sister, Ellen.

Ellen helped the new mother with the baby and taught her a few thinks about "mothering"—how to hold a baby, nurse it, change its diaper, swaddle it for sleeping, and keep it warm in the coolness of February. Of course, Georgia Ann wrote her mother and sisters in Mississippi about the birth of her new Sarah Ellen Bell. Little Sarah grew and developed into a charming baby girl.

By now, regular correspondence was made with the Shepard family in Tinnin, Mississippi. They were kept informed of the marriage of Georgia Ann and birth of a granddaughter. They were always curious and loving about Ira. But none of the family traveled to Henderson County; Ellen didn't have any promising men to suggest to her younger sisters. The sisters were finding a few men without leaving home to do so. Some were less than promising "husband material," and they admitted it. One of the men was described in a letter to Ellen (by one of her sisters about another sister's man) as "a whisky-drinking crippled fat man who used a wooden leg, which restricted his activities quite a bit"—not exactly the best of men in terms of what the sisters wanted. Pa did not like him. And as things went, he was soon sent disappointedly on his way.

Ellen had become aware that there was a Presbyterian church in Athens. She remembered the Presbyterian church in Brandon where she met Jasper. She decided to take Ira and visit there for services on a Sunday morning. Everything went well. The people were nice. The pastor had a sermon about the love of God and inclusiveness of the church—it sounded good to her. It was quite different from Flowing Waters Chapel and Brother Yonah with his scary "hellfire sermons."

Ellen sought to learn more about the church. She asked the pastor, Reverend John McIntosh, if she could talk with him about the church. He said yes and agreed to come to the Bell home to do so. She learned the congregation had been organized in 1855 (one year before Athens was incorporated as a town). At first it had met in a home and then a schoolhouse, and as it grew, it had built a church building.

A couple of different pastors had served the congregation on an interim basis until 1869, when Reverend

McIntosh was called. He was a seminary-trained man who came from Boston but had spent some time studying for the ministry in Edinburgh, Scotland. Reverend McIntosh had a wife and two children. He told Ellen that the love of God was supreme and that his church focused on seeking thoughtful solutions to the challenges we face. Pastor McIntosh talked about peace, grace, and love and that the church should be for all people and accepting of people who may be different.

He talked some about Jesus Christ. But that always confused Ellen a little. She thought, *Why not deal directly with God?*

Overall, Ellen really liked McIntosh's approach— steady, calm, and educated. He was very respectful of Ellen and didn't "hit on her" or in any way show disrespect for women.

Ellen and Ira continued to attend the Athens Presbyterian Church to help them decide what they would do in terms of church. They participated in several activities, including potluck meals. Ellen found those meals interesting, as some of the foods were a tad more western than she was accustomed to in Mississippi. Of course, she took some of her comfort foods for the congregants to enjoy. She met and became acquainted with several of the women in the church. Ira developed some childhood friendships that lasted for several years.

After careful assessment, Ellen decided to leave

Flowing Waters and get involved at Athens Presbyterian. She was not quite ready to join this church because she still had memories of Mason Chapel in Tinnin. Ellen did not tell Brother Yonah of Flowing Water about her decision right off. Additionally, she asked Nelson and Georgia Ann Bell if they would like to go with her one Sunday. Of course, Ira would go as well, as would the Bell's baby daughter, Sarah.

It was now mid-1878. Georgia Ann was pregnant again. Her pregnancy went well; she did not know of any problems. She had not seen a doctor or done anything special during the pregnancy. Nelson and Georgia Ann were excited about the soon-to-be new family member. They had chosen the name for the baby. If a boy, his name would be Calvin Jasper; if a girl, her name would be Anna Rachel.

Georgia Ann and Nelson had thought about letting Ellen assist with the delivery and saving what they would pay a midwife. When they asked Ellen, she didn't like the idea and smartly said so. The due date was now rapidly approaching. Georgia Ann went into labor. Midwife Candy was quickly brought in to help with delivery; she had done so with the earlier birth of their daughter.

Things with Georgia Ann and giving birth didn't seem right to Candy from the beginning that day. The baby was in a breech birth presentation. The head was not appearing in the birth canal; its buttocks were beginning to appear. Candy worked feverishly to reposition the baby for delivery. She was not successful. She urged Nelson to quickly go into Athens and get Dr. J. B. Bishop, a new doctor in the area, to come there and assist with the birth.

Dr. Bishop came as quickly as he could to the Bell home—within an hour. He examined the situation and said there were problems. He used forceps to try to reposition and deliver the baby. That did not result in a good outcome. The baby boy was finally delivered dead; Georgia Ann also died at the time. No explanation is known for the cause of death, though Dr. Bishop said it was likely a combination of high blood pressure and excessive bleeding. This was a sad day for Nelson and Ellen. Sarah Ellen also lost her mother, but she was too young to know the meaning of death.

Today, if we think back to 1800s, women died more frequently in childbirth than today. They and their partners did not know that they could prevent pregnancy—maybe they didn't even understand how it happened or what caused it; or maybe they didn't want to. Could it have been that the status of men in the community was based on the number of children they fathered? Prenatal and other medical care wasn't that good—if it were given at all. Babies were often born in homes with a midwife present. Medical doctors might not be available. Women might have eight to twelve babies during their married lives. With that number, a complication was, unfortunately, likely to occur. Some women continued to have babies until giving birth resulted in their deaths or the destruction of body organs so they could no longer conceive.

The situation with Nelson Bell was quite somber. He had lost his wife and son, who was to have been named Calvin Jasper Bell. He had a one-year-old daughter to raise. Of course, Ellen stepped forward to help.

Brother Yonah got word of what had happened. He came to the house to console Nelson, hug Ellen—though coolly—and offer to preach the funeral. He never missed preaching if a dollar or so might change hands. It was at this time that Brother Yonah was told they were now attending another church.

When he heard this, he scoffed. "After all I have done for you. How could you do this?" he said, adding a couple of choice words normally not openly used by preachers. With that, he left in a hurry, his horse kicking up a great amount of dust. Ellen's mind flashed to those times he had tried to take advantage of her; she didn't owe him any favors. Good riddance!

Arrangements for Georgia Ann and son, who was named Calvin Jasper, were handled by a funeral home in Athens. The body lay in state in the Nelson home and was moved to the Presbyterian Church in Athens for the memorial service. The service was led by Reverend McIntosh, pastor of the church. In his remarks, Reverend McIntosh talked about Georgia Ann as devoted to family and God.

He further spoke of the nature of Georgia Ann in word and deed and her love of life and nurture of family. He spoke kindly and sincerely and in a comforting message. Burial was in Smith Cemetery, the cemetery where Jasper was buried.

Ellen, just as always when times were tough, gave extra effort. She pitched in to care for one-year-old Sarah Ellen. Of course, Ira was now ten years of age and capable of doing some good farmwork, which he did, and he could do a little looking after the baby. He didn't go to school but learned simple reading, writing, and arithmetic from his mother. There was never any mention of a school in the Willow Springs community. Maybe there wasn't any. Athens, the nearest town, was fairly new, itself having been chartered in 1850 and then, mysteriously, unchartered. A few years later, it was incorporated. Its population was increasing. This brought a few stores, services, and improved school to Athens.

Ellen, as she would say, "took pen in hand" and sent a letter back to her Mississippi family, telling them about what happened. Sad. No one in the family traveled to Texas, though several sympathetic letters were sent. Ellen still had to be strong, wise, and motivated with life.

Ira and Ellen continued to live in the home with Nelson Bell. Nelson had to work hard to care for the farm and provide needed income. Of course, Ira was now old enough to help in a serious way as a farmhand. Folks in the community were somewhat aware of the situation. Some of the attention was not always what Ellen liked. She wasn't the kind of woman who now had to have a man around. She had been married. She had given a major commitment in her marriage to the man she loved. She felt that women could achieve goals and be successful without men, though it wasn't always easy in a society that valued the role of men and had laws that were restrictive of women. These laws and customs bothered Ellen, particularly as evident in the probate of Jasper's estate.

Amazing things happened! Ellen's cousin Susan Ratliff (from Tinnin) was now living not far away. This was the cousin who had gotten Ellen to go to Brandon in Rankin County in 1863, where she met Jasper at a barbecue and singing at the Presbyterian church. A couple of years later, Susan married John P. Walston, and they had moved to the Lovelady Station area of Texas. Somehow, maybe through shared family connections in Mississippi, they had heard of Ellen's plight and whereabouts. So, John Walston wrote a letter to Ellen. He intended it to be a letter of encouragement and with an uplifting future in mind.

The letter John sent to Ellen read, in part, "We heard that you were in Henderson County. Ellen, that is a poor county. You had better come down here. The land is good and we have all lived in good health here these past six years. You can get to Lovelady Station in three hours. We are nearly in sight of the station."

With Ellen's situation in life, this was a compelling statement. There is no evidence, however, that she ever went to Lovelady Station—even for a short visit, much less to live. No doubt she thought about it. Was Texas going to be her home for the rest of her life without Jasper?

With the schism between Pa and Ellen now subsided, letters from back home in Tinnin kept pulling at her. She was intrigued by what was going on. She even gave some thought to returning to Tinnin. But she did not go. She regularly wrote Ma and Pa but did not inquire about the possibility of her returning to Tinnin. She kept thinking that maybe, just maybe, an appropriate man would emerge. She also received word about unsettling conditions in the area near her Tinnin home.

One of her sisters sent a letter about a race riot in Clinton. She described it in some detail. She said some folks called it a massacre. It happened in September 1875. The Republican Party planned a rally in Clinton on September 4, 1875, with the goal of continuing to expand the role of freed men in the political process. Some 2,500 people gathered and enjoyed an afternoon of picnicking and politics. Amazingly, some seventy-five white people were present. Some Democratic Party candidates showed up and were given the opportunity to speak. Heckling of the speakers soon got out of hand. Violence erupted. Her sister explained that a group of white liners came with the intent of storming the town. They went about shooting at black people, "just the same as birds," she said. Some of the people were from Northern states; this didn't calm the white Southern hardliners. Her sister went on that some of this was a result of hard feelings over "reconstruction" efforts in the area. Before it was over, the letter noted that more than fifty people had been killed in a day or so.

Amazing! Clinton was considered the top town in Mississippi educationally—with two institutes of higher learning (colleges). One served women, and the other, men. Being separated by gender may be a clue to failed opportunity. Further, these institutes were run by rather conservative religious organizations. The town had a collection of relatively educated religious leaders. Where were they in seeking peace and human love in post-Civil War race relations? Most people suspect these institutions were established to serve only white people. Were any black people or Native Americans enrolled? None appeared to be.

A few people felt the institutes of higher learning actually carried out discrimination against black and Native American people. They failed in a wonderful opportunity. It was about a century later before Native Americans were visibly enrolled and another quarter century beyond that before black people attended. Certainly, different leadership roles would likely have served the community well. How do the roles these institutions took serve to further principles of religion and human decency?

All of this frightened Ellen. She thought it would be risky to go home at the present time and into such possible violence. She thought people who had different traits needed to find a way to get along and live in harmony. Questions arose: Why would she take her son into the fray? How could she live there until things settled down a bit? How could she make a living?

Maybe Ellen would be taken back by her parents into their home. And as always, after grieving the death of Jasper, she thought a good man might be around in Henderson County.

10
Sweethearts and Traditions

Ellen didn't really understand how much her siblings loved and missed her. As she was the older sister, they viewed her as their leader—a role model. They always looked up to her. This didn't appear to change when she left home in March 1864. For years, her siblings had such special memories of her. She had been gone from the family about a decade. Her siblings wanted her advice. Could Ellen help her sisters find romance?

Through the efforts of Nelson Bell, Ellen reconnected with her parents and siblings in 1872. Special bonds quickly redeveloped. Of course, Ellen's sister Georgia Ann made the trip to Athens in spring 1874—ten years after Ellen had left her home. Unfortunately, Georgia Ann died in childbirth in 1878. Ellen now filled a more important role in caring for her niece, Sarah Ellen Bell.

Whatever direction Ellen might take in the future, she would choose among directions torn by emotion. Sisterly love and loyalty would pull her toward caring for Georgia Ann's surviving child. She would also have the pull and desire to return to her childhood home in Tinnin to see her parents and sisters and surviving brother. At times, she thought an acceptable man might emerge in Texas. If so, she would stay there.

Ellen was a single, smart, widowed, attractive woman in her mid-twenties. Several men in the community eyed her. Maybe she stayed in Texas because of possible romance with one of them. But at least until 1875, she stayed to honorably probate the estate of her deceased husband. No romance emerged.

Just as men in the Henderson County community took notice of Ellen, her sisters back in Tinnin received plenty notice of their own. It seemed men always paid attention to the Shepard girls—Rachel, Margaret, Georgia Ann, Sarah, and Naomi—as they reached adulthood. And, without surprise, the girls sometimes took notice of selected men. Pa and Ma, particularly Pa, tried to keep their selections reasonable and of high standards. Maybe Pa understood the motivation of men a little better than this group of young women. He generally didn't feel the young men his daughters had brought around would make good marrying material. He wanted the very best for his daughters.

Most men in Henderson County were farmers, farm laborers, or in similar vocations. A few worked jobs for the county government. A few others worked in local stores and offices. Some worked in the cotton gin, but that was seasonal. A small number of men were wanderers and lived with only occasional day work and scavenging from the land; they would move on to the next town after a short while. But Ellen never knew when a man was eyeing her.

On a mid-October day as the sun was beginning to set, one of the men who worked with county government stopped by the Bell house to see Ellen. She didn't know him but had seen him about. He introduced himself as Sam Johnson and told her about his work with the county. He said his wife was dead–she'd died in childbirth. He told her there was a traveling carnival coming into Athens by railroad, and he wanted to know if she would go with him. The carnival was setting up for the weekend near the courthouse.

Sam gave some details about himself and promised to pay all expenses for going to the carnival. He talked about the carnival's midway, saying it had food, games, and activities. He told her there were a couple of side-shows she might like; one featured magic, and the other was an old-time fiddle music show. He said it would be his great pleasure if she would accompany him. He would meet her at her home in his carriage, they would take in the carnival, and he would safely return her home before midnight that evening. The offer caught Ellen a little by surprise; maybe this was a good opportunity, or maybe it was a setup for a bad ending. Sam was a good-looking, courteous man who had a job. Ellen thought carefully while talking about herself. She decided she would not go—too much risk. She thanked him for asking her and said goodbye.

Women rarely worked outside the home or away from a family farm except for the few who lived a "town life." Formal education attainment was low among both men and women. Often, mothers or older sisters (and sometimes a father or brother) would teach younger children the fundamentals of reading, writing, and arithmetic. That was the case with her family.

Maybe some of Ellen's notions were tempered by the values of her father; his roots were in the Midwest and reflected greater appreciation of formal education. Some would ask, "Why did he move to the South with his background?" Remember, it was opportunity in the land available as a result of the Choctaw Cessation and the potential returns from cotton as a cash crop.

Communication with family back home had not occurred for eight years beginning in 1864. Now that Ellen and family had reconnected, communication was helping repair relationships. About the only form of communication was to send handwritten letters. Most letters were mailed in three-by-five-and-a-half-inch envelopes with small sheets of writing paper of five by eight inches or ten by eight inches folded down the middle. Letters typically had two sheets of paper. The writing, ink or pencil, usually extended to the edge of the paper. Sometimes two letters by different sisters would be in one envelope. Cost for postage for a letter was two cents from Clinton to Athens and vice versa. Only a few days were required for delivery of mail from either location to the other. Railroads hauled mail, and except for crossing the Mississippi River, the route was fairly direct from Clinton to Athens.

In writing this book, a trove of old letters, receipts, and other documents were retrieved from tucked-away places in old trunks and shell boxes in the attic of the Shepard-Lee house. These documents were accessible, as the last Lee to live in the house died in 1962. The documents begin in the 1840s. Some were letters Ellen had received in Texas in the 1870s and brought back with her when she returned to Tinnin. Others were statements about medical care, drugs prescribed, and receipts for purchases such as food products, cloth, shoes, and farm tools. Regardless, careful study has allowed reconstruction of family history rich in high moral standards and integrity.

The writing style was consistent, regardless of who

wrote the letter. The interior had a return address and date. Addresses were simple—the person's name, county, and post office (typically the name of a town; no one had heard of zip codes). Ellen was nearly always addressed as Mrs. Ellen Lee, even by her sisters.

The letters typically began much as the one dated November 3, 1873: "My Dear Sister Ellen, I again seat myself to answer your kind letter which came to hand a few days ago. I no [stet] I ought to have written sooner but I have been very busy picking cotton in the week and on Sunday I go to the singing. My sweetheart came with me the past 2 Sundays."

The letters demonstrated good penmanship, some wording issues, and no paragraphs. When the subject was changed, the writer would repeat the name of the person that letter was addressed to, such as "My Sister Ellen."

Letters often ended with an expression of affection. For example, the last few lines of the letter of November 3, 1873, had this: "I will close for this time as I have a chance to send it to the office. Kiss little Ira for me. I remain as ever your true and affectionate Sister until death. Write soon and often. So, good by for this time. From Naomi R. Shepard to Mrs. Ellen S. Lee." Some words were spelled by sound and others were misspelled but largely the writing was quite good, considering the Shepard sisters had very little schooling outside the home. Words that were used less frequently were more likely to be spelled incorrectly.

For example, one of the newly married sisters thought she had recently had a miscarriage, and she spelled the word "mistcarage."

Ellen's sisters often sent letters sharing their experiences in finding a man. They asked for Ellen's advice and help. Ellen identified a few in Texas who they could take a look at if they came there to visit her. One was the young man in whose home she lived—Nelson Bell, who was born about 1849. His age would be about right for some of her sisters. The first sister who laid eyes on him wanted him for her man.

The subjects in the letters touched on various aspects of life, particularly farm life. Most were written by girls and women, so the subjects were naturally reflective of female interests. As a farm family trying to make it after losses during the Civil War, everyone had to work in the fields at least a certain amount to compensate for the loss of labor. Sometimes, a girl would include something about the progress she was making in trying to care for an orphaned calf or other animal. The letters might also talk about weather, crops, harvests, or other situations, such as animal health and sickness. Unexplained deaths of residents in the community would occasionally be included. Letters might report on romance (or the lack thereof). No letters ever reported troubles with law authorities, as the Shepard family was always law-abiding and of high moral character.

Since Ellen and Ira lived in the Nelson home, mail to Ellen was addressed "In care of W. N. Bell." Such an arrangement might have created some suspicion or at least curiosity among her parents and sisters back home. Maybe Ellen explained it shortly after Jasper's death, when she and Ira had to move from their farm home. However, that subject never came up, even though Nelson was an individual Ellen had in mind as a marriage-eligible man for one of her sisters.

On November 3, 1873, Ellen's sister Mag wrote a letter from Tinnin to Ellen in Henderson County talking about herself and her sisters picking cotton, going to singings on Sunday, and sometimes being out with their beaus/ sweethearts. The letter stated:

> I had a very pleasant evening yesterday … me and my beau took a ride. Rachel and another young man took a ride … she doesn't claim him as a sweetheart as he is only 19 or 20 years old. My [Mag, the writer] sweetheart's name is Sibley. I expect to marry him this winter about the first of January. I don't reckon the old folks will be willing but I can't help that Mr. Sibley and I are engaged. Pa won't hardly speak to him though Sibley is very friendly. He is very stout and uses an artificial leg. He has a splendid education and

can teach school or farm or get into most any kind of business. He was raised not far from here near Raymond. Most of the young men around here drink too much whisky. Sister, I would be the gladest in the world to see you and Ira but if I marry I don't expect to. If I could see you I could tell you a heap. Sister, I don't believe Pa and Ma ever will be willing for any of us to marry. I think we ought to marry. They are getting old. Just suppose they were to die and leave us with just Ira. What would become of us?"

Note: This Ira was the youngest child and brother of the Shepard family sisters and not to be confused with Ira Jasper Lee, the son of Ellen and deceased Jasper H. Lee.

The sisters commonly distinguished between the men in their lives with two terms, *beau* and *sweetheart*. A beau was a man new to the sister or who she really didn't think would work out in the long run. For lack of another man, a beau was someone to go to a singing or barbecue with. A sweetheart was a man who a sister liked and likely wished for a longer relationship with—someone she might have considered marrying material. A sweetheart might have been someone the sister would go riding with. Riding would give a couple some time alone together for talking, embracing, and the like. But the Shepard sisters were not into premarital sex. After all, the Shepard family was of high moral character.

Letters occasionally addressed whether they would go to Texas to see Ellen and Ira. In some cases, their beaus/sweethearts would be a reason not to leave for a while. Goodness, the beaus/sweethearts might find another female while they were gone!

Was Ellen identifying some possible men in Texas and telling her sisters about them? She suggested the sisters might come to Texas to take a look at them. But to do so, they would come there to visit with Ellen and Ira. In one letter, her sister Mag wrote back, "Sister Ellen, you can tell the young man you spoke of waiting for me that he is a little too late. You can tell him that there are some other girls out here that I expect would marry if they had a good chance. Sister Rachel says she would like the best in the world to go to Texas but cotton has gone down so low she don't know for certain whether she will have the money to go or not."

Ellen was aware that all of the sisters back home knew some of what was being written; anyone in the family receiving a letter shared it with everyone else. Those who wrote told about what they said. Georgia Ann became very interested in going to see Ellen and, maybe, a man or so she had heard about. Georgia Ann did not have a beau/sweetheart to keep her at home. She started saving money as she could by knitting and selling socks, making quilts, and the like.

How much notice Ellen gave to Texas men is unknown. Maybe she did give a little notice; maybe just a little eye contact or twinkle. Most of the time she was too busy with life to think of another man. After all, who could replace Jasper? She remained single through the decade of the 1870s, even though some suitors apparently came around. The young men who Ellen identified as potential marrying material for her sisters were probably also marrying material for Ellen herself. After all, personable Ellen was only in her mid- to late-twenties during most of the decade of the 1870s.

Here is a letter exactly (with minor editing) as she received it in 1872:

Mrs. Lee,

The undersigned after compliments and looks takes this method of approaching you on the subject of matrimony. Of all the female sex under my knowledge you are my first choice. If this meets your approval, will you please answer me as soon as practicable.

I am truly yours,
S. B. Lusk

PS.
You are forever and constantly
Impressed upon my mind
It seems predestinated that together we
Should be combined
If your mind should be so impressed
That I should be thine
Let me know by writing me a line
That you are also desirous to become mine
And we will be joined together in
Holy wedlock by some devine
You may fix the time
Excuse me for writing with lead pencil
For I had run out of ink on hand
It looks so pail
But my love for you will not fail.
Sammie

Did Ellen know this man? Did she date him? Was he an honorable person with good intentions? Was he wealthy? It seems that he had at least some education to write such a letter and add a post script poem. We do not know if Ellen ever responded. Records do show that S. B. Lusk married a different woman in 1876.

In 1876, two of Ellen's sisters back home had men named "Pink" or "Pinkney" (Pinkney was usually short-ened to Pink) in their names. One had the last name of

Bunyard, the other of Gary. In a letter dated December 1, 1876, Ellen's sister Naomi wrote about her man. She said, "I have a Pink much more handsomer than hers [referring to sister Sallie], and I think more suited for me. He will be 21 in January. He has 3 more brothers and they are all nice looking boys. Sister Ellen, do you think it best for a girl to marry or live single?"

But Naomi did not say that her sister Sallie had already married on October 19 to her Pink.

Rachel described the wedding of Sallie and Pinkney Gary in her letter:

> She and Pink Gary looked very well the day they married though Sallie had been in bed all the week before that day with the neuralgia. She didn't eat a single meal at the table until the wedding supper. We had a very nice time. Everybody enjoyed their selves so much. We had five large cakes and lemonade. We had a beautiful bride's cake to cut. Sister, the same person got the ring that got it when Mag was married …The old folks had to be willing for she said she would marry him regardless … Sister Ellen, I tell Mag that she is fattening slowly; she says it ain't so.

Now, for one sister to be talking of fat on another sister isn't much of a way to promote good family relations! Maybe the "fat" news wasn't shared.

Weddings were typically big social events in a family and the local community of the 1870s. Most wedding ceremonies were held in small churches or chapels or in large rooms in homes. A minister or judge would conduct the ceremony. The location might have a few flower decorations set up by family members or friends. Members of the family would work together to prepare for a meal or reception. They organized, cooked, set up tables and chairs or logs (if outside) for sitting, cleaned, and greeted guests. A family member good at sewing or the bride would make the bride's dress. In some cases, a ready-made, store-bought dress might be worn. A family member or friendly neighbor might do the bride's hair. Celebrations before and after were in various community facilities, such as a dance hall, picnic barbecue area, or schoolhouse. People were typically hesitant about the wide use of alcoholic beverages.

Brides wanted to look beautiful! After all, a wedding (even in those times) was the time when a young woman got a man for a lifetime commitment. The bride expected the groom to provide for her, keep her safe, and father their children. Brides also expected respect from the groom and for him to forever be faithful. Grooms expected brides to honor them, follow their instructions, have and care for babies, run the home, and be attractive and submissive. Sometimes grooms expected brides to do some fieldwork and work related to the vegetable garden and taking care of a runabout flock of chickens.

Bathing and personal hygiene often needed attention by both the bride and the groom. Most homes had no bathroom. Bathing was often little more than sponging to wipe the body with a wet cloth in the winter. In the summer, bathing might be in a creek or spring pool, where the water was often cold. A few places had waterfalls that could be used. Deodorant and similar products were quite limited. No bride or groom wanted a wedding with the strong presence of body odor! So, they did the best they could under the situation. Some folks have said that a bride might like body odor on her groom, as it was a sign of manliness. Really? Maybe times change, as does tolerance of body odor on another person, regardless of romantic association.

Brides and grooms might buy or make clothing for their weddings. Some would wear clothing they had; guests often wore existing clothing. Trying to have clothing reasonably clean was a challenge. A cast iron wash pot filled with water might have a wood fire started around it to heat water for washing clothing. Other times, clothing might be washed near the water in a creek—preferably a creek with clean water. To dry, clothing would be spread out on bushes or tree limbs. Not many folks had wire fences or clotheslines. Getting odors and stains out of dirty clothing was about impossible.

The wedding night would often be at the home of the bride or, less frequently, at a relative or friend's home. Sometimes it was at the home where the bride and groom were going to live. Spending the night in a hotel or guest house was a tad pricey for most couples. Not many such places were even available in the South during and immediately following the Civil War. Honeymoons, if there was one, were only a weekend or a couple of days. Newlyweds often had to quickly get back to work tending crops or livestock on their farms. Regardless, no one spent very much on a wedding—there was daily living that had to take place afterward.

By the late 1870s, all of Ellen's sisters had found men and were married, had been married, or were deceased. One of her brothers, James Alexander Shepard, was deceased (he died at six years of age). The other, Ira W., was a good-looking young man approaching twenty years of age. In his young life, he had a few favorite young women. And by 1880, he had a serious sweetheart who he referred to as the "Belle of Rankin County." The "Belle" didn't last until marriage; situations and compatibility resulted in changes in sweetheart status. This might have been just as well for Ira W., as he, a decade later, took Mary Ella Collier as his bride and moved to Sunflower County, Mississippi. In his new home, he had a good life. His farm and the businesses he started prospered. The prosperity extended over to future generations.

Most of the marriages went as well as could be expected. One experienced a major issue. The man one sister married was, at the same time, involved with another woman. This man fathered one child with her sister, and she experienced another pregnancy and miscarriage before it was found out. When known, the sister and her child went running back to the safety of the Shepard home in Tinnin. The man then drifted off to Louisiana with another woman. Counting the number of women he had is not easy—maybe four or more. The number of children he fathered is also unknown, as the extent of his communal relationships is a mystery. The sister never married again. The situation with the man who was her one-time husband is unknown. (These were the kind of things Pa was trying to protect his daughters in his attempts to screen out the bad men they brought around.)

The sisters typically settled within fifty miles of their home place. Some lived on farms; others lived in towns or cities as the wives of store owners or clerks. The lives of two were prematurely ended in the 1870s in a yellow fever epidemic that swept a portion of the South. Even the best medical care of the time could not cope with some of the diseases and health maladies that appeared on the scene. Clinton and Bolton usually had one or two doctors; much larger, Jackson had several doctors. And, since slavery was over, the outbreak of a communicable disease could not be blamed on slave behavior.

Ellen began to feel life was slipping on by. She had never met the husbands of her sisters (except Georgia Ann, and she was dead) or their children. This was just about always on her mind. She went about the routine of running the home she shared with Nelson; his daughter, Sarah Ellen; and her son, Ira. This wasn't easy and had become more difficult from the standpoint of a long-term situation—it had already been a decade!

Ellen would also wonder what Pa and Ma thought of her living in a home with a man who was not her husband. Would they understand the relationship? Nelson and his parents had been supportive and helpful in times of crisis. Certainly, he understood enough of Ellen to allow her (and her son) to continue living in the home until her situation in life was worked out. And without Ellen, how would Nelson cope with raising his daughter? But what Pa and Ma thought living hundreds of miles away was probably easy to discern—they didn't think it was proper. A widowed woman should not live in the house with a single man. There were too many opportunities for unwanted relationships to develop. Regardless, Ellen didn't have a lot of choices. She had been without a home, and the Bell family had taken her and her son in and given them a place to live and provided food to eat. Ellen did a lot of work for Nelson and provided care for his daughter.

Some folks in the Tinnin community said that Pa and Ma should actively pray for Ellen and her son. Pa and Ma, particularly Pa, were not "prayers." Yes, they would say little prayers of thanks, but they felt that situations in human life that were created by humans should be solved by humans and not dumped on an invisible god to solve. Pa and Ma hoped they had taught Ellen how to go about life in a positive, uplifting manner. Pa and Ma always thought that how a person lived, along with the kinds of relationships he or she had, was indicative of his or her fundamental values. (Of course, Ellen's marriage to Jasper didn't really reflect consideration of Pa and Ma's input .)

Ellen tried to continue some of the traditions of the Shepard family, particularly as related to her sisters. These were things she remembered from her childhood in Tinnin. Special days and holidays were recognized as best she could. She also wanted to fill in for her deceased sister, Georgia Ann, raising Sarah Ellen with the traditions of her grandparents. Her son, Ira, also benefitted from her continuing the traditions. This suited Nelson just fine, as long as he had no responsibility for them.

Birthdays, Christmas, and the beginning of the New Year were important traditions Ellen tried to keep. Maybe Ellen continued them around Nelson with the notion that a romantic relationship might develop. She had always resisted any hints or advances or romantic inclinations on Nelson's part. Of course, Nelson shared many of the same holiday traditions as Ellen and, no doubt, appreciated what Ellen did to help mark the special season and times in the lives of family members. These were appropriate in the lives of Ira, as well as Sarah Ellen. Ellen's sisters continued Shepard family traditions with their men after marriage, though most were tempered by the traditions their men had before marriage.

Ellen was always able to come up with small gifts for birthdays and Christmas. Sometimes, Christmas included one small, useful gift such as clothing and a large orange or apple; other times, a small amount of hard candy or some kind of nuts, perhaps pecans or English walnuts, might be included. A tradition was to have some sort of decorated tree. A native cedar about four to five feet tall with a reasonably symmetrical shape would be cut about mid-December. It would be stood upright in a gallon bucket filled with soil. Decorations of various sorts would be placed on the tree. Sweet gumballs, pine cones, and small branches with red berries from holly trees would be used, depending on what was available. Candles were not used on the trees Ellen prepared, as they were costly. And, if lighted, she felt they would pose a fire hazard. The few gifts would be placed around the tree's base on the floor. The gifts were opened on Christmas morning.

Birthdays involved homemade cupcakes, cookies, or a cake (Ellen was somewhat limited by the cooking stove she had). Often, a piece of homemade clothing would be included as a birthday gift. Ellen was a great believer in giving something a person needed and would use in some way.

Celebration of the beginning of a New Year might have been the event Ellen most liked to celebrate with traditional foods of the Shepard family for that time. Though a part of Pa's upbringing in Indiana, pumpkins were not included in his Tinnin traditions; nor did Ellen use them in Texas.

On January 1, 1880, Ellen prepared a special meal to commemorate the New Year. Her fixin's included dried peas, baked sweet potatoes, greens, cornpone, and a dish called hoppin' John with molasses lightly poured over it. Her greens weren't exactly as her Ma would have prepared in Tinnin. Ellen did not have collards, cabbage, or mustard greens; she had rutabaga greens. The rutabaga had been planted in the fall to grow roots, but this year the tops were very nice and she used some of them before the roots developed (she left the plants so root development would continue). The greens were cooked with a few slices of fresh hog jowl for seasoning and meat. Convincing Sarah Ellen, going on three years of age, to try some of these foods was a challenge for her father, Nelson.

Nevertheless, Ellen maintained some sort of family structure in her household. She wanted Ira and Sarah Ellen to experience a family orientation, though their families had been destroyed by the deaths of their parents.

She often thought about family traditions with her sisters. She thought Ira could experience more valued traditions if he were in Tinnin with the Shepard family. A presence in Tinnin could not possibly be a part of life at this time. Maybe the future would be different.

11

A Big Decision

Years were passing by. Ellen felt lacking. Was she missing out on life? She spent hours thinking and dreaming. Her parents were getting older. Her sisters were into young adulthood and marriage. She had not seen her brother since he was little more than a toddler (her other brother was dead, as he only lived into couple of years). Her son would soon be a teenager. Time was moving on.

The first event after the New Year in 1880 that got Ellen thinking was a letter from her brother, Ira W. Shepard. He was only about two years of age in 1864 when Ellen and Jasper had married. After the marriage, she was forbidden by Pa to ever bring Jasper to the Shepard home. What her brother knew about her was primarily what had been shared with him by Ma, Pa, and their sisters. He wrote a letter to Ellen on the last day of December 1879, that partially read as follows:

Mrs. Ellen S. Lee,

Dear and most affectionate sister, I once more in life seat myself to try and write you a few lines to inform you that we are all well at present ... Sis we had right smart at Christmas and I believe most everybody here did and I hope you had a heap of Christmas ...your sister Mag's husband is doing well with his store ...We made a very good crop ... I will be nineteen years old the twentieth of next March and weigh only 140 pounds. I have a fine bunch of hogs ...I haven't told you anything about my sweetheart. She lives in Brandon in Rankin County and her name is Miss Lizzie Boggs. She is the Belle of Rankin County ...Sister Ellen, do you ever expect to come back to Mississippi? If you want to and do not have the money to come home with, write to me and tell me and I will raise the money for you. I want to see you and Ira very badly. Tell Ira and little Ellen howdy and kiss them for me. Tell Mr. Bell I would like to have him come here to live. Well, I will bring my letter to a close by asking you to write soon and often. Excuse my bad writing and spelling. So, goodbye for this time.

Ira W. Shepard.

(The letter from Ira repeats some of what a sister had told her earlier but this reconfirms the sweetheart matter.)

This letter from her brother really tugged at Ellen. It brought back a lot of memories of Tinnin and her family. Her memory of her brother was as a toddler just beginning to walk and run around a little. Now, he was an adult. She immediately wanted to see him and others in her family. She had heard he was a smart, good-looking, and well-mannered young man. Maybe his relationship with his sweetheart would develop into marriage. No doubt, Pa would like some grandchildren with the Shepard surname. Maybe he would take over the Shepard farm in Tinnin when their Pa was no longer able to manage it.

The second event that really got Ellen thinking about the situation was the visit by the census enumerator for the 1880 Federal Census. Nelson Bell was the head of household and gave the information. Four people were in the household—Nelson Bell (age thirty-one), Sarah Ellen Bell (age two), Ellen Shepard Lee (age thirty-three), and Ira Jasper Lee (age twelve).

After the enumerator left, Ellen had a certain sadness come over her. She remembered that Jasper H. Lee, her husband, the love of her life and the father of her son, had given the information to the last enumerator in 1870. Interestingly, there were also four people in the 1870 Lee household! It had been almost a decade since Jasper had died. She sat alone in a chair on the porch of the house and stared off into the distance. Her eyes moistened, and a tear rolled down each cheek. There, vividly in her mind, was the image of her man. She missed him dearly. She thought of opportunity in Henderson County. She thought of family and friends in Tinnin who she had not seen in sixteen years.

In a flash, her mind thought, *I want to go home—to Tinnin*. She wondered if going home would be possible. She had the responsibility of running the household for Nelson. She also had the responsibility of caring for her two-year-old niece and twelve-year-old son. Life in Texas had not been comfortable since Jasper's death. Maybe sometime Nelson wanted to have a romantic relationship, but that didn't suit Ellen.

Another concern was the future of the Mississippi farm property. Her sister Mag had once sent a letter to Ellen that created concern about ever going home to Tinnin. In the letter, Mag said, "Pa says if he can possibly sell the place he will and move to Louisiana next fall. I would rather move to Texas. If we should move to Louisiana and your side of that big Mississippi River we will certainly go to see you all then for it won't take so much money."

Maybe Pa had become weary after a decade of poor farm production and extra hard labor following the Civil War. Getting farmworkers and sharecroppers was a challenge that came around routinely each year. Pa might have also been observing what was happening in soil erosion on the hills of loess soil. Plowing laid the land virtually bare. Hard downpours of rain would wash the top and most fertile loess soil away. Gullies were beginning to form in some hills. Loss of fertile topsoil by erosion reduced the productivity of the land.

The Shepard children were growing up and leaving home, taking their work productivity with them. Son, Ira W. Shepard, had said he wanted to go farm in Sunflower County, Mississippi. This flat, fertile land of the Mississippi River Delta in the state of Mississippi was said to be the best cotton land around. So, if Ira did go to Sunflower County, he would not be taking over the Shepard farm in Tinnin. That would leave a need for someone else to do so. But none of the daughters had married men who appeared to have the interest or stamina. Maybe grandson Ira J. Lee could do it as he became an adult. A lot of thoughts stormed through Ellen's mind.

To help in the process of making a decision, Ellen quietly had a talk with Reverend McIntosh of the Presbyterian church in Athens. She respected him a lot, as he always appeared levelheaded and reasonable. He raised some good questions and offered support for Ellen in reuniting with her family. The reverend did not personally see much future for Ellen and Ira in Henderson County. Society and Texas laws were harsh on single women. The reverend did suggest she share her situation with two or so trusted church members to get their opinions; she did, and they were supportive of her going home (but did not want to lose her from their church community).

After a few days of quietly contemplating her future and going about work as usual, Ellen made up her mind to contact Pa and Ma. Beforehand, she quietly spoke with Ira. She went over in her mind what would be involved in going home. She knew she would need to talk with Nelson. It wasn't simple; things were more complex than merely picking up and leaving.

She began thinking about the letter she would write to Pa and Ma. What would she say and how would she say it? Of course, she wanted to ask if she and Ira could come back to live with them.

Before Ellen wrote the letter, she told Nelson early one morning that she wanted to talk with him when he came in from the field for lunch. All morning she thought about how to tell Nelson. After all, he and his parents had been so good to her. They had taken her in when she had no place to go. And there was Sara Ellen, who would need motherly care.

Noon came. Nelson ate, and Ellen said she had something to say. She said that Nelson and all of the Bell family had been very nice to her, and she greatly appreciated what they had done. However, it was now time for her to move on in life. She said she was writing her family in Tinnin to ask about returning. She wasn't sure but felt they would allow her and Ira to do so.

Nelson, though kind of shocked, said OK but immediately asked about Sarah Ellen's future. Ellen didn't have a good answer. She thought aloud that maybe one of Nelson's sisters would take Sarah Ellen into her family or that maybe Nelson could get a live-in housekeeper. Of course, there was always the notion that Nelson might marry again. But that didn't appear to be something that would be happening anytime soon.

Nelson had always been a source of advice, comfort, and confidence for Ellen. She asked him for suggestions in writing the letter. Together, they came up with a general approach. Be tactful, loving, and humble—none of this "I am going to do so regardless of what you say," like she had done when she'd chosen to marry Jasper. She would first offer proper greeting and indicate that she loved and missed her family. She would talk about their twelve-year-old grandson, Ira. She would indicate that the death of Jasper left her unsure of direction in her life. The process of settling the estate had been long and had left her with virtually nothing. (Fortunately, the Bell family had taken her in.) She would indicate that she felt that going to her Tinnin home would be best for her. She would ask how they felt about her and Ira working and living with them. She would indicate that she hoped to hear from them very soon.

The letter was written and mailed. Ellen waited for a response. After a couple of weeks wait (which seemed like an eternity), a response was received. Ellen hurriedly opened the letter. "Yes, you are welcome to come back to Tinnin and live in our home," it read. "Please do so soon. We miss you. We want to see our grandson Ira."

She shared the letter from Ma and Pa with Ira and Nelson. Details for the return needed to be worked out. Ellen began planning. She knew it would take some time.

But first, she would write her Pa and Ma and thank them for offering for her and Ira to come there. She indicated it would be about another year before she could travel to Tinnin. She would keep them informed of her plans. She welcomed hearing from Pa and Ma with anything she needed to know.

One additional matter was shared in a letter Ellen sent to Pa and Ma: What would happen to Sarah Ellen Bell? She was the primary caregiver of this daughter of her sister Georgia Ann. She did not know how Nelson would cope if she left the child in his care. He was a good father, but he had a lot of farmwork to do. Pa and Ma did not think Sarah Ellen should come to Tinnin with Ellen and Ira if and when they returned. Pa and Ma kind of felt that the needs of Sarah Ellen might keep Ellen in Texas. Of course, Sarah Ellen was a granddaughter of Pa and Ma who they had never seen.

Ellen's letters to Pa and Ma were shared among her siblings, particularly those living at or near their home. Some of them wrote Ellen with encouragement. Of course, the decision to allow Ellen to come back to Tinnin was one for Pa and Ma.

Ellen thought about living arrangements in the Shepard home in Tinnin. There were four large rooms with very high ceilings downstairs on each corner of the house. A wide enclosed hallway went between pairs of rooms. The front of the hallway was used as a place for greeting and sitting with guests. The back was used as a dining room. The upstairs, though not all finished, contained considerable space that could be used with a little improvement. And there was the large closet room under the stairs that Jasper had used in courtship days when he'd stayed overnight at Ellen's home.

Next, Ellen thought about the people who would be living at the house if she and Ira returned. There would be Pa and Ma; her sister who had returned home because her husband was unfaithful (she had one young child); and her youngest sibling, brother Ira W. There would be plenty of room in the house. She also thought her brother might marry and leave. Or he might marry and bring his wife into the home so that he could take over the farming operation as Pa and Ma aged. There would be enough room either way.

Ellen spent almost the entire year of 1880 preparing to go back to Tinnin. Of course, she also continued to manage the household for Nelson and provide care for Nelson's three-year-old daughter, as well as her own son.

She began getting ready for the return by assessing how to do it: What transportation would she use? How much would it cost? What could she take with her? How would she dispose of what she couldn't take? How would she tell friends and family goodbye? She realized that, once she left, she would likely never see them again.

Letters were received from back home with suggestions on transportation. Some were from family members; others came from friends who remembered her. They asked what she was going to try to bring with her, such as a bed and other furniture. Ellen soon realized she couldn't move the few items of furniture she had; she sold them for a few dollars. Some of the letters asked if Ellen had enough money and offered to send money if she would let them know what she needed. The estimate in one letter said that sixty dollars would likely be enough for both to ride the cars (train). The fare for Ellen would be thirty dollars, and for Ira it would be fifteen to twenty dollars. Ellen immediately thought she needed more than sixty dollars—there might be some things she needed to buy along the way.

A letter from her brother (now nineteen years of age), dated September 22, 1880, offered his suggestion on the best way to return to Tinnin. The letter stated information on travel he had gotten from a friend: "Mr. Walter Baskins says it is the best for you to come by way of Palestine, Texas, through Arkansas in a stage coach and to St. Louis and take a barge down the Mississippi to Vicksburg. You can ride on a car (train) to Clinton."

Another suggestion in the letter was to take a boat from Shreveport, Louisiana, to New Orleans and take a barge or boat up the Mississippi to Vicksburg. Some of these options seemed a little flamboyant and less than economical. Ellen wanted a route that was easy and manageable. She also wanted a short route that was safe and affordable on her meager money supply.

Ellen asked around Athens about transportation for herself, Ira, and their possessions. It made sense to her to ride the train from Athens to Tallulah, Louisiana. This was the same route she and Jasper had used to come to Athens seventeen years earlier; now she was reversing the direction of travel. In Tallulah, they would get a ride to the ferry to cross the Mississippi River into Vicksburg. In Vicksburg, they would catch a ride in a wagon to the depot for the train to Clinton. She carefully saved money, including small income amounts from the sale of property she could not take back with her. She needed to buy train tickets and pay freight for one large box of personal belongings. She did not ask her family for money, though they offered to send money to her for to make the trip.

She didn't have much in the way of physical possessions. A few things could be taken. Of course, they would take clothing and the like. She began by disposing of a few things. She asked Nelson if she had anything that might be useful to him. She identified items that might have some value that could be sold. It was not easy to part with some things—sentimental attachment caused her to want to keep them. Among these were the cedar bucket Jasper had bought in 1869. She had room for moving only a few things to Tinnin. And how was she going to transport what she kept?

The possessions she was taking with her had to go into a big wooden box. With Nelson's help, she and Ira got twelve-inch board planks and constructed a box that was approximately a four-foot cube. The box held a good deal of stuff and would offer some protection from damage. Once filled, it would be sealed up by nailing planks over the top. The box would be shipped as freight on the passenger train. Between the weight of the wood and the contents of the box, it became too heavy for one person to lift. Train workers would load and unload the freight.

Ellen had a trunk that she had acquired from a woman who was selling it secondhand after she and Jasper came to Texas. She would take it as baggage on the train. The trunk would have clothing, a few items for remembering

Henderson County, and letters and papers (some of which were later found and used in family research). She also had the two old travel bags she and Jasper had used sixteen years ago, and these could be used as luggage. Ira would have one of them for his clothing and personal items—not much.

Moving was also emotional for Ira Jasper Lee. He had always lived in Henderson County. He had a few friends from his involvement with the Presbyterian church in Athens. One of these friends was a girl who could likely have become a sweetheart later as she and Ira became young adults. And she would have been a good one! She was likely one who Pa and Ma Shepard would have approved of. School really wasn't an issue; not much by way of formal education was around, and Ira Jasper didn't attend a school. This part of Texas wasn't much into schools at this time. Some folks might say he was homeschooled, though that notion didn't exist at that time.

One of the things Ira and his mother would give up was the aging horse that had pulled the wagon for trips to town and was used for riding. Ira loved this horse dearly. It would do about anything Ira would ask. Ira and Ellen had named the horse Captain. Captain was a proud horse, who could follow commands quite well. Maybe Ira could find and identify with a new horse after they got to Tinnin. Ira loved Captain. Nelson was going to keep Captain, and that helped them feel better about leaving him; they knew Nelson would take good care of him.

The year of 1880 was passing on. Ellen and Ira were preparing for the travel to Tinnin. Not all would be complete in the year. It would be 1881 before they would depart on a journey that would change the lives of several people. Maybe Ira would grow to have a family and manage a farm. He had a lot to learn. He had a good teacher in his mother, Ellen, but more was needed. She felt he needed a man, such as Pa, around to teach him.

The time for their departure grew near. Ellen tried to wrap up all details at the Bell house. She told friends goodbye; she spoke with Brother McIntosh thanked him for his guidance and support and said goodbye. He announced in a church service that Ellen and Ira would be leaving, and members of the congregation wished her well.

Ellen wrote to her parents a few days before she was to leave, stating her plans and train schedule. When the letter was received in Tinnin, everyone paid attention to the details. She thought some of her siblings might meet her and Ira in Vicksburg. But no. Her sisters had left home and were not available to meet her and Ira in Vicksburg. She would be met by Pa and Ma, however, in Clinton.

The day of departure arrived. Final details were discussed with Nelson. Saying goodbye became emotional. Ellen and Nelson hugged and said their farewells. She expressed her gratitude for all he and his family had done for her and Ira. Sarah Ellen was given a big good-bye hug and several "smacky-on-the-cheeks" kisses as small children often enjoyed. Ellen offered some words of inspiration for a three-year-old girl. Sarah Ellen no doubt got a sense that she was losing something in all of this, as Ellen had been like a mother to her. Nelson had earlier agreed to take Ellen and Ira to the depot the day they were leaving.

Nelson took them to the depot in Athens in a wagon pulled by Captain. Ellen bought tickets to ride a passenger car. They all hugged goodbye again. Ellen and Ira boarded the car (train). Their luggage and baggage was placed aboard, and they were on their way. They waved to Nelson and Sarah Ellen as the train pulled out of sight. Nelson and Sarah Ellen started the ride back to their home; Ellen and Ira saw the wagon go out of sight. Tears ran down both their faces. They realized that they would likely not see each other again. Sad!

The train was pulled by a coal-fired steam engine. It traveled through the countryside, over creeks and small rivers, and into the towns. Ellen and Ira watched for fields, pastures, animals, houses, and features of the country-side. They wanted to have good memories of the lay of the land. The train made several stops in the towns. On the fourth stop near Shreveport, Ellen reached into her bag and pulled out two cornpones she had cooked the previous day and brought with her as they traveled. She had two more that would be saved until later.

After some time, the train traveled out of the hilly countryside into the low, flat land of the Delta. This was a sign that they were passing through Monroe and weren't too far from Tallulah, Louisiana, where they would leave the train. With luggage and baggage, they caught a ride on a wagon going to the ferry landing on the Mississippi River. It had been seventeen years since Ellen had seen the Mississippi River; Ira had never seen it.

As the ferry was being tied up at the landing in Vicksburg, Ellen and Ira gathered their belongings. They got off the ferry, and one of the crew members unloaded their baggage and freight. Though the depot wasn't far away, Ellen and Ira arranged to be transported there in a wagon. Their baggage and freight were too much to carry.

Ellen bought tickets for herself and Ira to travel on the train from Vicksburg to Clinton. The train departed on schedule and made its way through steep hills, over creeks, and across the Big Black River near Bovina. In a bit, they would pass through the small towns of Edwards and Bolton and arrive in Clinton.

What a glorious day! Just ahead down the tracks was the depot with a sign that read, "Clinton." The train arrived on schedule. As it pulled to a stop, they looked out the window. Ellen saw Pa and Ma standing on the platform waiting; that made her feel wonderful. Ira had never seen them and didn't know who to look for. Ellen pointed them out.

Ellen and Ira quickly gathered their belongings. It was a clear, sunny day—just right for a reunion. Gee, Pa and Ma looked good to have aged more than seventeen years since Ellen had last seen them. They got off the train. Hugs. Kisses. More hugs and kisses. Pa and Ma would get to know their grandson Ira, who was barely a teenager but would need to grow up fast on the Shepard farm. They checked to be sure their luggage and baggage had been unloaded before the train pulled out for its next stop at the depot in Jackson.

Ellen had arrived in Clinton. But the journey back to Tinnin wasn't complete. Pa and Ira loaded their luggage and large freight box on the wagon, and they all headed north to Tinnin. Pa drove the wagon and talked about many things along the way, such as Monroe Street, which was developing into a place where people built their homes in Clinton. The horse pulled the wagon on out of town and toward Tinnin. They passed Sumner Hill, Stafford Ridge, and Kickapoo and proceeded down a long trail through the Shepard Hills.

Pa had questions. "What happened to your husband, Jasper? Why did he die?"

Ellen wasn't expecting that question on this day of reunion. She could tell Pa still wasn't quite over the marriage. Ellen explained that he had become quite ill on

November 15, 1870, and had died the following day. She said the doctor had come three times to the house and had treated him, but he'd died anyway. The doctor thought he'd had a heart attack or something. His body was buried in Smith Cemetery.

After this, Pa asked, "Did you ever learn about his past?"

Ellen said, "Not much."

Pa said, "Well, I did. You might be surprised. I won't share the details today. I know you want to remember him as a man dedicated to you and his marriage. I will talk sometime to you in private."

Ellen really didn't want to know. It was sad that Pa had brought up this subject; maybe it was to ward off any future ideas of matrimony that Ellen might have after getting back to Tinnin.

After a bit of riding, the horse turned onto the drive that curved downhill toward the Shepard home, which was on a ridge after crossing the bottom of a small valley between the hills. They passed by a dug well that provided some of the water for the home (remember Pa had been a well digger in Indiana before he'd moved to Mississippi; he had a knack for getting good water wells into service). Pa spoke and said it was the best well around and kept water year-round. Another well just behind the house provided water on a daily basis.

The wagon pulled up to the big porch on the front

of the Shepard home. Glorious! Ellen was thrilled. She shouted and jumped for joy. Ira was very pleased to see his grandparents' home. But Ellen quickly thought about her siblings. She was enthusiastic about seeing the home place without them around as children but saddened because they were gone. All were gone except the sister who had returned after a marriage in which her husband was unfaithful and her youngest brother, Ira W., who came running in from his work in a cotton field to greet and hug the new arrivals. Ellen hugged her sister and her sister's small child. Everyone hugged Ellen's son, Ira—the only young Lee around.

To Ellen, some things were different. Her parents had aged. There was no Bummer or Ritz, but there was a new dog name Howl. (Ellen wanted to know how the dog had gotten that name and was told it was because he howled at full moons.) One thing new was six honeybee hives just south of the fence around the house. Trees had grown and aged; some had fallen. Buildings had deteriorated; one in the animal lot had a collapsed roof. Slave housing had fallen in or been torn down. A couple of new sharecropper cabins had been built. Some of the steeper hills had signs of gully erosion. Things looked so different. Ever so quickly, a flash came into Ellen's mind: *You can't go home.* There is no such thing; home changes. Many things change over time.

Ellen was so happy to see her parents and brother and sister that all else was forgotten—including what had caused them to be apart for seventeen years. Ellen was glowing with happiness. Getting back to Tinnin was now partially achieved. Next would be adjustment and the final adaptations.

12

Adjustment to Return

The year was 1881. Ellen and Ira were now living in Tinnin. She tried to fill the emptiness she had experienced in her life and seek happiness in Tinnin. What would it take for satisfactory adjustment to life in Tinnin? Maybe it would involve a greater role in the plantation for Ira.

After being away about seventeen years, she would need time to adjust. Would she have a satisfied life in Tinnin? Considering their relationship in 1864, would she be able to get along with Pa? Could she accept the maturity and aging of her family? After all, her parents were older; she was older. Pa was now sixty-seven years of age, Ma was fifty-one, and Ellen was thirty-four. Her siblings had reached adulthood, married, and moved away. So many changes influenced Ellen's ability to readily adjust to Tinnin.

It was Ellen's nature to pitch in and strive to make the best of situations. She knew she and Ira would be expected to do their share of work around the farm and home. A surprise she first learned about the farm was that the amount of land was now much less. Hard times after the Civil War had resulted in her father selling and losing acreage. Some of the Federal reconstruction programs seemed to have taken advantage of Pa and the plantation. Representatives of the Federal government were thought to sometimes be unscrupulous. Could this be a product of carpetbagger activity? Carpetbaggers were Northerners who had come south after the Civil War and for their own personal gain and had taken advantage of Southerners.

Without sufficient income to cover some debts in which land had been used as collateral, Pa had lost acreage by foreclosure of the lien holder. Altogether, the farm acreage was now close to four hundred—a decline of some eight hundred acres while Ellen was living in Texas. She wondered if, had she been there, she could have done something so the property wasn't lost. Maybe she could have helped Pa make smart decisions and not have to sell or lose land for failure to make loan repayments in a timely manner. Oh well, the water was under the bridge; there was no turning back. Plus, four hundred acres should be sufficient for the smaller family that now needed support.

After their arrival, Ellen and Ira got somewhat settled into a large room that would be theirs. A couple of small beds and not much else was in it, though there was enough for them to get by on for a while. Ellen then went outside the house and showed Ira around. This was a good time for her to see things that had changed. She showed Ira the water well and went over how to draw water to keep it clean and safe to use. She showed him the privy, the animal lot and outbuildings, the smokehouse, the chicken yard, the beehives, and the garden that had a few things growing in it. The same site for a garden was used for many years; it was good for cool or early season, midseason, and late-season vegetable crops, depending on the kinds they were. Then they walked down to the spring branch that brought good water within a hundred yards of the house from a spring on a high hillside. After they'd looked around a bit, it was late afternoon and time to go back to the house. Ma would soon have dinner. Ellen pitched in to help finish getting it ready.

Dinner was simple. Traditional food was prepared for an evening meal of the Shepard family—boiled dried peas seasoned with ham hock, cornpone, fried salt pork meat, raw onion, and pickled zucchini relish. Seven people were at the table—Pa and Ma, Ellen's brother Ira W., Ellen's sister Rachel and her daughter, and Ellen and Ira Lee. There was no longer need for a separate children's table. Pa said a quick blessing that included thanks for bringing Ellen home safely.

Conversation was nice for their first meal home. A lot

of reminiscing took place. Ellen got brought up to date on her sisters. Ira W. talked a little about his sweetheart in Rankin County, but somehow the feeling was maybe it wasn't going to be a long-term relationship. Talk about neighboring families revealed a lot of change over the years Ellen was gone. The school had a few months of class each year. Mason's chapel continued much as before, with an itinerant preacher named Pastor Murrow. Pa talked some about the farm and challenges with finding labor and managing sharecroppers. He said the hill land was just not as productive as it used to be—back when he'd first gotten it in the mid-1840s. No doubt, erosion of topsoil was taking its toll. Soil conservation practices needed to be used.

Ellen and Ira were tired and sleepy from the long trip. So, it was time for bed. The window shutters were folded shut and fastened. The outside doors of the house would be latched securely by the last person to come inside, Pa usually.

Pa thought Ira needed a little instruction about his approaching manhood. He didn't check with his mother before doing so. He thought men knew men better, and after all, Ira was now thirteen years of age. He took him out on the front porch. He talked about the budding whiskers on his face and the hair beginning to grow other places on his body. Pa indicated that he might want to shave his face a little. But some whiskers, if trimmed and neat, would be OK on the farm. He talked about bathing and washing areas where body odor may readily develop. Frequent sponge bathing may work, Pa said. This would be done with a cloth, soap, and a wash bucket of water. Pa said to never use the drinking water bucket for bathing. Ira needed some of this man-to-man talk. Neither his mother, Ellen, nor his uncle, Nelson, had talked about such things.

The discussion continued. Pa asked his grandson if he liked girls. Hesitantly, but for no apparent reason, Ira said he did like them but that he was kind of shy around them. He said there was a girl he'd left in Athens who appeared to have potential but that he might never see her again. No one had ever talked to Ira about such topics before.

Pa asked if he knew about animals and their lives; Ira said yes (all young folks on a farm with animals "know" about them). Pa said humans were sort the same as farm animals but were mostly very private and cautious about what they did. Pa told him he would talk some more soon about being a man and how to relate to girls and young women. "Always be kind and respectful," he said, "and never take advantage of females." Pa further said that some things were only for married folks. Now, Ira had a lot of questions in his mind. Boys were usually always ahead of parents and grandparents when these subjects were brought up. Sometimes adults waited too long for this conversation, but this was not the case with Ira.

Pa ended by talking about his before-going-to-bed pee each night off the porch (just as he had done most nights since 1857). This was probably something Ira didn't need to be told a lot about. But since Ira was a new man in the Shepard home, Pa felt he had an obligation to do so. Anyway, Pa believed "off the porch" (either the front or back porch) was better than wondering around the yard in the dark (you might step on a snake or a pile of fresh dog crap) or using the slop jar in the bedroom, which, he said, was mostly for the women. He told Ira he had learned that women didn't like to use a slop jar that had earlier been used by a man—something about the odor. Of course, it could be emptied and rinsed out, but that was a morning task for the next day. Pa told him to go to different places around the porch—not the same place each time—and never on the porch floor. And that was the end of Pa's instructions for the night. And it was off to bed.

The first thing Ellen wanted to do the next morning was take a ride around the farm and Tinnin community. She got permission from Pa (he was still controlling about certain things) to use a horse and the one-horse wagon to do so. Ira helped her with the hitching (he knew how to do it, but he needed to learn the way things were done on the Shepard farm). She had Ira drive, and with instructions from her, they rode to the fields on trails used to get around on the farm property. They talked a little about the fields, the creeks that ran through them, and how overflowing creeks such as the Bogue Chitto Creek could ruin young crop plants.

Some fields were now planted with different crops than before Ellen was gone, and she said that Pa would give him the details. As the passenger, Ellen got out of the wagon and opened and closed gates along the way. She told Ira to always close any gate he opened—leave gates the way you find them. On their ride, they passed five fairly new sharecropper houses and a couple of falling-in former slave cabins. The other slave cabins Ellen remembered had been torn down.

Ellen showed Ira where the Union troops had come onto the farm and camped. She told him about how the family had prepared for the arrival of the troops and the threat to burn the house. Ira wanted to know why it hadn't been burned. Ellen explained that Pa had been raised in Indiana and had views on slavery, the Civil War, and how to relate honestly and fairly to all people that were different than the views of others in the area. He'd truthfully told the troops he had voted the Union ticket and that no Confederate soldier lived in the house. That, without doubt, had saved the house.

After they had looked around the farm for a little while, it was time to explore Tinnin. They rode back to the house and up the driveway to the main dirt road and turned right. To Ellen, it seemed that fewer houses were being lived in and more were getting into a bad state of disrepair.

They rode by the Zachariah Ratliff Family Cemetery. Ellen told Ira about some of the people buried in it and that Pa and Ma wanted to be buried there when their time came. One of the things Ira noticed was that some graves appeared to be outside the bounds of the cemetery. He wondered who they belonged to; he wondered if they had been slaves. He might have been surprised to learn that a couple of them were his distant relatives.

Next, they rode by the schoolhouse and Mason Chapel. Ellen told Ira that she had gone to the Tinnin School a few months each year for eight years. The school usually had one teacher, and all grades met together. She said he was likely beyond the age to go to school. A teacher's home was next to the schoolhouse so the teacher, who was paid very little, would have a place to stay.

Mason Chapel was somewhat run-down but still served a few families in the community. It needed major repairs, including a new roof. Ellen and Ira stopped at it and went inside. Surprisingly, the preacher, Brother Murrow, was there. Ellen introduced herself and explained that she used to go to church there but had been away in Texas. Brother Murrow welcomed her back to Tinnin and indicated that she and Ira would be welcome to come to Mason Chapel. Brother Murrow said that George and Sarah Shepard and some of their family attended. Services were on Sundays with even monthly calendar numbers. Preaching began at 11:00 a.m. Sometimes, there were special events, such as singings and barbecues—it sounded like old times to Ellen. Brother Murrow said he would visit the Shepard family on Saturday afternoon and looked forward to seeing them as well.

Ellen and Ira next headed for Ratliff Store, which was about like it had been when Ellen had gone away in 1864. She told Ira that his great-grandparents, the Ratliffs, had started the store and operated it for several years. They stopped the wagon out front, hitched to a porch post, and went inside. There wasn't much to see. It was typical for a small country store. The small amount of goods for sale was in stark contrast to the larger mercantile stores found in Vicksburg, Jackson, and a few other Mississippi cities.

The store had a few food items, such as sugar, salt, coffee and tea, which were kept in pottery jars on shelves. Several bolts of cloth and sewing supplies were on a large table with a cabinet at one end. Limited ready-made clothing and shoes were near the back. Tobacco products; moonshine liquor (on a shelf out of sight); and a few things used as medicines, such as paregoric (an opium product), were near the cash box. Behind the counter with the cash box were bullets and gunpowder. Small pieces of hard candy were in a pottery jar next to the cash box. Several small wooden containers had common small-seeded vegetables, such as turnips, radishes, and carrots. Larger boxes held pea, butterbean, okra, and squash seeds. There were bins of corn meal that had been ground at a water-powered stone mill on the Bogue Chitto Creek.

Ellen introduced herself to the person running the store. Ellen told her that she had grown up in Tinnin but had been away for seventeen years—had just gotten back. She asked if she had been in the area long. The store clerk said she'd been there for about fifteen years. She'd moved from Brandon, where, for a while, she had been a house-keeper at Sister Annie's Boarding House. Further, she said that place had some very interesting people—some were scary and others were nice. One wonders what the store clerk really knew about the men at Sister Annie's. Ellen didn't ask her about the men.

Ellen then asked the store clerk if she knew a few folks in the Tinnin community, including Samuel Echols, Rufus Tilman, and Margie Mason; the clerk knew two of the individuals Ellen had named. After a few minutes of talking, they discovered a distant kinfolk relationship with the parents of her mother, who was of the Tinnin family for which the community was named. Now, that kin relationship was special to Ellen. The discussion and relationship would prove quite meaningful to her in the years to come. Ellen tried to explain the kinfolk relation-ship to Ira, but it wasn't very clear to him. He would learn more in the next few years.

Now, it was time to head back to the Shepard house. They passed a couple of homes, and Ellen told Ira who had lived there when she was growing up in Tinnin. So many changes made it difficult to explain the community. How life in Tinnin had changed since 1864!

Ira had a question for his mother, and it kind of caught her by surprise. "Do you have any old sweethearts around here?"

Ellen thought. She said, "A couple of beaus but no sweethearts. I am sure they are all married, moved away, or dead. Your daddy was the only sweetheart I ever had."

Then Ira wanted to know if she was interested in finding another man. Ellen hedged her response and never said a flat-out no.

The next Saturday afternoon, a one-seat, horse-pulled buggy came into sight up the hill from the Shepard home. Brother Murrow was coming for the visit he'd mentioned. Everyone gathered on the porch to welcome Brother Murrow. He said a prayer and read a short Bible passage. They talked about different things, with emphasis on the return of Ellen with her son. Brother Murrow wanted to know if Ira had been baptized.

Ira quickly spoke up, saying, "No, but I might want to be."

Then they talked about church experiences in Texas. After a few words about Flowing Waters Chapel, Ellen talked about the Presbyterian church they had attended in Athens, Texas. She said the church community was about peace, love, hope, and joy. She said that the Presbyterian preacher didn't preach about the hot fires of hell and scare everybody. Interestingly, Brother Murrow's sermons didn't get into hot fire subjects very often, though he was somewhat oriented in that direction. He wanted people to know that sin had consequences. The visit ended with a prayer, and the family said they would be at the next service.

The pace of activity would soon pick up on the farm. Crop time was at hand. Some fieldwork had already been done. Ira needed to learn the details from his Grandfather George and his uncle, Ira W. They were more than willing to have another person to help in the fields and to manage the sharecroppers. Ira was quite willing. He viewed his new life in Tinnin as a great opportunity that he should seize and develop. He wanted a good life on a farm. He knew of the hurt his mother had experienced when the farm she and his father had was repossessed.

Ira had some farm experience from living with Nelson Bell in Texas. Ira's father had died when he was too young to be taught farming. He knew a little about cotton, corn, and other common crops. He was ready to learn more and become more important on the Shepard plantation. His mother, Ellen, assured him she would be around most of the time to help keep him on the right track. She strongly wanted him to be successful; she did not view failure as an option. Maybe she was an overprotective mother!

The Shepards mostly used mules as draft animals.

Ira learned a lot about mules the first summer. Between the teachings of Pa and his mother, he learned they were a cross of a male donkey and a female horse and were smarter than either parent. Good care of the mules was a must. He was to provide feed, including corn or oat grain and grass or good quality hay, and water, along with rest; and he was never to abuse them. They were valuable animals that could work for long hours at a steady pace.

By the time Ellen got back to Tinnin, things had changed a great deal on the plantation. It had been through hard times. Buildings, fences, and barns were in poor repair. This is the old mule barn that had been on the plantation for many years.

Pa stressed the importance of having a good relationship with an animal you expected to do work. He would say, "Treat 'em right, and they will treat you right."

Ellen would reiterate with, "Be kind to animals, and they will be kind to you."

Maybe Ellen and Pa shared some of the same sense of how to go about life and get things done. Anyway, Ellen wanted Ira to learn the right ways of doings things—likely for his future benefit.

Ira had learned how to hitch horses, oxen, and mules to wagons from his mother and Uncle Nelson in Texas. These wheeled vehicles had tongues that extended forward alongside or between (in case of two) the animal(s). Now, he would learn how to hitch animals to various equipment, including plows and cultivators. Ellen explained that it was all more complicated than he probably thought. He first learned about hitching one mule to a singletree to pull a turning plow or cultivator in a field or log in a forest. He learned about putting collars, hames, trace chains, bridles, blinders, bits, lines, and belly bands on mules. He learned how to hitch a pair of mules using a doubletree to a middle buster plow or disk harrow. The process was similar to that of one mule but was complicated by having two animals that had to be hitched to work together. The Shepards did not use more than two-mule teams on implements.

Along with all of this, he learned how to manage mules by giving commands. Ellen reviewed the most important commands in field work, such as *get up* for "go," *whoa* for "stop," *gee* for "turn right," and *haw* for "turn left." He learned how to use the plow lines to help direct a mule and motivate it to exert effort and pull whatever it was hitched to. Holding plow handles so the plow point would go in the soil just right—not too deep—took some time and strength and helped develop his arm muscles. Holding the handles of cultivators so the soil was tilled and weeds destroyed and not damaging or destroying crop plants took greater care.

The first cropping season provided many learning opportunities for Ira. Planting seed required soil preparation, and that was early in the growing season. There were differences in how cotton and corn were planted. He learned to identify crop plants and distinguish them from weeds. He learned to use a hoe to chop cotton without damaging the plants and cut weeds from growing corn. He learned that chopping was to thin cotton plant populations to promote growth and development, remove weeds, and loosen the soil. Harvest required even different skills.

In late August, the newly hired teacher at Tinnin School came by. She introduced herself as Miss Sloan and said she had recently graduated from a college in Jackson and had been hired as the teacher at Tinnin School. She'd been told a boy had recently moved here from Texas. She wanted to talk about enrolling him in school. She said school would begin the first of October after much of the cotton crop had been harvested. She would be teaching reading, arithmetic, writing, and beginning science (something new at Tinnin). Ellen and Miss Sloan talked about ages, costs, and school days. Ira didn't think he wanted to go; he thought he was too old and knew enough anyway. Miss Sloan said most students quit school by age fourteen, but that was a little early. Miss Sloan said goodbye and told them to let her know. She got on her horse and left. Ellen talked with Ira and thought it over; he would not be going to school.

Ira had a little experience picking cotton in Texas with Nelson Bell, so that wasn't totally new. Ellen usually picked side-by-side rows when Ira picked. Getting cotton harvested was viewed like getting cash in your pocket. Pulling a pick sack, ever so quickly removing white seed cotton from the bolls, and quickly putting the cotton into the pick sack required fast and repeated motion all day long. The faster you went, the more you could pick. Once full, a pick sack was weighed (usually 60 to 70 pounds) and emptied into a cotton house—a small building on the edge of a field for storing cotton after it had been weighed and picked until there was a bale (about 1,100 pounds). And it took a far greater mass of cotton than you would think to make a bale! Once there was a bale, it would be hauled to a gin in a wagon. Ira liked driving a loaded wagon to a gin. He could wait around for an hour or so for ginning and go to a store to get a special candy snack or something.

Most things on the farm appeared to go routinely the first crop year. Pa and his son, Ira W., ran things. Grandson Ira carefully observed the goings-on. He would sometimes talk to his mother about the events of a day. Ellen was proud of the way her son went about work and learning. She often offered encouragement for him to learn new things and bragged on him when he did. In the back of her mind, she thought that one day her son might be the boss of the Shepard farm.

The cropping season ended in late fall. Most of the sharecroppers had worked out well. The cotton harvest was good—twenty-three bales. so was that of the other crops, including sweet potatoes and pinda. It was at that point that Ira W. began to reflect on his future. He was now twenty years old with a promising adult life ahead. Hill land required a lot of work. Productivity of the soil appeared to be going down. Where would he have the best future?

A change was on the way for the Shepard farm. Ira W. Shepard decided he would strike out on his own. He had found a young woman he wanted to marry. Together, they talked about their future. They decided to leave the hill land in favor of the nearly level and highly fertile land of the Mississippi Delta in Sunflower County, Mississippi. Ira W. had heard it was the best cotton land on Earth.

Ira W. talked to Pa about his tentative plans. Pa was a bit surprised, for he had thought his son would be taking over from him in a few years. But that appeared not to be the case. Ira W. told Pa his grandson, Ira, was young, smart, and energetic and that, with a few more years on the farm under his direction, he could take over, and the farm would continue.

On December 1, 1881, Ira W. Shepard (age twenty) married Mary Ella Collier, and moved to the Sunflower County community of Caile, near Inverness, Mississippi. It was a big move for a young man who had no wealth. But Ira W. had a lot of smarts about farming and success in business ventures. As of this event, the Shepard family no longer had a child who had not married, though two had married, gone away, and moved back home for different reasons. In both of those cases, the two no longer lived a married kind of life.

Operation of the Shepard plantation was now solely in the hands of Pa, and he was reaching the age of losing some of his stamina and interest. Maybe some of what Ellen had in mind for a "complete" return was now unfolding. And it related to the advance of her son, Ira, in taking over the farm. But he had a lot to learn. Ellen encouraged, taught, and worked beside him and asked Pa to do the same. She wanted him to be able to do a good job.

After Christmas was over and the year 1882 was beginning, Pa asked Ira to come talk with him. Ira was approaching age fourteen. Though Ira was not yet an adult, Pa felt he could be a lot more involved on the farm. Ellen wanted in on the conversation as well; she had a vested interest in her son being successful. After all, she would work with him side by side as needed in order to help

Ira learn the ropes. So, the three of them sat on the front porch in the late afternoon sunlight, wearing coats and hats to protect themselves from the chilly January breeze in central Mississippi.

The conversation dealt with how to make the farm more productive—and have more money at the end of the year from the major cash crop of cotton. Several things were discussed. Among the first was labor to do the required work. There were very few people to hire who would work hard, and money would be needed to pay their wages. They talked about using sharecroppers. Ellen mentioned how sharecropping had helped her and Jasper get their start in Texas. Pa indicated that a couple of sharecroppers had been used over the past few years. Maybe it was now time to expand a little in that direction.

Over the next few days, they decided to continue with the two sharecropper families from last year and add another for the 1882 crop year. Each would have about fifteen acres of good cropland. Some ten to twelve acres would be planted with cotton and a couple of acres, with corn. Any remaining land could be used as the sharecropper wished for gardening and other crops. They arranged with the sharecroppers from last year and told them to put out the word that they were looking for another sharecropper.

Ellen felt there should be a written agreement between Pa and each sharecropper. So, she talked around and got an example of an agreement used by another farm owner.

They were able to use that agreement to create one for themselves. Of course, everything was handwritten, not very legalistic, and had little detail; but the paperwork was helpful. Ellen drafted what they might use; Pa agreed with it. Contact was made with the two sharecroppers of the past year. The use of a written agreement seemed OK to them; they thought it better than an oral agreement, though Pa Shepard was a man of his word. A new sharecropper was located and agreed with the use a written agreement. He thought a written agreement would be good, as he felt that his previous landlord had cheated him.

A major issue with written agreements and sharecroppers was that they could not read and write; one had a wife who could read a little. Ellen would read the agreements aloud. Each sharecropper signed with an "X" (they could not write their names). The signing (X-ing) was typically witnessed by a Shepard family member. Nevertheless, the sharecroppers were very trusting of Pa and his family. Pa had earned that trust through years of being honest and fair. He tried extra hard to be a person of high integrity.

The sharecropper agreements typically contained the parties' names, the date, the cropping year, the kind of crop, the field location on the farm, the number of acres, and the work responsibilities of the sharecroppers. The agreement included the division of crop yields. Most sharecroppers worked on thirds—this meant they got two-thirds of the money from the sale of cotton, and the landowner got one-third. If they worked for Pa on other things, such as building fences or cutting stove wood, they were paid a daily amount in cash. Most of them had very little, and the daily work was important. The rate was typically one to two dollars per day for a hard day of labor.

Part of the agreement dealt with Pa providing "furnishings" to sharecroppers. Furnishings included what they needed to live on—primarily basic food items and occasionally money for clothing, including work boots. Small cash amounts would be advanced to the sharecropper. Ellen kept a record of the advances in a small paper tablet. The amounts would be totaled and deducted from the sharecroppers' portions of the cash from cotton sales. The Shepards didn't have much extra money for making advances. If they needed to, they would themselves borrow money. Ellen was very careful to keep all records honestly and accurately. What the sharecroppers received was meager but very important to them. Since most could not read and write, it would be fairly easy for a dishonest person to manipulate records to the detriment of the sharecroppers. Ellen never wanted this sort of thing to happen.

The farm operation continued much the same through the 1880s. Ira (Ira Lee, as Ira W. Shepard had married and moved to Sunflower County) matured in farming and management skills; Pa was being slowed by aging, but his mind was still sharp. Of course, Ellen was always around to advise and assure things went well.

Though the cash crops were doing OK, Ira felt the farm needed to be more self-sufficient; Ellen agreed. The goal was to produce more of what they needed to live and, maybe, help the sharecroppers as well. The first action was to add new, young fruit trees to the orchard. The orchard was still much as it had been during the Civil War; the trees were getting old and some had died. Ira and Ellen ordered a few two-year-old fruit trees (peach, pear, and apple) from an out-of-state nursery. In addition, they got four improved pecan trees from a nursery in south Mississippi.

The fruit trees were brought to Bolton by train by a man named Arthur Stone, who worked for the Green Tree Nursery Company in the mountains near Asheville, North Carolina. The train transported the trees as freight. A time was set, and Ira and Ellen went in a two-horse wagon to pick them up at the depot in Bolton. When they arrived at the depot, three other people were there to get trees and were soon gone. The only trees that remained were those that belonged to Ira and Ellen. They had brought the cash to pay for them and the freight.

Ellen noticed that the man who'd brought the trees was a nice person who apparently had some education. They chatted briefly about how to set out and care for the trees. For some reason, Ellen and Arthur clicked. He was a single man and appeared interested in romance. In her mind, Ellen wanted to know more about Arthur. She asked a couple of questions, such as where he lived and if he had gone to school. He asked her a few questions, including whether she was married and where she lived.

Arthur had to go on to Vicksburg and deliver another batch of trees. He would come back through Bolton on his way to North Carolina. He told her that, if someone would meet him in Bolton when the train came back, he would go to the farm and help set out the trees. He indicated that a shovel and some old horse manure from the barn would be needed to set them out. He said he would help shovel the manure into a wagon and help mix it with the soil to assure that nutrients were available for the trees to grow. He also said the trees would need to be watered so the roots were moist. They checked on the schedule, and the train was due back the next day at 9:36 a.m.

The next day, Ira and his mother went back to the depot to meet Arthur. He was going to help get the trees set out right to assure they would live and grow. When Arthur was boarding the train, he touched Ellen's hand as a sign of interest in her; it made her feel good as well. Back at the farm, they unloaded the trees and put a little water on the wrapped roots to keep them in good condition until the next day, when the trees were to be set out in the orchard.

So, the next morning they were off to meet the 8:30

a.m. train. They didn't know if Arthur would show up but felt that his help would be good to have. He said he would do it without pay—as appreciation for their buying the trees. The train arrived on schedule; Arthur got off with a small overnight bag. They rode to the farm. Arthur got right to work; he was fast and organized. Ellen and Ira helped. He knew how to use a shovel to haul horse manure and dig holes. He tried to follow good practices in setting out the trees—he dug the hole twice the size of the root mass, mixed the manure with the soil, filled the hole, and created a small dike around it to hold water. Ira brought buckets of water from the spring branch. Pa came to the orchard and met Arthur just about the time the work was finished.

After they were finishing planting the twenty trees (five apple, ten peach, and five pear), Arthur commented that this orchard site was an excellent location for fruit trees. He suggested that the orchard be expanded to produce fruit crops for the local market. He particularly liked peaches and apples for this area. He said he would be happy to work with them on developing an orchard plan and getting it underway if they were interested. Pa said he would talk with Ellen, Ira, and others about it.

It was now getting near noon. Arthur had to be back in Bolton for the 4:15 train that afternoon. Ellen asked him to have lunch and said they would drive him back. Ma didn't have anything special prepared, but Arthur ate.

He and Ellen sat together at the lunch table. There might have been a little twinkle in their eyes.

Over lunch, they talked about various things. The Shepards wanted to know about life in the mountains and about Arthur's family. He indicated that his wife was dead, and his three children were adults and now gone from home. He said he was now forty-five years of age. Pa was inquisitive, as he had been in the past. He wanted to know details relating to a few things, such as Arthur's work history, church attendance, and relationship with the law. Arthur had been in the fruit tree business for about twenty years. All in all, he sounded pretty good to Pa and, of course, to Ellen.

Then it was time to take him back to the depot in Bolton. They made it on time, and he caught the 4:30 train that would take him east, where he would transfer to another train to go north to Asheville. Ellen told him to write her; likewise, he asked her to write him. They waved at each other as the train pulled out of sight.

Six days after Arthur boarded the train, she received a letter from him. Arthur was proposing that he come to Tinnin in a few weeks to talk about how to expand the orchard and add nut trees—specifically pecans. She quickly wrote him back and said to come on; just let her know so that she could meet him in Clinton (closer than Bolton). Ellen quickly told her family that Arthur was coming to talk about fruits and nuts. As soon as those words were out of her mouth, Arthur was labeled the fruit and nut man. Ellen didn't think it was too bad of a name—if he actually showed up and provided good advice.

Maybe there was also something romantic developing. Arthur came. They talked about increasing the number of fruit trees and adding a few nut trees (specifically pecans) to the orchard. He gave the family specific suggestions about the kinds of trees to set out, how far to set them apart, how much manure to use in the holes that were dug, and how to water the small trees to ensure they lived. He said he would send another letter once he was home detailing the kinds of trees and offering a quote on cost.

Ellen did have a few minutes of alone time with him in the orchard area near the dug well. Mostly, they talked about getting Ellen to travel to Asheville and visit the area where the fruit tree business was located. Exciting! Maybe romance would blossom in her life once more.

In about a week, she got another letter. But as she opened and began to read the letter, she saw it was different from what she had expected. Arthur said he would be happy to help get the orchard expanded with quality fruit trees. He went farther and said that he was now renewing a long-term relationship he'd had for several years with a woman who lived west of Asheville in a little place called Waynesboro. That sort of deflated Ellen and left her with an empty feeling for the rest of the day.

Regardless, when Pa talked to Ellen and Ira about

expanding the orchard, they decided not to do so. Ellen had a range of reasons, including lack of workers who knew about fruit production. No contact was made back with Arthur. The orchard was never expanded. Maybe a good opportunity was missed, but the timing didn't seem to be right.

Ellen was seeking more in her personal life. Farm life was going well; she was very proud of her son's progress.

After going to Mason Chapel for a few years, Ellen decided to venture into Clinton to the large Baptist church, operated in association with the institute (which would later become Mississippi College). The trip would take fifteen to twenty minutes in a horse-drawn wagon.

Wow! The church was very different from the Presbyterian church in Athens and from Mason Chapel. The Clinton community did not have a Presbyterian church, which she would have preferred.

The Baptist church had a large congregation. Ellen observed that it appeared to superbly meet the strict faith and social needs of most of its long-term members—others, not so well. She observed that how well the needs of people were met varied depending on the commitment of the individuals to the Baptist doctrine. She observed only one color of skin among its members—white. She thought a lot about skin color. She often pondered, *Aren't those people who had other than white skin entitled to choosing a place to worship that met their needs?* She observed that people with other than white skin had a few places of their own "color" for worship. Occasionally, Ellen would talk to sharecropper families about faith and what it meant. No doubt, some of her feelings on skin color were shaped by the teachings of her Midwest raised Pa.

Ellen also observed that only men were involved in leadership roles with the church; she always felt that women could do as well as men (and better than some). Certainly, she felt, God would not place men in positions of superiority over women and keep women from using their abilities. Right or wrong, she came to the realization on her own that long, long ago in Christianity, the men themselves had structured things so they could assume superior positions. She figured the men never relinquished the power they had established and enjoyed keeping women subservient. She thought this difference between men and women and their respective authority was taught as the way it was to be, and these beliefs spilled over into secular laws and family living.

Some of the church members in Clinton were farmers. But most had nonfarm jobs with the institutes (colleges), schools, local stores, government, railroad, and cotton ginning. Overall, their level of education was a little higher than the average of the white people in the community. They had organized Sunday school classes, Sunday school papers, and other resources for learning. This experience helped Ellen further realize that churches were made up of people with different personalities, values, and beliefs—though all of the members pretty well followed Baptist doctrine.

Preaching services involved music; announcements about upcoming events or happenings, such as recent deaths or marriages; Bible reading; testimonies; and a prepared message by the preacher. During the sometimes fiery sermons, one or more men might shout, "Amen," or, "Tell 'em."

Of course, there would be a time to take up collection—the preacher would even talk a minute or so about giving to the "Lord's work." The preacher said he liked to see folks digging in purses and pockets for contributions.

No service was complete without an altar call, also known as "come to Jesus time" and being "saved." Every week or so, one or two people would go down front and make a profession of faith. There would be a prayer, and the people who had just been saved would be told about a future baptism. The individuals would be introduced to the congregation and asked to stand near the exit door after the service to be greeted by church members. Ellen didn't always agree with the conservative tone of the sermons, but nevertheless, they were usually well prepared and provided useful information for her life.

Several groups were active at the church. Of course, she joined a Sunday school class. She was asked to assist the ordinance committee and help in other ways. Ellen could not be a committee member because she was not a member of the church. This didn't dampen her participation. She never had joining this church in mind. The ordinance committee prepared for communion, baptism, and similar special services at the church. Communion involved using tiny pieces of bread, along with a small amount of wine. Ellen was a good worker. She would sometimes bake the unleavened bread used in communion. The wine was really only grape juice, though sometimes it might be on the borderline of fermentation.

Being involved with the ordinance committee gave her the opportunity to meet and work with a number of people. And there was an unmarried male member of the ordinance committee who dressed well, was neatly groomed, and spoke in a way that signaled education beyond normal in the local community. He apparently worked a job with the local college and earned fairly good income. Ellen was intrigued by him and wanted to get to know him better.

His name was Rufus Provine Nelson. Maybe something would develop!

13
Another Life

Since arriving back in Tinnin, Ellen had experienced a renewed life—one that was energetic and held potential for the future. But she was always seeking new opportunities to better herself, her son, and her parental family. Getting involved with church activities at the Baptist church in Clinton resulted in her meeting new people and having more social contacts outside her home family and the Tinnin community.

This led to her becoming involved with groups or clubs; some were religious, and some were not. The adoption of new methods in the home and on the farm was often initiated in these clubs or groups. Some focused on education for a better life on the farm and in the home. She kept thinking about what she could do to help Ira and Pa have more income and produce more food.

Nothing gained greater enthusiasm from Ellen than changes taking place in farming and home food production. Some of the new implements and methods took years to get into the rural areas of the South.

Just prior to the US Civil War, factory-made agricultural equipment had begun to come on to the farm scene. The US Civil War, however, delayed its adoption in the South. Its use expanded rapidly outside the South. Before the war, labor was plentiful on most Southern farms, with little need for reducing the amount of hand labor required. The Northern states did not have a labor advantage but had a big advantage in the use of new technology. The factories were opening there, and labor was not so abundant.

Some would say that the first American agricultural revolution occurred between 1862 and 1875. No doubt, equipment promoted recovery from the war in the 1870s and 1880s once it reached the South. As more equipment was used, labor needs decreased. The loss of slaves as economical labor was an incentive to use equipment. Animal power had largely replaced human power in preparing land and tilling crops. It would still be half a century before engine power would begin to replace animals.

With a draft animal and an implement such as a turning plow, one person on the Shepard plantation could be much more productive than before. So, by 1890, many things were available and being used based on animal power. The Shepards already had iron plows and side-row cultivators. Based on her observation of displays at fairs and similar events, Ellen encouraged Ira and Pa to get a two-horse straddle-row cultivator, a spring-tooth harrow, and seed drills/planters. Using these developments allowed them to produce more with less human effort.

Agricultural leaders of the time were well aware of labor reductions. In 1850, it took seventy-five to ninety hours to produce a hundred bushels of corn (2.5 acres of land). By 1890, only thirty-five to forty labor hours were required to produce a hundred bushels of corn on the same amount of land. Labor hours per bale of cotton went down about the same, though cotton still required much more labor than corn. That kind of information really impressed Ellen. She wanted to adopt all the new technology that would help the farm and family life. She was innovative in the use of a lot of new technology based on animal power.

A limited number of new implements was available for the farms in the cotton South. Ellen and Ira would acquire what they could afford that had potential to improve productivity and reduce the need for hard labor. The production of the sharecroppers had become a major part of cash income on the farm. There were four share-cropper families in the early 1890s. It was Ellen's notion that the sharecroppers needed to be treated with respect and helped in their work.

Ellen's role in operating the farm was expanding. She and Ira regularly supervised the sharecroppers in the fields and at the barely more than shack houses. Most of the families had three or so children. Ellen often had contact with the women, who maintained the home and worked a good deal in the fields. She sometimes would talk about health, food, and other family issues. She might help sick children get the needed care of a doctor. She was very saddened when one family had a few-months-old baby get sick and die without medical care. Lacking resources, the family quietly buried the baby just off the front porch of their house near an oak tree. Ellen only found out by asking the mother about the baby. No marker was placed, though people familiar with the family knew what was under the little mound of earth in the yard.

Ellen was helping Ira develop abilities in managing the sharecroppers. She wanted him to care just as much for the well-being of them and their families as he did for the farm productivity of cotton, corn, and a few other crops. Sharecroppers were good people who had spiritual needs just like other people. With this in mind, Ellen helped sharecroppers organize and establish a small church, Wells Church, very near the Shepard farm. It affiliated itself with the African Methodist Episcopal Church. She donated a little money to help get it going. At first, it had a minister who led a service once a month. Other share-cropper families in Tinnin were also served by the church.

Ellen got into home food preservation. Using what was produced was important to her. She studied home canning using glass Mason jars, a method invented in 1858. It took many years for glass jars and canning techniques to become widespread in the South. Families had to have the money needed to buy the jars, and they needed to know how to safely use them in food preservation. Glass jars were certainly handy when compared to the pottery containers used in some methods of food preservation, such as fermenting, salting, and sugaring.

In the early 1890s and as an outgrowth of being involved with the church, Ellen got into a canning group. They learned how to prepare food items, use heat, use wax to seal jars properly, and store canned foods until needed. The group also learned the differences in foods and how this affected canning; for example, tomatoes were said to be acidic, and snap beans were not. Keeping the food from spoiling and safe to eat was also discussed but not fully understood. They learned the role of heat in the canning process—it destroyed harmful bacteria that might cause the food to spoil and make you sick.

Jellies and preserves were popular items made from wild berries, such as blackberries, and farm-raised fruits, including peaches and apples. They were prepared with heat and a great deal of sugar. The sugar acted as a preservative to prevent spoilage. Covered with a wax seal (layer on top), the sugar-based foods would keep for several months up to a year. People liked the sweetness of jellies and preserves. They were good when spread on bread.

To some extent, Ellen became a local canning leader among people in the Tinnin community. She taught some of her relatives and friends. People would ask her about the process and how to carry it out. She was sometimes asked to demonstrate in another person's home or bring a sample of something she had canned.

A canning tragedy struck one day with a woman who had talked to Ellen about canning. She had prepared the beans and put them into jars. The jars had been heating for a while in the small oven of a woodstove. She opened the door of the oven to check on things. A cool burst of air blew inside the hot oven, instantly resulting in one of the jars exploding. The force sent glass all around the oven and out the door. Part of the hot, jagged, sharp glass hit the woman's face, causing deep cuts and burns.

The woman was placed on a pallet in the back of a wagon and, as quickly as horses could go, was transported to a doctor. He examined the burns and cuts and cleaned away the broken, jagged glass. There wasn't much more he could do. He sent her home and said she should take it easy for a few days. He suggested applying a bit of butter every now and then to soothe the wounds. Gradually, the cuts and burns began to heal. It was obvious that her face would forever have deep scars—reminders of this canning tragedy. Word spread rapidly through the community. No one ever heated jars in an oven again. A hot water bath in a large canning container was typically used until newer devices such as pressure cookers became available.

The canning accident got Ellen's attention. She went to see the woman several times (she lived only a couple of miles away and attended Mason Chapel). From then on, she was always very careful when telling people about heating jars. This accident frightened Ellen, and she took a less active role in promoting canning in the community. However, she continued canning for her own home use. As leader of the family, she was responsible for having food available at all times.

Ellen refocused on farm operation in the early 1890s. She always kept the records carefully and accurately. She learned how analysis could be used to identify crops and fields that produced the greatest cash returns. She had heard there were specialists in such matters at the new Mississippi A&M College who could offer guidance in keeping and using records, but she did not make contact.

Except for a little home canning, Ellen was no longer an advocate of the preservation in in the community. She began analyzing possible farm alternatives. She occasionally mentioned her thoughts to Pa and Ira—some of which sounded pretty good to her.

The Shepard farm, she thought, should begin producing more vegetables for the "city" market in nearby Jackson. The city had somewhat recovered from the destruction it had suffered at the hands of soldiers during the US Civil War and was making steady growth. Many people lived in town and, except for small yard beds, had little garden space. Their jobs also used up much of the time needed to grow a garden of much size. She counted at least a dozen grocery stores that might be interested in selling fresh vegetables; it didn't seem that any other farm was regularly trying to meet potential demands. These were in parts of town on Capital and State Streets and Robinson Road or on side streets that crossed them. Many of these residents worked in state government offices, at banks, or at related regular-paying jobs. It did not count those minority-owned stores in the Farrish Street area mostly frequented at that time by residents with lesser discretionary income.

Ellen put together an informal plan and took it to Pa and Ira for their input. Ma wasn't involved; her health was deteriorating fairly rapidly and much more so than Pa's. Ellen described the potential of beginning fresh vegetable production for the Jackson market. She named the stores she had identified and described how no farm was regularly providing fresh vegetables. She also stated that residents in the central part of Jackson had no opportunity for gardening of much size.

Next, Ellen listed potential vegetable crops to grow by season of the year:

- Spring—greens, potatoes, carrots, snap beans, English peas, and squash
- Summer—peas, butterbeans, okra, tomatoes, and squash
- Fall —greens, root crops, and late English peas

She then went into the advantages of the land they had—fertile, loose soil that was relatively easy to till but experiencing mild erosion. She said that sharecropper families could be hired on a day basis to help produce and harvest the vegetables. Now, what did Pa and Ira think?

Pa was concerned that the vegetable production would cut into the cotton and corn production. Ellen explained that most of those crops were produced on a sharecropped basis, and she didn't see how the vegetables could cut into their work. Of course, they might be hired occasionally as day laborers. Ira was interested in how any vegetables might be delivered once produced. By horse and wagon, Ellen said. That meant that he might get to take the wagon into town and go to various stores; he kind of liked the idea. Pa also wanted to know if the stores would actually buy vegetables from them for selling to customers. Ellen didn't know but agreed to check with a few next week when she went to the Hinds County courthouse to pay property taxes for the year on the plantation owned by her father.

The discussion ended with an agreement to try a few vegetable crops the first year and expand if the initial enterprise worked out OK. They would need to determine which fields to use and decide which vegetables to plant. Pa suggested yellow crook neck squash; pole snap beans; okra; and, maybe, tomatoes. He also suggested they plant a few acres of sweet potatoes for fall harvest and delivery to the grocery stores.

Several possible approaches were discussed. Income had to cover the costs.

14

Family Progression

A few years later and after a few years into the decade of the 1890s, Pa and Ma seemed to be slowing down. Their health was gradually deteriorating. Aging was catching up with them. They were less able to move about. Their knees were not as strong as they'd once been; nor did they bend as well as they had in the past. Their feet were sometimes sore in ways they were not accustomed to. Memory and body functions were deteriorating. They seemed forgetful and put things in the wrong places.

Occasionally, they would attempt to do things they shouldn't, such as the time Pa was going to empty the slop jar into the water well, thinking it was one side of the two-holer; Ellen saw what was about to happen and rushed outside to stop it. He said he was just trying to be helpful. Though not contaminated, water was not used from that well for a few years. Sometimes both Ma and Pa suffered shortness of breath and weakness. Occasionally, Ma had fainting spells. Ellen had to keep a close eye on them. More of the farm responsibilities were now on Ira's shoulders. He could handle it; he was now the farm manager.

Pa's health seemed to fail rapidly in the later winter and early spring of 1895. By May, he could no longer walk on his own; nor could he control body functions. Dr. W. S. West of Clinton was called to the house. He said Pa appeared to have something he was just learning about called senile dementia. He explained that Pa's brain no longer did what it was supposed to do in human life. In the meantime, Dr. West said to keep him comfortable, provide food and water, feed him by hand as needed, and try to remind him to frequently use the slop jar so his clothing and bed would not regularly get soiled. That was about a full-time job for Ellen. But she, as with past situations, put forth extra effort.

On May 10, 1895, Dr. West was sent for, and he came to the house. He examined Pa and pronounced him dead. Pa was eighty-one years of age—he'd lived a long life for a man born before 1850. Ma was beside herself; she just could not understand how her life could go on without Pa. She had sat by his bed almost continually for the last few days and offered food, water, and comfort. She slept very little. She loved George deeply. She had worked side by side with him for years in running the home and farm. But she herself was already showing more signs of failing health.

Pa's funeral involved keeping the body in the home for visitation. A mortician from Baldwin Funeral Home in Jackson assisted with arrangements, including dressing and moving the body to Mason Chapel and then to the cemetery. In this case, the family parted from the tradition of bathing the body and dressing it in the home. A simple casket was used. It was placed in the front room with a fireplace. No one was currently sleeping in that room, and it had become sort of a parlor. A couple of neighbors took turns sitting up with the casket and body all night—a tradition in the community. Neighbors dug a grave in the Zachariah Ratliff Family Cemetery in Tinnin. The grave was located in proximity to Ma's parents but with space for Ma to someday be buried between Pa and her parents.

The Shepard children were notified, and most arrived in time for the funeral. Ma, with help, was able to attend the service and go to the cemetery. Some family traveled a hundred miles or so to be present. All wanted to pay special tribute to their pa. A few people brought flowers from their yards to place on the burial site.

It was May 15 when the service was held. Early that morning, Ira went to check on the crops. Quite a coincidence occurred that day: The seasonally very early first cotton bloom of the year had opened. It was a beautiful white in the early morning, and he knew it would turn pink by the time of the funeral. Never before had there been such a beautiful single bloom this early in the year! Wonder why it occurred on the funeral day for Pa—the man who had farmed the land a little over fifty years?

Ira picked the bloom and took it to Mason Chapel for all to see. He placed it on the lapel of the jacket Pa wore—touching! It was closed in the casket and buried with the body. This was very fitting; life all these years in Tinnin had depended on cotton to produce a crop that could be sold for cash. Pa would always say, "You have to have blooms in order to have cotton, and the more the better."

Brother Murrow held a funeral service at Mason Chapel, followed by a short graveside service at the cemetery. He talked about how George W. Shepard was a man of high moral character who promoted equality among all people—even though it wasn't the popular thing to do—and a good farmer and steward of the land. One of the things he mentioned was Pa's love of farming, especially cotton. He said an interest in cotton farming was amazing for a man from Indiana. Then he told those gathered about Ira picking the first cotton bloom of the year from the field earlier that day. Was it a sign of some sort? Did it signal a loss? Not a dry eye remained in the crowd. He had a dignified service that included the congregation singing a couple of hymns, including Pa's favorite, "Amazing Grace."

Ellen increasingly became the leader of the family. Without Pa, Ira, at age twenty-seven, would become head of the household. This was quite important in those times when men enjoyed greater authority than women. Regardless, Ira always deferred to his mother, Ellen. She was wise, experienced, and could make good decisions. Her life with her husband Jasper and living as a single woman for over a decade after his death in Texas had taught her a lot about the world. Ira and his mother never had differences of opinion that resulted in heated situations.

Almost immediately after Pa's funeral, Ma had a spell, and Dr. West was summoned to care for her. Ma was under the care of Dr. West for much of the summer. She needed more care in July and August 1895. In those two months, the doctor made fourteen house calls to the Shepard home to administer to her needs and see if something could be found to reverse her failing health. Ellen stayed close to her bedside, except when one of her sisters could be present. But Ma's health was in serious condition. The physician found it difficult to be specific about her health issues. Maybe she was suffering blood sugar issues, kidney failure, or circulatory problems.

Dr. West visited four days in a row the last of August and pronounced Ma dead on August 31, 1895. No death certificate was filed because it was not required by law; therefore, the cause of death is unknown. Ma, in general, had deteriorating health and failed to thrive. Dr. West charged $2.50 for each house visit but only $1.50 on the day he pronounced her dead. No records of any medicines were kept. It is possible he administered some medicines as part of the care during his visits. The last days of her life might have included the administration of paregoric to lessen pain.

Plans were made for Ma's funeral. She would be buried alongside her husband and near her mother and daddy in the Zachariah Ratliff Family Cemetery. A walnut wood casket lined with velvet was bought at Baldwin Funeral Home in Jackson and delivered to the Shepard home. A mortician would handle details such as bathing and dressing the body. Plans were to have the body lie in state in the home for two days before burial. As with Pa, a couple of neighbors sat up all night with the body. All of her daughters and son were notified, and they made every effort to attend the funeral, along with spouses and children. Overall, Ellen greeted mourners at the home. Ira assisted as he could. Neighbors in the Tinnin community were very supportive in this time of loss and sadness.

The morning before the service, Ira went to one of Ma's favorite places on the spring branch near a cotton patch. Ma would sometimes work in the patch when she could get some time away from the house. It was a kind of cool, restful place with a couple of shade trees not far away. Ira picked an open cotton boll with glistening white locks of seed cotton. He placed the open boll in the casket on her right shoulder similar to what he had done with Pa and the cotton bloom.

As with Pa, Brother Murrow conducted a memorial service at the Mason Chapel Church. Held on September 3, 1895, the service included an opening prayer, Ma's favorite Bible scripture—Psalm 23—a couple of her favorite hymns, a message, and a closing prayer. The message included facts about Ma, such as her place of birth, the name of her husband, the number and names of children and grandchildren, and her strong role as a mother. The preacher mentioned that an open cotton boll had been brought from a patch near her favorite spot on the spring branch. A short graveside service followed. Ma was buried in the space left between Pa's grave and that of her father in the Zacharia Ratliff Family Cemetery in Tinnin, Mississippi.

Engraved granite markers were ordered and installed at both graves. The engraving included full names, dates of birth, and dates of death. The two markers were placed on solid ground. After about four years, the settling of the graves resulted in the markers leaning and tipping over. Ellen saw the condition and, the next day, dispatched Ira and one of the sharecroppers to upright and stabilize the markers. They tried to do the best they could with this job, but settling continued. Maybe it was also due to the shifting nature of the earth (loess soil over limestone rock) in the area.

The Shepard home at one time was home to a large family—sometimes an extended family. Now, for the first time, no Shepard lived there. Ellen and Ira were the only two people who lived in the home. Their last name was Lee, though Ellen could profess she was a Shepard. Things around the house became kind of sad. There wasn't much activity. Their minds began to turn to thoughts of what might be in store with the turn of the century. The year 1900 was only a few years away.

Ellen was quite busy with closing the estates of Ma and Pa, as well as keeping the house up. Ira was busy with the crops and overseeing the sharecroppers.

Neither Pa nor Ma had a will—not a good idea. Ellen knew they should have one but she had not been able to persuade either of them to have one prepared by a qualified lawyer. They would say it cost too much money. Or, maybe Pa and Ma found it difficult to make decisions about their possessions and distribution among their children. One might feel shorted.

A couple of months after Ma's death, the group of siblings gathered at the home to discuss final estate details. Personal effects were fairly easy to handle; each child or child's heirs got something. Furniture and the like stayed with the house. Animals on the farm and unharvested crops had value and needed to be settled. Ira and Ellen moved ahead with the sharecroppers harvesting the crops. Since Ira and Ellen already owned some of the animals, there was no urgency to deal with them. But those they didn't own were to be purchased or sold. Money derived over the fall from the farm was to be divided among the heirs. Ellen and Ira were to keep records of all harvests and sales.

Ellen knew the importance of properly handling the estate. She had experienced a bad situation in Texas when her Jasper had died. She talked with a lawyer in Clinton about the legal aspects of settling the estate. They agreed he would prepare the needed paperwork and guide them as they went along.

The major estate item was the farmland and the home and outbuildings on it. Ellen and Ira needed the home for living. No decision was made at the time. They agreed to discuss it at another time. Until then, Ellen and Ira would continue just as they had been.

Another year passed, and the siblings had a reunion. They again talked about what to do with the farm.

A range of opinions was offered but it was agreed that Ira, with support from his mother, would go about buying out each heir's share of the property. Each would have an equal acreage of equal value based on the going rate of farmland. Georgia Ann was dead, so her spouse at the time of her death in 1879 would be the heir. Ellen would help Ira get things figured out. He would use the services of a bank to borrow the needed money with a few years for paying it back. Everyone seemed to agree, so Ira began.

Ira was able to make land payments so that all was covered by the end of 1899 or shortly thereafter. His mother did not ask for a payment. The approximately four hundred acres of farm property that remained would be all his; this sounded nice to him. Making the payments might require extra attention to saving money all year. A receipt in the family records from B. F. Mulholland of Brandon dated January 14, 1899, shows the following: "Received of Ira J. Lee the sum of seventeen dollars and fifty cents, this being the amount due as interest on the Shields boys portion of the Shepard estate at 10% for the year 1898." Documents also include banking receipts and statements from the Bank of Brandon and the Bank of Pocahontas.

The Shepard surname would continue in the Mississippi Delta though the big house in Tinnin had none. Ira W. Shepard, who lived in Sunflower County, wrote Ellen on July 11, 1898, that he had a new son born June 30. The birth was difficult. They'd had to summon a Dr. Donald from Indianola to deliver the baby. The letter indicated that the doctor put Ella under the influence of chloroform and used instruments to make the delivery. The baby weighed eight pounds. Dr. Donald charged twenty dollars, which Ira W. stated was good money spent; otherwise, Ella would have died.

In the same July 11, 1898, letter, Ira W. Shepard wrote

about the war between Spain and the United States. Apparently an acquaintance from Sunflower County was in the army involved in the fighting. His letter stated "Sis, the war is getting very hot. I am afraid the whole world will be in before it ends. The Spaniards are making it pretty hot for the Americans. They had a very bloody fight last week. A great many Americans were killed. Surely, England will go with us." Ira W. was referring to the Spanish-American War over independence for Cuba. But how did it come to be that this war and its details were on Ira's mind to such a great extent? The war, prompted by the sinking of the battleship *Maine*, in the harbor of Havana, lasted ten weeks in summer 1898. Hostilities spread around the globe. The Spanish empire collapsed afterward. It is amazing that Ira W. was so well informed on the war when he lived far away in rural Sunflower County! Maybe telegraphy or a letter from a friend in the army gave him the information.

Ira J. Lee appeared to be developing a health issue. He was increasingly having difficulties breathing. He was only thirty years of age when Dr. W. W. Farr of Bolton, Mississippi, wrote a medical statement on November 12, 1898: "I hereby certify that Mr. Ira Lee is within my charge as a patient and is unfit for road service." Though not in this statement, it appeared his health issue related to asthma and not tuberculosis. Statements by family members (now deceased) who knew him spoke of his bouts with asthma. Road service had to do with citizens keeping up the roads (trails) that were in rural areas. County governments did not have road departments that maintained rural roads. It appears that medication and lifestyle allowed Ira to live another forty plus years. And he took on other responsibilities—the subject of the next chapter.

In the years immediately after the death of Pa and Ma, some changes were made on the farm. The number of sharecroppers was reduced to three. The Davis Trimm family decided it would no longer sharecrop on the Shepard farm. It had found another farm and moved. This saddened Ellen and Ira. But they kind of thought it was a good idea because of the need for supervision, and only Ellen and Ira were available. Ellen also provided family support and the furnishing that was made available throughout the year for living.

The production of vegetables was about ended, other than those for the family. Labor to produce them simply was not available. Ira didn't have time to make the delivery to the grocery stores in Jackson. In addition to the vegetable garden, sweet potatoes and pinda were grown. These were popular with the sharecroppers. Ellen and Ira also liked them. Other farm-produced food crops included honey, chicken and guinea eggs, cow's milk, and pork, but only in cool months of the year because there was no refrigeration to keep it from spoiling. In the cool months, pork could be smoked and salted as ways to keep if safe to eat.

A possible new crop they considered was sugar cane. They had some land they thought would be productive in sugar cane. Sharecroppers could possibly be hired as day labor to grow, harvest, and process the cane into syrup. Some new equipment would be needed, such as a roll juice extractor and large pan over the wood-fired oven for cooking the juice. Ellen and Ira agreed he would investigate the possibilities, including costs.

Something was happening in Ira's life that caused him some distraction from farming. He had met a young woman who stirred a romantic flame in him. A serious courtship developed in 1899 between Ira and Carrie Cheers Hendrick, a young woman who lived on a farm in a nearby German community in Madison County. Ellen thought this relationship was probably a good idea. She had met Carrie but did not find her very personable. Nevertheless, Ira was now thirty-one years of age and should be sufficiently mature to be able to make good choices of a life partner.

Ellen encouraged Ira to see that any plans he and Carrie might make could include life on the new Lee farm. Yes, the name had changed when Ira had paid off the Shepard heirs and changed legal records in the Hinds County Courthouse. Ellen was proud that this had been done. This helped assure the future for the old Shepard place that was now over sixty years in the being. And, of course, Ellen planned to continue living on the farm in the big house her father had built in 1857.

Was Ellen about to give up on romance in her life? A man she met at the Baptist church in Clinton briefly got her attention—as mentioned at the end of the last chapter. His name was Rufus Provine Barker, and there was a hint of potential romance.

What about the seemingly nice man? She talked with him a little; he was a gentleman with an education and good job, and he appeared to be considerate of others. Things never clicked between them, however. He was too "churchy," Ellen thought. She knew to watch out for that sort of "over-expressive churchy" individual. Such individuals were likely hiding some sort of mean spirit, such as she had seen in Texas. Ellen was busy with things in Tinnin and did not give the time for in-depth assessment of "Mr. Churchy."

Of course, she had Mason Chapel there close to her home and was now much more involved with it once again. In 1902, a new Methodist church was opened in the tiny cotton ginning town of Pocahontas. She and other family members sometimes attended.

15

A New Household

Ira and his sweetheart became engaged in May 1900. Carrie Cheers Hendrick was an attractive eighteen-year-old farm woman. She was born in Coahoma County in the Delta area of Mississippi and grew up in the hills of a German community in Madison County known as Gluckstadt. Though she was physically attractive and had some wonderful traits, she could have certainly used some skills in how to be nice and get along with people.

The courtship lasted about a year. Ira and Carrie were busy with plans for their future together. Their planning involved moving forward with the new Lee farm and living in the old Shepard house. During the course of the year, Ellen's sister Rachel and her twelve-year-old daughter, Addie Conrad, had moved back because of a failed marriage. Two additional individuals took a little more space out of the house, but it was still plenty large for a newly married couple.

In June 1900 the US Federal Census enumerator came by the Lee place in the Tinnin community. He gathered information from Ira, who was now the head of the household. The census report indicated that four people lived in the house—Ira, Ellen, Rachel, and Addie. For most of the past quarter century, a blended generation family had lived in the house. In another year, there would be an additional person. And beyond that, maybe a new, younger generation would emerge.

Ira and Carrie were married on August 7, 1901. Her mother, Louvenia Stone Hendrick, attended; so did Ellen, Rachel, and Addie. This situation raised some questions in Ellen's mind. Where was Carrie's father? His whereabouts were not discussed. Ellen likely never knew. (That same 1900 US Federal Census reported that Carrie's father, William Hendrick, was in the Mississippi Insane Asylum at the time of the wedding. Why he was there is unknown. Maybe he was seeking mental health care, or maybe Louvenia had him "put" there because of an indiscretion. He apparently died shortly afterward and was buried on the grounds of the facility in an unmarked grave. The unmarked graves became a big issue in the early 2000s, as buildings were to be constructed on the site of the graves. Once the first grave was uncovered, construction was stopped until provisions were later made to move the graves.

No honeymoon travel was in store for the newlyweds; trains and ships were big in some places but not in Tinnin. They would be at their home. There wasn't much time in the summer to take a break from work on the farm, but early August provided a couple of weeks of slower work pace. The crops were mostly laid by, and harvest would get underway in early September. The slower pace allowed them to get everything all set in their part of the home for their "comfortable" living.

One day, an interruption came from the mule barn when a belligerent mule kicked Ira on the right thigh; at least that is what he said happened. It was a hard kick—knocking him down and temporarily taking his breath away. He couldn't get up. He rolled over. No one was in the barn, so he lay there until he was able to stand. After a few minutes, he regained his ability and crawled to a divider in the barn where he could pull himself up. He wondered if his leg was broken, but he was able to stand. He decided it was a deep bruise in the muscle.

Some folks wondered if the bruise wasn't due to a severe lick inflicted on Ira by Carrie with a hard piece of oak firewood. The mule kick story was a cover to protect her and their relationship from an early marriage disagreement. People were curious about what he was telling them. Regardless of what happened, it didn't seem to make much difference in their honeymoon.

Ellen, Rachel, and Addie adjusted to a newly married couple being present in the house. Of course, Ira had lived in the home for about twenty years and had grown to adulthood living in it. With the new bride, somewhat of a division of responsibilities was thought to be needed. But making it work was not so easy.

A challenge for Ellen was how to get along with Carrie, who could be very sweet and nice in one moment—she could really turn on the charm—only to have her unpleasant personality evident in the next. This happened from nearly the beginning of the marriage. It appeared Ira's new bride would not be easy to deal with. Rachel and Addie also saw this side of Carrie. Ira appeared to always get along with her reasonably well—she deferred to him as the male head of the household. Wasn't that what all women were supposed to do in 1901?

Adjusting to Carrie took more effort from everyone, including the sharecroppers (she occasionally made unnecessary negative statements to them). In addition to not being able to get along with people, Carrie also preferred not to do much housework and cooking. A few housekeeping issues arose related to her and Ira's part of the house. These included not sweeping the floor; letting the fireplace and wood-burning stove accumulate too many ashes; and allowing the current guard dog, barn cat, and a few hens to occasionally venture inside the house. Carrie would do enough cleaning to get by in the quarters where she lived and not much elsewhere in a house that five people shared. Most cleaning was left to Ellen and Rachel. Of course, Carrie found ways to avoid work on the farm and around the barns. She was sometimes grumpy with the sharecroppers and their families, and this did not build goodwill. Making friends in the community was a challenge for her. Ellen began to wonder if this marriage was going to work out; she didn't want Ira to have a failed marriage. There was never any notion that Ira did not have a strong commitment to Carrie and that the two of them did not see eye to eye on most things.

Fall was moving toward winter. Life on the farm revolved around cropping seasons. By now, most crops were pretty well harvested. Some of the cotton, though picked, still needed to be ginned. Sweet potatoes and pecans needed to be harvested. A couple of nice quality, extra fat pigs were being fed to reach over 150 pounds by November in preparation for slaughter once the weather was cold, and that was usually about late November or early December. Cold weather was needed to maintain the meat until seasoned or smoked to prevent spoilage. Christmastime would soon be at hand.

Just about the time folks were somewhat adjusting to Carrie in the house, she announced after a little over three months of marriage that she thought she was pregnant.

That kind of changed some of the attitude toward her. Ellen was excited to know she would soon be a grandmother. Ira was happy—he was looking forward to a son. Carrie's pregnancy progressed normally, though there were times when she took advantage of her "condition," and, as some people said, she raised hell. Ellen was hoping that, if the baby was a girl, the name would include Ellen and, if it was a boy, it would include Jasper. Although there was a midwife in the community, Ira tried to get his mother to assist; she said no.

Ira found that a new baby required a little money. He went about operating the farm much as usual in the 1902 cropping season. Sometimes Carrie would seek attention as a pregnant woman and disrupt things a bit. They took some advance income on cotton to buy a few things needed for the baby. One thing in particular was a wooden crib with rockers and a thin pad on the bottom. The rocker crib would serve this baby and future babies and the generations that followed.

When Carrie appeared to be going into labor, the midwife was summoned. She observed the situation and announced that a doctor was needed. Dr. E. B. Poole came from Clinton to deliver the baby on August 20, 1902; he charged twenty dollars for the home delivery. The baby was a healthy girl. Carrie and Ira had decided ahead of time that it would be named Ellen Louvenia Lee if it were a girl; they also had chosen a name for a boy if needed.

Everyone was happy about a daughter/granddaughter, though Ira had said he wanted a son. No doubt Ira was hoping for a boy who would grow up and become a major part of the farmwork. Grandmother Ellen was happy with the name.

Carrie was twenty years of age when she became a first-time mother. The baby's father, Ira, was thirty-four years of age when baby Ellen was born; new Grandmother Ellen was fifty-five. Both were a tad older than they thought they would be with a firstborn child and grandchild. Generations change; ages of marriage and parenting change. For example, Grandmother Ellen was approaching nineteen years of age when her son, Ira, was born—close to the same age as Carrie. Men tended to be several years older than women in marriages; younger women supposedly liked older men because they brought security to a wife. Grandmother Ellen was sixteen, and Jasper was thirty-seven when they were married. With a newborn, some age differences did not dampen spirits or interest in caring for the baby.

Carrie provided basic care for new baby Ellen Lee. She nursed her, changed her diaper for the first few days, held her in a comforting manner, and otherwise cared for her. Then she grew impatient and tired of some of the routines required in mothering. She got other people to care for and rock the baby. Maybe she was depressed or suffering from something that many years later would be called "postpartum depression." At first, Grandmother Ellen was happy to be involved. Later, she tried to teach and motivate Carrie as a mother to do what was needed; success in doing so was slow. After all, the baby was the responsibility of Carrie and Jasper.

It appears that Carrie grew up in a dysfunctional home. She did not have a decent father around. Her mother had a few babies that provided some basis for Carrie to learn about baby care, as well as their idiosyncrasies.

Somehow, it seemed that Carrie did not want to do any more than was essential for the health of growing baby Ellen Louvenia. Of course, she breastfed the baby; no wet nursing was involved (there was a sharecropper woman on the farm who could have served as a wet nurse). One biological factor that was likely fortunate for Carrie and Ira was that lactating tends to reduce fertility and delay the next pregnancy a bit.

As baby Ellen developed, began walking, speaking a few words, and the like, Grandmother Ellen would take her to church or to stores in Tinnin, Clinton, or Pocahontas. They developed quite a bond. Grandmother Ellen was trying to help baby Ellen grow and develop a personality of kindness and caring. Sometimes, baby Ellen would get a new dress compliments of her grandmother. Before they knew it, she was a beautiful two-year-old little girl!

Ellen observed that attendance at Mason Chapel had dwindled to a very few individuals. All appearance was that the church would soon close; some members had already started going into Clinton, and others traveled to Pocahontas. Ellen and Rachel decided that they would become involved with the Pocahontas Methodist Episcopal Church. It was a tiny community where they took cotton for ginning, bought supplies at a mercantile store, and had gotten to know some of the people.

The Methodist church had begun several years before in a vacant house on the Lane plantation. In 1902, a new church house was built in Pocahontas. It really looked like a church of the time—with a steeple; a double front door; and large, ornate windows. Men's and women's privies were to one side behind the building. A new cemetery was being started several yards behind it. Pocahontas was a bit longer wagon ride from home to church than Mason Chapel, but it had some appealing features.

Soon after going and aligning herself with Pocahontas Methodist Episcopal, Ellen invited the minister to have Sunday dinner with herself, Ira and Carrie, and Rachel and Addie Conrad. The minister, Reverend Presley, accepted the invitation. Ellen worked hard on the Saturday before getting ready for the preacher. To some extent, Ellen's mind drifted back to Easter Sunday in 1863 when her parents had had the minister over for dinner just before the Union troops came storming through. Ellen just about had everything ready. Food preparation was well underway—every preacher was served fried yard-bird chicken and vegetables to go with it. She knew some last minute things would need to be fixed on Sunday, such as boiled rice. The floors were clean, cobwebs swept from the ceiling on the porches, and a fresh Sears catalog in the privy.

For some reason, Carrie did not like what Ellen was doing and the notion that the preacher was coming to the house she lived in (but not to her living quarters). Ellen had invited everyone who was at the house to be there for lunch and had talked with Carrie about how she was preparing. In somewhat of a fit of rage, Carrie took a pan of dirty dishwater and poured it over the floor around the dining table. Ellen became furious at this, but she didn't confront Carrie about it. Ellen got a mop and started cleaning up the floor. It took a while to get the floor back to reasonably clean. Fortunately, there were no more in-cidents at this time.

Everyone, including baby Ellen, went to Pocahontas Methodist Episcopal that Sunday morning. They partic-ipated in the worship service and departed quickly after-ward for home. Of course, Ellen checked with Preacher Presley to remind him of the dinner. When home, Ellen worked feverishly to get everything ready, while Carrie sat on the front porch with baby Ellen. Rachel and Addie also helped; Ira was out checking on crops or something.

About 1:30 that afternoon, Preacher Presley came down the hill in a nice one-horse carriage. (Why is it that preachers around there always had nice horses and carriages?) He pulled up to the front gate and hitched the horse. He walked to the front porch and was first greeted by Carrie. Oh, how she hugged him, poured out her personality, and told him how wonderful his sermon was and that she was so happy to have him at her home for dinner. Every other person greeted Preacher Presley afterward. He was invited inside to the dinner table, where everyone took a seat.

Carrie began as if she were the hostess entitled to welcoming the preacher, asking him to say a blessing, and offering food to him, beginning with the fried yard-bird chicken. Ellen let her get away with this behavior; she thought it was far better than a confrontation while the preacher was there. As the meal ended, the preacher thanked Carrie for the wonderful meal and thanked all the others there for inviting him. Ellen and Rachel washed all the dishes and utensils after the preacher had left. Carrie went back to sit on the front porch in a rocking chair.

In early 1905, Carrie was again pregnant. Ira just knew this baby was going to be a boy. All went well during pregnancy. With the help of a midwife, Carrie gave birth to a baby girl on May 20 of that year. The baby was named Sudie Willie Lee. No one knew where Ira and Carrie had gotten the name; it was not used in the family. Ira was upset that Carrie had had a girl—probably something she had eaten, he said. He vowed to change what Carrie ate before another baby. Anyway, Sudie Willie thrived with limited care from her mother. But of course her grandmother was always there. Baby Ellen was now reaching three years of age.

It was Ira's contention that girl babies just resulted in more fieldwork for the men. Maybe this was the case not so much at a young age, but as they got older, they required more clothing, food, and the like. A girl was not expected to work in the fields as much as a boy. Some women worked part-time in the fields; however, they could not usually work full-time because they had responsibilities around their homes.

Grandmother Ellen enjoyed watching her granddaughters grow and develop. She continued to take Ellen to special little places. But, there was work to do to maintain the home, prepare meals, gather eggs, and help look after the garden. Just as in past years, Ellen continued to support the sharecropper families and help them to have a better life. For some reason, though, Ellen did not feel as energetic as she had in the past. Still, she felt good and went about her daily chores. Ira suggested that she see a doctor, but she chose not to.

Before long, another baby was on the way! About the time Sudie was fourteen months of age, Carrie was again pregnant. After a couple of babies, the newer ones didn't seem to get as much attention. When the date of giving birth was a couple of months away, Ira began trying to make certain the new baby was a boy. He thought he had all the girl babies he wanted.

On one of Ira's trips delivering a wagonload of sweet potatoes to a couple of grocery stores in Jackson, Mississippi, he rode along Farrish Street. He saw a Gullah store and two voodoo and hoodoo shops. Though the distance from New Orleans and Atlanta, where voodoo queens were well known, wasn't that great, these probably weren't much more than cheap fortune teller places. They were touted as being operated by "qualified" voodoo queens. One shop had a lot of signs, among them "Get Rich," "Stay Healthy," "Have Good Crops," and "Catch the Big Fish." One that really got his attention was, "Get the Boy Baby You Want." Ira stopped the wagon, hitched the horses, and went inside. He had never seen anything like it. The shop had unusual pottery and paraphernalia on its shelves around the walls that, together with silk cloths and burning incense, created a unique atmosphere. He learned that hoodoo was more associated with religion. It was the power of voodoo that he wanted.

The voodoo queen, in an apparent or imitated trance, was selling and administering magical powders and charms. She had a big glass ball and was dressed in a way he had never before seen. The queen spoke in language he had never before heard but could understand. The queen asked if he had matters to be discussed or things he wanted advice on. She said she could do most everything a New Orleans voodoo queen could do based on African spiritual folkways. For a dollar, she would give the answer to one of his questions. So, he wanted a boy, and no one would miss the dollar. After payment, the conversation began.

The voodoo queen wanted to know the matter.

Ira said, "I want a baby boy. I only have girls."

The voodoo queen asked if he had a wife.

He said, "Yes."

She asked if his wife was "with child."

He said, "Yes. She told me she was with child."

The queen proceeded by saying that, since Carrie was already with child, the baby was "set." But he could certainly do some things (she never said that what he would do would make a bit of difference; Ira was gullible about this).

The voodoo queen, speaking with very strong confidence about getting a boy baby, instructed Ira that his wife should be very choosey about the kinds and sources of the foods she ate. The voodoo queen said she should eat cooked pig's liver from a male hog. This was the most important thing. She should eat the liver regularly or at least several times a week. in addition, Carrie was to only eat other meats from male animals—roosters and bulls. The voodoo queen gave Ira a small package of some sort of granular powder for his wife to sprinkle on her food. The queen mumbled something about the powder containing ground ram horns and salt.

The voodoo queen told him she would tell him more for another fifty cents. Everything she'd said had been sounding so good to Ira that he dug the additional payment out of his pocket. She continued with instructions. In addition to Carrie eating only meats from male animals, she should also dig a few sassafras roots in early February and boil them in water to make tea. The tea was to be seasoned with a small amount of tallow from a male animal. The queen also gave Ira a very small amount of a shredded leaflike material to sprinkle on his wife's tea. It was said to be from the leaves of a male gingko tree.

In the end, the voodoo queen poured a bit of fragrant incense into a small bowl and blew on the surface of the liquid so the fragrance increased. As the incense was rising, she majestically waved her hands and magic wand above it. She said a goodbye and told Ira to keep a positive attitude about the baby. Ira felt happy all the way home. She also said he might come back for another session with her the next time he was on Farrish Street. The special treatment she could provide next time would only cost a dollar. She further said the treatment had guaranteed results, but she never said what the results would be.

Had he done what he needed to do to have a boy baby?

The horse and wagon made the trip back to Tinnin in a little less than three hours. Ira told Carrie what to eat and went so far as to slaughter a small male pig to get the liver and other flesh. He made her some sassafras tea and sprinkled some of the ground leafy substance on it. He also put some of the potion of ground ram horns on the only small piece of male pork liver he was ever able to get her to eat.

Soon, time for the delivery of another baby was at hand. Would Ira's magical efforts to get a boy work? He was concerned that his wife hadn't followed the instructions very well. On March 1, 1907, Ivie Carrie Lee was born. Just as with the previous two babies, she was born right there in their home and was healthy. Ira could not believe the baby was a girl; he felt he had done all he could but admitted that he didn't understand all that was involved in the gender of a baby. He felt the voodoo queen had let him down (but he never told anyone about this silly encounter on Farrish Street).

Three babies created additional demands on the household. Plus, changes were taking place with other people. Addie, Rachel's daughter, got married and moved to live with her husband in the Mississippi Delta. Rachel decided to go live with them, as their first baby was due. Rachel thought maybe she could help with the baby or on the farm her daughter's husband was starting. Maybe she wanted to escape some of the noise, activity, and rudeness she had been living among under the same roof as Carrie.

More than three years went by before Carrie again thought she was pregnant. Ira asked her how she knew; she mumbled a few things. He reminded her that, while she was "with child," she should regularly eat liver from a male pig and eat only meats from male animals (such as roosters and not hens). He wanted a boy but resigned himself to taking whatever came. He had talked to some farm folks in the community about a curse on him for having only girl babies. They had several thoughts as to what to do but none that he thought would work. He figured that, if voodoo didn't work, nothing would. Anyway, he had grown to love and adore the three daughters he had. If he could just get them old enough and motivated to go to the fields!

On August 20, 1910, a baby boy was born. Ira was so proud to have a boy; he took a peek between the newborn's legs just to be sure. Yes, all appeared to be there! Ira harnessed a horse to the one-horse wagon and dashed around the Tinnin community telling everyone he saw, "I have a boy! I have a boy! I have a boy!"

The boy was named Jasper Henry Lee in memory of Ira's father. Ellen went on and on about how wonderful that name was. She talked about her husband, Jasper, and how the new baby's name was the same as Ira's father's name. Further, Jasper was a long-term given name used with the Lee surname all the way back to England.

Now, there were four babies in the home. Managing them could be a challenge. They had a mother who wasn't always energetic, patient, and considerate. One of the things Carrie did after the babies were several months of age was to put long dresses on them—both girls and boy. As an aid in baby management, a bedpost or other heavy piece of furniture would be sat on the tail of the dress. The baby could tug, scratch, cry, and exert itself to roam about but was kept confined within a range of a few inches of the bedpost. At the same time, the child would get some exercise but could not wander off and get into something dangerous, such as a fireplace or hot stove.

Ira and Carrie had an increasing family. Ira had to figure how to produce more food to feed the family and crops for cash so he could buy what little they needed. Three sharecropper families remained. Maybe he should go back to producing more vegetables; maybe he needed to start producing sugar cane, as he his mother had discussed nearly ten years earlier. After discussion with family, Ira agreed to do both—a few more fresh vegetables for the grocery stores in Jackson and a few acres of sugar cane to try it as a crop and produce molasses for sale and home use.

The sugar cane, in particular, would require a source of seed or planting joints with buds. Planting was in early spring in plowed land. Maturity would be reached in October. Harvest would require cutting the cane and hauling it for juicing and evaporating. As Ellen had noted would be needed years ago, a roller juicer connected to a long pole and turned by a walking mule was bought to mash juice from the harvested stalks. The juice would be collected in a barrel. A cooking pan over a fire pit or oven would be needed to evaporate excess water from the juice. Gallon syrup cans were ordered through the DeWeese Store in Pocahontas. All was on hand and ready by the time of harvest in late October.

Unfortunately, this time coincided with cotton and corn harvest. But Ira was able to work it out, using share-croppers as day laborers to do the work. The syrup produced the first year was very good. Folks around the community bragged about how good it was. Ira was able to sell about 125 gallons.

The years between 1910 and 1913 passed quickly. Farming continued much as it had been. The children were growing. Ellen Louvenia was now over ten years of age and approaching her teenage years. The other girls were coming along well.

In mid-1912, Carrie was again pregnant. More or less, having babies was becoming routine for Carrie. Ethel Naomi Lee was born on April 28, 1913. And as Ira said in announcing the new family member to people in the community, "I have been blessed with another girl." Ira's thoughts about girl babies had changed. One of the girls, Ellen Louvenia, was now old enough to help care for the new baby.

Another year went by on the farm. And there was no need for guessing; Carrie was pregnant again. On April 4, 1915, she gave birth to a boy who was named Ira Nelson Lee. This name reflected the man and family who had rescued Ira and his mother in Texas in the 1870s—Walter Nelson Bell. This was the sixth baby born in the family. Ellen sent a letter to Nelson Bell's daughter, Sarah Ellen, in Texas telling her about the naming.

The baby was sickly, and a doctor was summoned from Clinton. Dr. W. D. Potter examined Ira Nelson at about two years of age and gave him some kind of medicine that had little positive influence (the charge was ten dollars to travel the five miles from Clinton, including medicines that he left). Ira Nelson died a few days later, having lived two years and two months since his birth. The cause of death was unknown. So many childhood ailments went around the countryside, and medical care was quite limited. Maybe his death had something to do with his mother not keeping their rooms in the house clean. Ira Nelson was buried in the Zachariah Ratliff Family Cemetery in an unmarked grave (though the initial intention was to permanently mark it).

Ira and Carrie were heartbroken over the death of their baby. They had been fortunate with their previous five babies and were thankful for the health of these children. Ira Nelson had lived long enough for the family to love and appreciate his two-year-old abilities. Fortunately, the firstborn son (fourth-born child), Jasper Henry, was living and healthy.

The death of Ira Nelson stirred feelings among the sharecroppers. One or two from each family turned out for the short burial service held for him at the Zachariah Ratliff Family Cemetery. Grandmother Ellen was deeply appreciative; she hugged them. Now, not often did a person such as Ellen hug a sharecropper, but Ellen was unique. She appreciated and respected all people, regardless of color and other differences. She had always shown courtesy to sharecroppers, including when one of their children would die. The model of respect Ellen had shown was returned to her on this sad occasion.

Up until this time in the marriage of Ira and Carrie, she had been pregnant or lactating at least thirteen of their fifteen years of marriage! And the number would likely increase. There would likely be more children. Ira no longer insisted on boy babies. He had learned that girl babies are pretty darn nice.

Ellen's health continued to show signs of causing her to slow down. She had put up with a great deal of stress, tragedy, and poverty in her life. Yet, she maintained a happy, pleasant disposition and was always cheering on other people. No doubt, these things make some sort of impact on human health. Ellen was also saddened by the death of her sister Rachel in the same year as Ira Nelson's death. Rachel was her last surviving sister. Only her brother Ira Wittie Shepard (the youngest Shepard sibling) survived longer than the sisters.

Ellen's wisdom helped many people. In about the last year of her life when she was still a fairly sharp thinker, her granddaughter Ellen Louvenia Lee sought her advice. Ellen Louvenia was in her middle teen years and somewhat ready to strike out into the world for herself. She told Ellen she couldn't get along with her mother, Carrie. She wanted to know what to do.

Ellen Louvenia was thinking of completing what schooling she was taking and heading out into the world. She said she had a beau and that he might become a sweetheart. His name was Glen. During the conversation, Ellen's mind thought back to her own years at home with Pa and her wonderful sweetheart who Pa had rejected and forbidden to come to the house. Ellen encouraged her granddaughter to assess her possibilities very carefully and always go about doing nice things for other people.

Ellen Louvenia was smart to get an education, but she would need a job when she left home. She was thinking that maybe she and her sweetheart would strike out. But that didn't happen for another little while, as they were later married in Clinton and lived there a short while. They went on to have successful careers.

Grandmother Ellen was beginning to get forgetful. She could put something down and not remember where it was. Sometimes, things were put in the wrong places. She or other members of the family would search for them. One day she put kitchen scraps in the pie safe. Another day she went to the garden to get eggs from the hen nests. Most everyone except Carrie tried to be helpful and patient. Carrie would avoid her, and if she saw something unfortunate about to happen, Carrie wouldn't stop it but, rather, would go ahead and let Ellen suffer the consequences.

The ravages of age were depriving Ellen of the ability to move about. Some of her joints were stiff or didn't want to move. Balance was occasionally a problem, particularly after first standing up or getting up out of the bed. She would hold onto a chair or the head of the bed or prop against the wall. And with time, it was getting worse. Only a couple of times did she fall, and fortunately, she did not suffer any major injuries or bone breaks.

Ellen Loretta Shepard Lee died March 21, 1918 (she was born September 7, 1847); she was seventy years of age and would have been seventy-one on her next birthday. She lived about forty-seven years after husband Jasper's death. She had done so much for so many people; she was always thought of as a very nice person. Little did she know that she would not live to see all of her grandchildren. Ira and Carrie would have four more children—three girls and another boy who died at birth. Ellen would have been proud that most all of her grandchildren grew up to be good people and have responsible careers.

Even with her decline, Ellen had maintained that lovable, friendly smile and personality and kind disposition that had endeared her to so many people. But death is usually always sad. Regardless of how religious clerics try to explain death, death means that life has gone. The body decomposes to become minerals that return to the Earth.

Ellen's wake and visitation was at the Shepard (now Lee) home. Baldwin Funeral Home was in charge of delivering a casket and bathing and dressing the body. Usually, a family member dressed the body, but there was no one in the home to do it—certainly proud, disagreeable Carrie wouldn't do it. Ellen's body lay in state for a couple of days in the front parlor of the house. A number of people stopped at the house to greet the family and pay tribute to Ellen. She was a wonderful person who touched many lives. Of course, there were a few in the community who did not appreciate her friendship with the sharecroppers and others of lesser means. Many of those who stopped by brought a dish of food of some type to leave for the family.

A couple of sharecroppers dug the grave in the Zachariah Ratliff Family Cemetery. They said this was the least they could do for an honest, considerate woman. Ira Wittie Shepard, Ellen's brother, came for the funeral from his home in Caile, located in the fertile farmland of the Mississippi Delta. A few nieces and nephews also came. The absence of sisters left sort of a hollow feeling in the family (all Ellen's sisters were deceased). Of course, Carrie and Ira's children were there, in addition to a few community citizens.

A short service was led by Preacher Presley of Pocahontas Methodist Episcopal on the front porch of the house. A few people sat (Carrie was one). The casket with the body was on the porch. The service included statements about the life of Ellen, a reading of Psalm 23, and a group singing of the hymn "The Old Rugged Cross." The preacher closed the porch service with a short prayer.

When the preacher gave people a chance to say something, two people spoke—Ellen's brother Ira Wittie and one of the sharecroppers. Both said very touching things about the love and kindness Ellen had for people around her, even when the people had markedly different skin appearance, lived in shabby houses, and went to different churches. Tears rolled down the cheeks of most every adult on the porch, including Carrie's.

Sharecroppers served as pallbearers and transported the casket and body on a wagon from the house to the cemetery. That was unheard of in this part of the South.

After a short statement and prayer at the cemetery by Preacher Presley, the group sang "Amazing Grace." The sharecroppers then lowered the casket and body. They began to slowly fill the grave with shovels of earth, remembering all the while that Ellen was one of the few people who had ever been nice to sharecroppers. No doubt, her kindness and respect was learned from her Midwestern father, George W. Shepard. A half dozen people had brought flowers from their yards. These were placed on top of the earth mound of the filled grave.

Ira, her son, was heard to say, "My mother Ellen is home. She came back to Tinnin and is now going home to be with the Lord."

Yes, she'd made it back to Tinnin!

16

Afterlife Presence

Ellen was now dead. Her physical body had been buried in the Zachariah Ratliff Family Cemetery. A local preacher might say that "a separation of soul and body had occurred." This was in March 1918.

Family members were still in mourning. Ellen continued to have a major influence on her descendant family. With almost everything they would do and the decisions they would make, they would ask themselves, "What would Ellen do?" If not said aloud, the question would be in the back of their minds.

Though she had died, it seemed that Ellen's values and teachings were still very much alive. Some of her descendants were having a hard time getting over her death. They wondered why she had to leave Earth. After the funeral,

Brother Murrow told Ira to contact him if he could be beneficial. Ira sensed a need. So to help with grieving and adjusting to life without Ellen, he asked Brother Murrow to meet with family members and talk about adjusting to the death of a loved one. Ira and Carried arranged for him to come to their home on a Saturday afternoon. He did; several members of the family were ready to listen attentively to what he had to say.

Ellen Loretta attended the Pocahontas Methodist Church in the later years of her life. The church structure was built in 1902 and was taken out of service in 1987. It stands today in the tiny cotton gin town of Pocahontas, Mississippi

Ira welcomed Brother Murrow. He had the adults and older children seat themselves in somewhat of a circle.

Brother Murrow sat in one chair in the circle. He began with a short, comforting prayer. He mentioned the wonderful life of Ellen, which had ended on Earth on March 21, 1918—just a few days ago and the first day of spring. He talked about how she was related as mother, grandmother, and mother-in-law to members of the group. He said she had loved each and every one of them. He further mentioned the most appropriate celebration of her life that the family had held with her funeral.

Calling on his Methodist religious teachings, Brother Murrow went on to say, "We will all be with her again in heaven."

Some of the older children were thinking that rejoining her would be wonderful, but doing so was frightening because it would require that they also die an earthly death. They were not yet ready to die, and some doubted they would ever be ready. They thought of death as scary; it was the end of earthly enjoyment and of being with people they loved.

Brother Murrow, using his church background, explained, "When she died an earthly death, her soul was raised into heaven to be with God. This is because she was a born-again Christian and had become a faithful member of the Pocahontas Methodist Church. It was her immortal being, or as some would say, spirit. We will all have the opportunity for our souls to join her one day in heaven when our physical lives end." What he was saying was raising more questions with the children than it was providing answers. They began to think about the need to be baptized into the church and living lives that merited being in heaven with Ellen.

Brother Murrow continued talking about death and how it was hard to explain in a comforting way. He said he was not a medical doctor and could not explain death in those terms. "But," he said, "based on my studies, death occurs when the body is permanently unable to do what is needed to carry out life processes." He added, "Death can be explained in several ways, such as biology and brain activity. If the heart stops or breathing ceases, death will likely occur quite soon." He went on to talk about how the decline of Ellen's health over the past months was preparation for her family and friends to know that the death process was gradually occurring. She was losing her ability to go about life as she had in earlier years.

As the discussion continued, Brother Murrow asked each individual to remember at least one special thing about their departed dear family member and speak it out loud to the group.

Ellen Louvenia, the oldest grandchild, began by stating that she really liked how her grandmother would take time to listen and help in making choices. Sudie mentioned how her grandmother had taken time to teach her about cooking and other things a young woman needed to learn in running a home. The other older grandchildren also made statements. Last up was Jasper Henry (now called Henry), who indicated he had a good sense of how to identify and use new ways of farming. Then Ira, her son, talked about several of his mother's wonderful qualities, including her ability to be strong in bad situations. Carrie, her daughter-in-law, did not make any statements—in her typical manner, she remained pouty and sullen.

After family comments, Brother Murrow indicated that the family had offered wonderful ways of remembering Ellen. Then he wanted to offer a comment. He said, "I remember Mrs. Ellen Lee as a friendly, moral, and supportive member of the church who sought to do God's will. Though she did not agree with everything I preached about, she was always carefully listening and thinking about what I said as the word of God."

Realizing he had taken enough time, Brother Murrow said, "This family is healing from the death of a beloved member and, given a little time, will be fine. It is good to have memories, but we can't let memories overcome our emotions. We must have a reasoned approach. Don't let your sorrow take over you lives; go about routines, and this will help you through. Occasionally visit her graveside for quiet time and reflections. I ask each of you to pray about your feelings over the loss of Ellen. God will help you through if you seek guidance." He then said a short ending prayer and told everyone goodbye. He got into his buggy and left. The family waved to him as he rode up the hill toward the main road.

Ira told the family he now felt a lot better. He indicated that Brother Murrow had done a good job helping the family understand how to adjust to the death of their beloved Ellen. He asked each person to think about what the preacher had said and to use it to guide his or her thoughts and actions. Ivie, one of Ellen's granddaughters, spoke up. "Yes, he said a lot, but I don't understand all of it. I am going to continue to think and pray about it."

The next morning, it was back to routine in the home and on the farm. Spring was here, and it was time to get the fields ready for crops. Sharecroppers were at work; a couple of hired hands and older children were in the fields as well. Fortunately, the weather was good, and over the next several weeks, all was readied and planted. Good showers and warm temperatures helped the seeds germinate and give a good stand of cotton, corn, and vegetable crops.

After Ellen's death, Ira and Carrie would have two more children. Edna was born on August 1, 1919, and Lyda, on April 19, 1923. These two did not have the opportunity to get to know their grandmother Ellen. They would certainly have benefited from her presence in their home. A couple of the older daughters gave much time to the care of Edna and Lyda; maybe they were surrogates for their grandmother in this regard. Anyway, seven of the nine children born to Carrie and Ira lived into adulthood and assumed productive lives as citizens in the communities where they lived.

Ellen had always felt that men had a big advantage over women. She'd had firsthand experience in that regard while settling the estate of her deceased husband, Jasper. Maybe Ellen was an early feminist or women's rights and suffrage advocate. She knew the women's suffrage movement had been underway for many years. Anyway, 1919 would have been a good year for her, and 1920, even better. Tennessee became the thirty-sixth state to ratify the rights for women amendment to the US Constitution. (There were forty-eight states in the Union; a three-fourths majority of the states was needed for ratification.)

Ellen's home state of Mississippi was not one of the states that voted to ratify the amendment. In fact, Mississippians voted in opposition to ratification on May 29, 1920. That action by voters in her home state would have been hurtful to Ellen, as she was typically an early adopter and progressive when it came to women's rights and new technology. Unfortunately, the nature of the voters in the State was to oppose progressive people and ideas. Some say the same notion has held back advancements in important areas for another century.

In June 1920, the US Federal Census enumerator came to the Lee home and farm in Tinnin. Ira Jasper Lee was head of the household—same as in the two previous census reports. One person was missing this time—Ellen Loretta Shepard Lee. Three new children were present. Individuals listed by the enumerator were Ira Jasper Lee (age fifty-two), Carrie Cheers Hendrick Lee (age thirty-eight), Ellen Louvenia (age seventeen), Sudie (age fifteen), Ivie (age thirteen), Henry (age nine), Ethel (age seven), and Edna (eight months). The family had certainly changed since the previous census in 1910!

A little more than four years after the death of Ellen and about one year before the birth of Lyda, Ellen Louvenia Lee announced she was getting married. In June 1922, she married Glenn Edwards. Immediately, there was a tremendous amount of wailing and crying by her mother, Carrie. Was this due to her sadness about her daughter moving away? Or was it due to the loss of her daughter as a source of household work? Maybe the sadness was due to both, but most likely the latter played a significant role. Some family members thought it might have been due to occasional bouts of mental illness Carrie was thought by some to suffer from.

The new Mr. and Mrs. Edwards lived a short while in Clinton and wound up living for many years in Montgomery, Alabama, where they were highly successful in business. To some extent, Ellen Louvenia Lee Edwards was viewed by other family members much as Ellen Loretta Shepard Lee had been; she was a person to look up to—someone who could make good choices and be successful. One indication of her success was revealed during the Great Depression of the 1930s. Ellen and Glenn took a cruise on a Holland-America ship from New York to Cuba and back to New York. That was virtually unheard of in the Tinnin community, where the only travel to great distances was as soldiers going to war. Ira, Carrie, and their children were always excited by a visit from Ellen and Glenn.

Most years were relatively routine with Ira and Carrie. One year that stands out, however, is 1923. On September 3, they bought a new Ford touring car (#8228213) from Flora Motor Company in the nearby town of Flora. Ira paid $469 cash at the dealership. He and Carrie had saved the money since the good farming years of World War I. This was the first vehicle of any kind with an engine the family had owned. Three of the older children went the day it was bought (Carrie stayed home, as she had baby Lyda to care for). The family rode in a horse-pulled buggy to Flora. For the most part, Sudie and Ivie drove the Ford car home, as Pa Ira did not understand enough of the mechanical devices to do so safely. Henry also wanted to drive it and did so for some of the distance (he was thirteen years of age at the time). Henry's main duty was to get the horse and buggy back home following the car. (Mississippi did not pass a driver's license requirement until 1938; the requirement of taking a test to get a license was put in place in 1946. Therefore, at the time, if you could operate a motor vehicle, you were qualified to drive it.)

Pa Ira tried to learn to drive. When he did get in the driver's seat, the car would jerk about and kick up dust; Ira didn't understand gears and clutches. He often killed the engine. The car would sometimes go off the pig-trail dirt roadways and wind up in a ditch or bumping into a tree. No family members would ride with him. Even animals were frightened. But that was likely due to the noise of the engine. In fact, Ira never learned to confidently drive a vehicle. His reasoning was that the front fenders covered the wheels, and he could not see the direction they were going when he turned the steering wheel. This was OK with the older children in the family, as they were anxious to drive if given the opportunity.

Ira and family had first looked at a Model T when Ellen was alive. She'd wanted them to get the car in 1917. Flora Motor Company had a salesperson demonstrate the car at the farm. The Lees hadn't bought at that time, as they'd felt the price was too high. But Ellen was always wanting to try new things. Maybe this was more evidence that she was an early adopter or innovator. Even with the Ford touring car, horses and wagons were still much used. The car was never used to transport products; in fact, it wasn't designed to do so. Ira had great pride in the family's first automobile.

Expansion of US agriculture during World War I to

meet demands in Europe resulted in overproduction and low prices for farm products in the 1920s. Agriculture was in a depression. The US Congress attempted legislation that would bring relief but without very good results. Nearly six hundred thousand farms, or one in four in the nation, were sold to meet financial obligations; fortunately, Ira was able to manage his farm so it survived. Times got really tight in the late 1920s, but Ira held on. He often thought about his mother, Ellen, and how she'd endured the hard times she'd faced. Hunker down and be self-sufficient; buy very little.

Tough times on farms in the 1920s resulted in more of the Lee daughters looking for ways out of farm life. They had heard that some towns and cities had thriving manufacturing industries with good jobs. Ellen Louvenia had married before the Depression was so severe. Now, Sudie and Ivie were each looking for a man who would take them away from the harsh reality facing Ira and Carrie. Each found a man about the change of the decade. But another and more extended Great Depression was on the way.

With Sudie's and Ivie's marriages, Carrie wept and wailed considerably; some folks said she had "weeping fits." To Carrie, the marriage of a daughter was like the death of a person she loved. As before, she got over the weeping about the marriages of daughters in less than two weeks of weeping episodes. Carrie and Ira realized the size of their family in the home was shrinking; Carrie was now beyond the usual age of producing more babies. She was a complainer and wanted people to do things for her that she should have done for herself. Maybe she had been spoiled as a child and never got over it.

A major event in 1930 was the opening of a bridge over the Mississippi River in Vicksburg. Prior to the bridge, ferries and boats were used to cross the river. The new bridge connected a roadway (Highway 80) in Mississippi with a roadway in Louisiana. Crossing the river had been a major issue for family members (and everyone else) for many years, including newlyweds Jasper and Ellen as they traveled to Texas in March 1864—nearly sixty-six years earlier. In 1880, Ellen and Ira had come back across the Mighty Mississippi on a ferry from their life in Texas to live in Tinnin.

The opening of the bridge across the Mississippi River was billed as a historic occasion in central Mississippi. Ira wanted to go and be among the first to cross on the bridge. Henry also wanted to go and would drive in their car. On May 1, 1930, they skipped out on farmwork and made the trip to Vicksburg to be one of the first cars to drive across the bridge. The roadway to Vicksburg wasn't a very good highway, but it was adequate. To great fanfare, the bridge was opened to automobile, pedestrian, and railroad traffic. With cantilever engineering, it was a major construction feat. The bridge was 8,546 feet long (a mile and a half), with 116 feet of clearance above the typical water level in the Mississippi River. Wow! Ira and Henry had a lot to talk about when they returned home late that day.

Crossing on the bridge gave Ira and Henry the notion they could later drive to Ira's birthplace in Henderson County, Texas. They could see the burial site of Ira's father and Henry's grandfather (Jasper H. Lee) and look around the area. Possibly they could see relatives who were still living in the area, including children of Sarah Ellen Bell.

Interestingly, no married daughter ever returned to live with Carrie and Ira, either as a newlywed seeking a first home or as a single woman who had experienced marital issues. The home lacked the loving vibrancy of their grandmother, Ellen. It had the unpleasantness of their mother, Carrie. Ira was there as the head of household, but he was very involved with farming. He had many of the gentlemanly qualities that his mother, Ellen, and her father, George Shepard, tried to teacher him. Carrie, however, set the tone for the home, and it was not always pleasant. Times were tight, money was short, and few modern conveniences were present in the home.

Money got so short that son Henry took a job with the railroad in the mid-1930s. He, by and large, gave up farming for a while to work in track maintenance and construction though he still lived at home. It was good to have a small paycheck for the Lee family.

One interesting thing Henry gained was social security through the US Railroad Retirement Board (RRB). In the early 1930s, President Franklin Roosevelt took office during very difficult economic times in the United States. He pushed legislation in 1934 that would aid railroad employees and serve as a model for later social security legislation. In 1935, President Roosevelt signed legislation creating the controversial (but very beneficial) Social Security Administration, which applied far beyond railroad jobs. Henry was covered with enhanced benefits until his death many years later. His social security number had an "R" at the end, designating "railroad."

Ira and Henry made their long-planned trip to Henderson County, Texas, in 1937 after Henry had gotten one of his paychecks for his railroad work. The bridge over the Mississippi River made it possible for them to drive. They were in the Athens, Texas, area only a couple of days, but that was enough time for them to see what they wanted. Ira got to see his father's grave marker in Smith Cemetery. The epitaph for Jasper Henry Lee mentioned he was the father of Ira; no mention was made that he was the husband of Ellen, but such was the status of women at the time.

It was interesting for Ira to visit the area he had known as a small boy in Texas and try to figure out where things had been when he'd lived there. Ira even thought about what his life would have been like if his mother had not gone back to live in Tinnin, Mississippi. Anyway, there was no going back to those times and events. They had been able to cope with the challenges of life in Mississippi.

Henry worked for the railroad for a few years but was being pulled away. The health of his father began to deteriorate, and Henry was needed to operate the farm. Ira had long experienced asthma and breathing problems. Now other health issues were apparently occurring. At that time in the Great Depression, few people sought the assistance of a doctor unless they were very ill—maybe too far gone to ever get better. Fortunately, his limited railroad work was sufficient to quality him for social security for the remainder of his life!

Henry always had a special fondness for his grandmother, Ellen. Maybe she showed him special attention when he was quite small. After all, he was her only grandson to survive beyond early childhood. Henry had some of her traits related to work and honesty. He also had some traits of his mother, Carrie. But, most of all, it was his father with whom he shared many things in common.

After his railroad work, Henry was at home on the Tinnin farm. He did not plan to ever leave or go anywhere. He would carry on the family farming tradition. He had a small place in the back of the main hallway for his bed and belongings. Henry really was not very comfortable in the house with his limited privacy. The marriage of a couple more sisters freed up space. So, he was able to occupy a larger front room. He lived in the house with his parental family and one younger sister who had not left home.

On a fall day in 1939, Henry was on the one-mile drive from the Lee home to the Ratliff Store for some Prince Albert Tobacco (yes, Henry unfortunately smoked roll-your-own cigarettes at that time in his life). He passed an attractive young woman who was out walking by herself between the Tinnin schoolhouse and the teachers' home. He didn't stop that day; he waved and tipped his hat.

A couple of days later, he was on the same short trip at the same time of day, and there she was making the school-to-home walk accompanied by another young woman. Henry couldn't resist; he stopped and introduced himself. They said they were new teachers at the Tinnin School and stayed in the teachers' home along with a couple of other teachers. Henry asked if they would like to ride to the Ratliff Store (only a quarter of a mile away) and get an ice cold cola. He thought for sure that they would say no, but to his surprise, they said yes. They probably assessed that Henry was an honorable young farmer who meant only good. Plus, he had a car to ride in. The got in, and Henry drove off—most likely with a big grin on his face.

They each got a cola (it came only in very small bottles then) and sat on the porch steps of the store. They talked a bit. One said she had a boyfriend; the other didn't mention anything about a boyfriend.

Henry observed that the one without a boyfriend appeared to be intelligent and was beautiful. She said her name was Doris Sloan. He drove them back to the teachers' home and asked Doris if he could come visit her the next day after school. She said yes, and that led to what became the romance of a good-looking young woman with another Jasper Henry Lee. (Sounds like a repeat of 1863/64, doesn't it?)

The relationship of Henry and Doris began and grew into a certain closeness that led to a marriage proposal. The celebration of the rites of marriage was held on August 3, 1940, with Brother Murrow officiating. The ceremony was conducted at the home of Edna and Brunner Huddleston (one of Henry's sisters and her husband) in Jackson, Mississippi. Edna and Brunner had been married about five years before. The big room in the farmhouse that Henry had gotten for himself a couple of years ago now belonged to the newlyweds—Mr. and Mrs. Lee. They would also get another room of about equal size for use as a kitchen and other purposes. Of course, the toilet was a two-holer privy out back.

Doris was no longer a schoolteacher. Two factors were at work. First, Mississippi State law prohibited married women from teaching. And second, the Tinnin School was closed because it had been consolidated with the

Clinton School. Doris was a full-time homemaker, and Henry, a farmer. By the first of October, Doris suspected she was pregnant. Pregnancy was confirmed in another month. So, Henry and Doris went about preparing for the birth of their first child; and, likely, there would be several more. They took an unusual step at the time for rural people by getting some prenatal care and planning for delivery of the baby in the Jackson Infirmary. Doris had a college degree and knew about health and maternity care.

Ira carried on work as long as he could. He began to lose weight and become lethargic. He would sit and rock for long hours on the porch of his home. Sometimes, he would fall asleep in the rocking chair. He would always dress neatly in a farm sort of way that included high-top shoes, long-sleeve shirt, long pants, and a hat, even while sitting in the chair.

Shock and sadness struck on January 1, 1941, with the death of Ira. The family somewhat expected his death because of his declining health. There was considerable grieving in the family about the death of Ellen Loretta Shepard Lee's son. Carrie whimpered and mourned, with occasional bursts of wailing. Was she sincere? Time would tell.

All the Lee children and their spouses began to arrive at the house. Conditions were rainy, wet, and muddy. The decision was made to bury Ira in the cemetery at the Pocahontas Methodist Church, rather than with his mother in the Zachariah Ratliff Family Cemetery. The mud was too bad to get to the family cemetery, which was beginning to suffer from neglect anyway. Ira's viewing was at his home. Brother Murrow, who had done about everything for the family for decades, delivered the eulogy in the Pocahontas Methodist Church.

The family worked to overcome the loss of Ira. Lyda was the only unmarried child at home. She was going to college in Clinton and played a big part in comforting her mother on the death of Ira. To some extent, they grieved together.

Late on May 28, 1941, Doris thought she was going into labor. Henry quickly drove her to the Jackson Infirmary, where a boy was born the next day. Henry was very proud to have a son, as he had grown up around all girls. Plus, Henry thought, when he was older, he could get the boy to carry on the farm and plan the transition of it to the next generation. Doris continued being a housewife and new mother to their son. Coping with the antics of her mother-in-law was a daily challenge and a source of anxiety.

The farming routine went as well as could be expected for the next year. World War II had broken out. Pearl Harbor, Hawaii, was attacked on December 7, 1941. All of Europe was at war, with countries fighting on one side or the other. Government rationing of food, clothing, gasoline, and other products was instituted to ensure plenty of resources for the war effort. These actions meant that Henry and Doris's home would continue to provide an austere place to live meagerly without modern conveniences of electricity, running water, heat, and plumbing for the kitchen and bathroom.

Things don't always go as planned; this was true on December 8, 1942. Before Henry left home that morning to go grind corn with a hammer mill at the Ratliff Store, he held his son high, gently raising him above his head into the air, and placed him back into his playpen. Henry kissed Doris goodbye. At the store, Henry and a helper positioned the steel-wheeled Farmall tractor in just the right place for the wide belt to transfer power from a pulley on the side of the tractor to a pulley on the hammer mill. All was up and going well. The belt and pulleys were turning at a high speed (was it too fast?). Corn was being ground to the proper size for meal.

Suddenly, the big rotating belt lunged off the flywheel and wrapped around Henry's right arm just above the elbow. The rotation of the heavy belt was powerful. In a twisting motion, it almost totally severed the arm a couple of inches below the shoulder. Henry was flung to the ground. He temporarily lost consciousness. His helper called out. People came running from the store and rushed to Henry's aid. Blood was flowing. The twisting motion of the belt that pulled the arm off had closed some of the blood vessels, which reduced the rate of blood loss and helped him remain alive. The bones in the upper arm were broken, jagged, and protruding from the flesh.

When Henry regained consciousness, he was able to stand up and walk in a staggering, wobbly way. As he walked, his right hand drug along on the ground. The skin and tissue that held the arm to the body stretched several inches long. He made it to an automobile that was used to rush him to the hospital in Jackson for care. Emergency room personnel went about amputating what remained of the arm and hand. The nub of bone that remained was covered with skin stretched from around it and sutured into place. Anesthesia was used at the hospital, but no doubt, he experienced a great deal of pain. He had a blood transfusion to replace some of what he'd lost. His body was in shock. Hospital care helped him survive. Doris stayed at his bedside around the clock.

After several days in the hospital, Henry returned home, where Doris provided tender care to promote the recovery of her man. Henry could no longer hold his son. He was not able to do farmwork of any sort for a while. Gradually, he regained some ability but was always handicapped by having one hand. He was a right-handed man who now had to exist with only a left hand. He now had to learn to do more things with his left hand. Fortunately, spring and the start of crops were a few months away.

Jasper's grandson, also named Jasper Henry Lee, visited his grandfather's grave in Smith Cemetery, Henderson County, Texas, in 1979 (110 years after the death of Jasper). Note that his right arm has been amputated.

Coping with the horrible consequences of this accident would not be easy. As was often the case, the spirit of Ellen would promote resilience in this traumatized young family. And, as you may surmise, there is a lot more to this story. Henry's life lasted forty-seven years after the loss of his right arm. In spite of the handicap, he was able to accomplish a great in his life of seventy-eight years.[2]

---

[2] The amputating accident is covered in detail in *One Gone* by Jasper S. Lee, published in 2018 by Archway Publishing of Bloomington, Indiana.

Epilogue

Ellen Loretta Shepard met and fell in love with Jasper Henry Lee in late 1863 and married him in March 1864. He was more than twice her age and was not from around her home area. His charisma had an amazing appeal to Ellen. She immediately fell for it.

Young women didn't have many potential husbands at the time, as the US Civil War was raging across the Southern states. Bloody battles killed thousands of young men and permanently maimed thousands more. Ellen was caught in that situation, as well as deteriorating conditions at home due to the loss of farm productivity and a way of life that were, unfortunately, built on slavery. Families also lost many possessions to the plundering by Union and Confederate troops. In the mid-1860s, the future didn't hold a lot of promise for many young people in the war-ravaged deep South.

So, when Ellen had a chance to develop a romantic relationship with Jasper, she did so. In a matter of weeks, they were talking about marriage and future life together. She had introduced Jasper to her family. Instantly, Pa did not like him or think he was up to the standard of marrying his oldest daughter. It seems Jasper was never able to answer Pa's questions in a straightforward manner with the kind of truthful information he wanted to hear. There were always unexplained gaps in his life. What had he been doing all those years? They moved ahead with plans to marry without Pa's approval—which, sadly, resulted in him rejecting both Ellen and Jasper by not allowing him to ever come to their home again.

Maybe Pa had some sort of special insight into Jasper; maybe it was the unanswered questions that gave him insight. Where was Jasper born and where did he grow up? Who were his parents? Questions about what he'd been doing during his young adult years weren't answered to Pa's standards. Had he had other women and fathered children? Had he been in Union or Confederate forces? Getting answers was not easy then and has not been easy today. By nature of his birth and childhood upbringing in Indiana, Pa was more of a Unionist than a Rebel during the US Civil War.

Diligent search of government records from the mid-1800s, DNA analysis, and review of old letters and documents kept by Ellen and other family members provided a lot of information. Exact information on Jasper is not available, but more reliable information than was available to Pa has come about. Best information is that Jasper was born in South Carolina in 1827. The name of his mother was Sarah Lee. His father's name is unknown. But according to current day Y-DNA testing of descendants, it was Faust.

As an older teenager or young adult, Jasper traveled with pioneers from his home (Richland County, South Carolina) in the late 1830s. Some have speculated that he was running from conscription in either the Union or Confederate military during the US Civil War. He traveled a bit and worked on farms and in other ways. Sometimes, he was thought to have hidden in the woods, barns, or other places. Mostly, he lived without resources. He traveled by hitching rides, walking, and riding a train. By the time Jasper reached Brandon, Mississippi, in late 1863, he had been married twice and possibly had lived in brief communal relationships. Evidence is that Jasper provided no support for the child he fathered.

Jasper and Ellen produced a son, Ira Jasper, who was born on February 3, 1868. There is no evidence that Jasper was ever anything more than a gentleman with Ellen–always kind and considerate of her.

They lived together as Mr. and Mrs. Lee for six years and eight months after marriage. A very short married life left Ellen a widow with a small son while still in her early twenties. Ellen was known as a wonderful, smart, kind, and considerate woman who appreciated all people regardless of skin color and other traits that made them appear different.

Tinnin was her home, and she went back to live there!

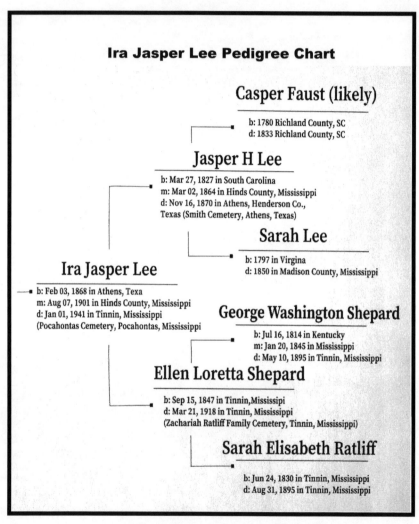

Ira Jasper Lee Pedigree Chart

Casper Faust (likely)
b: 1780 Richland County, SC
d: 1833 Richland County, SC

Jasper H Lee
b: Mar 27, 1827 in South Carolina
m: Mar 02, 1864 in Hinds County, Mississippi
d: Nov 16, 1870 in Athens, Henderson Co.,
Texas (Smith Cemetery, Athens, Texas)

Sarah Lee
b: 1797 in Virgina
d: 1850 in Madison County, Mississippi

Ira Jasper Lee
b: Feb 03, 1868 in Athens, Texa
m: Aug 07, 1901 in Hinds County, Mississippi
d: Jan 01, 1941 in Tinnin, Mississippi
(Pocahontas Cemetery, Pocahontas, Mississippi

George Washington Shepard
b: Jul 16, 1814 in Kentucky
m: Jan 20, 1845 in Mississippi
d: May 10, 1895 in Tinnin, Mississippi

Ellen Loretta Shepard
b: Sep 15, 1847 in Tinnin,Mississipi
d: Mar 21, 1918 in Tinnin, Mississippi
(Zachariah Ratliff Family Cemetery, Tinnin, Mississippi)

Sarah Elisabeth Ratliff
b: Jun 24, 1830 in Tinnin, Mississippi
d: Aug 31, 1895 in Tinnin, Mississippi

Pedigree chart for Ira Jasper Lee